BLOW ON A
DEAD MAN'S
EMBERS

Also by Mari Strachan

The Earth Hums in B Flat

BLOW ON A DEAD MAN'S EMBERS

Mari Strachan

CANONGATE

Edinburgh · London · New York · Melbourne

Published by Canongate Books in 2011

1

Copyright © Mari Strachan, 2011

The moral right of the author has been asserted

First published in Great Britain in 2011 by Canongate Books Ltd,
14 High Street, Edinburgh EH1 1TE

www.canongate.tv

British Library Cataloguing-in-Publication Data
A catalogue record for this book is available on
request from the British Library

ISBN 978 1 84767 531 6

Typeset in Goudy by Palimpsest Book Production Ltd,
Falkirk, Stirlingshire

Printed and bound in Great Britain by CPI Mackays, Chatham ME5 8TD

This book is printed on FSC certified paper

MIX
Paper from
responsible sources
FSC
www.fsc.org   FSC® C020471

I
Adam, Llio, Cai, a Rachel
hefo cariad mawr

1

Something is weighing on her breast, squeezing her heart. For a moment Non cannot move, not sure if she is awake or still in a dream. She breathes evenly to keep panic at bay, and her heartbeat steadies. The dream vanishes but the weight remains. She recognises it: it is a sense of dread that is becoming familiar, though quite what it is that she dreads she does not know.

She opens her eyes, then narrows them against the brightness streaming into the bedroom with its threat of another scorching day. In four, no, three days it will be the solstice, so it must still be early for the sun to be this low in the sky. When she is able to move and put her hand out to Davey, all she touches is the cool sheet on his side of the bed. Again.

The open sash window lets in the sweetness of the honeysuckle that clambers around it and the industrious drone of bees moving from lip to lip on the flowers. Non breathes deeply, stretches until her calf muscles tingle, then swings her legs sideways and sits up on the edge of the bed. She reaches for the small, dark brown bottle, uncorks it, tips out thirteen drops of the liquid it contains into a glass, pauses, then adds one more drop, pours water from the jug onto the drops and swallows the draught in one gulp, grimacing, as she always does, at the bitterness of it in the back of her throat. Every morning she hears her father's voice tell her that her lifeblood is less bitter than the death that will surely claim her if she does not swallow it, the death that is constantly at her shoulder. It is what gives you the gift you possess, Rhiannon, her father would also say. A gift that is as bitter as the drops, a gift that is no gift at all.

As she sits on the side of the bed her heart begins to calm, but the dread that woke her still weighs upon her. She feels as limp as a rag doll as she stands and walks towards the washstand. The heat is enervating; it lies like a thick blanket over every day. She pours water that is already lukewarm from the large jug into the bowl, and splashes her face and neck with it.

She remembers the time before the War when the quiet and warmth would engender a sense of deep contentment in her. It now seems far in the past, that time early in their marriage when she had discovered that Davey was impossible to wake in the mornings, when she would take up her book and tiptoe downstairs to sit in the kitchen or at the open door to the fresh morning garden, breathe deeply of the promise of a new day, and read – until it was time to put her coarse apron on over her nightdress to rack the range and light the fire and wake the house with the noise. A rumpled and sleepy Davey would descend from the bedroom and pretend to chase her out into the garden. That has all gone. The War has taken her husband as surely as if it had killed him, and returned a stranger to her in his place.

She lifts her hairbrush and draws it through her hair. Forty long strokes. Non has no recollection of her father teaching her that rule; that must have come from her sister. She gathers the hair together at her nape and ties it into a large knot. She pulls her work dress on, fastens the buttons with nimble fingers and neatens the collar in the looking glass above the washstand. She studies her reflection. She, too, has changed: she sees it in her eyes. She has turned into a timorous creature, as different from her true self as Davey is from his. You mouse, she tells herself, are you going to be defeated by this mystery, this puzzle of what is happening to your husband? She stands up straight. She, who has beaten off death every day of her twenty-nine years, will not be beaten by this.

2

Non makes her way downstairs and pushes open the kitchen door. The sunlight in the hallway streams into the room towards Davey who is crouched beneath the table. The fringe of the blue chenille tablecloth dangles in front of his face, and he peers out through it into the light, shouldering an imaginary rifle.

It is happening again. Is this what woke her? Is it this that she dreads? Non has grown used to the nightmares Davey has at times since his return from the War, when the bedclothes churn into a battlefield as he fights and thrashes and sweats his way through some private torment – nightmares that wake her and drive her from the bed but which Davey denies when she asks him about them. Now, it seems the nightmares have changed from dreams into something more real, more fearful. The first time it happened was Wednesday morning; she will never forget it, she thinks, not for a sparrow's heartbeat. She had woken to find Davey gone from their bed and found him sprawled under the kitchen table, deadly quiet in his concentration as he aimed his rifle at some unseen foe. Non had crawled under the table to him and he had given her a look that chilled her heart and froze her tongue. She had crept away and left him.

She knows that there is nothing to be done now except to leave him. But has she not just resolved that she will not be beaten by the mystery of what is happening to her husband? She knows that he betrayed her when he was away – and it pains her to think of it – but she senses, no, she knows that is not what is haunting Davey through his nightmares; it is something else, something that has to do with fighting the enemy. She draws a chair back from under the table, lifting it to stop it screeching on the flagstones, positions it so that she can see Davey, and sits on it. She smoothes the tablecloth with the back of her hand. Like life, she thinks, smooth and rough, worn thin so that it is almost a hole in places, plush as if it were new in others. She is uncomfortable. She does not want to sit here on a kitchen chair to watch her husband fight the enemy all over again under the table, but believes she must if she is to understand what happened to him.

This man on the floor is as unlike himself as possible. His hair and his clothes are dishevelled as he crawls around on the flagstones in the confined space. His eyes are wide open with the whites showing all around, as if he is mad with fear, like a horse Non saw when she was a child. The farmer had shot the horse, said it had turned wild and dangerous. Non flinches each time Davey fires the rifle he imagines he has on his shoulder, the recoil sending him sprawling backwards. He is sweating profusely, his shirt already soaked under his arms and on his back, from whatever endeavours he thinks he is attempting. He mutters and calls out, words and phrases Non cannot understand, which sound sometimes like commands, sometimes like entreaties. He shouts, 'Down, down', and flings himself face down on the flags. She hears his face thump on the stone and she cringes.

'Oh, Davey,' she whispers. Her Davey, the real Davey, is a small man, and neat, and this was part of what she had loved about

5

him from the first time she saw him. Small herself, she did not feel overpowered by him. He was far from being a moneyed man, but he had always made sure that the clothes he wore were clean, mended and ironed. His hair that had a will of its own, springing up from his head in dark brown spikes, was always carefully brushed, and his moustache with its glints of red neatly trimmed and combed.

When she first met him it was as if she had always known him, and yet, it was his son she knew first. Wil was in the Infants class when she came as a student teacher to the local school, as sturdy and quiet a boy at five and a half as he is now at fifteen. She remembers being saddened that first winter when he seemed unmoved by the sudden death of his mother from a cough that had turned rapidly to pneumonia. She had felt a greater sadness at some of the tales that came her way about Grace, tales of callousness and cruelty towards Wil and his small sister.

She looks down at Davey, lying flat now on the flagstones, his shoulders twitching as he sights down the length of his rifle, his forefinger squeezing on the trigger. She had not met him until the following spring; he had come to see if Meg could begin school a little younger than was usual. He had looked into her eyes and smiled at her and she had been lost. She had never thought that she would marry; she had never met a man she would wish to marry. And what man would wish to marry a woman like her who could not bear a child of her own for fear that it would put too great a strain on her weakened heart? Over the year he spent courting her, Davey told her that he had children, he did not need more. He wanted her, she delighted him by being so clever, so different.

And they had been happy, hadn't they? She loved Wil as if he were her own child. Meg she found a little harder to love. Davey's mother had been glad to relinquish Wil to them, but refused to part with Meg. She'll come round, Davey had said, but Catherine Davies had not done so for a long time. Perhaps there had been a little dark patch creeping in to dampen their happiness even then, Non thinks; perhaps that first year before Osian arrived had not been the idyllic time she had thought it was.

She starts. Are those footsteps on the stairs? She does not want the children to see their father like this. She jumps to her feet but before she can reach the door it opens and Osian comes through into the kitchen, dressed in nothing but his drawers and flicking his penknife open as he walks past her towards the back door. He stops when he sees Davey, and Davey retreats into a crouch, staring at the light glancing from the penknife's blade. Non puts her hand on Osian's arm to guide him away, although she knows that he will cry out at her touch. And so he does, a high-pitched scream that ricochets off the whitewashed walls and reverberates from the flagstones beneath her feet.

She turns to look at Davey as she draws Osian through the door into the garden and sees him fling himself flat again onto the floor beneath the table, yelling as he prostrates himself, 'Down. Whizz-bang coming. Down, Ben, down.'

3

Osian's scream ends as suddenly as it started once they are through the door and Non lets go of his arm. The garden shimmers already but the sun has not reached into the back of the house yet. There is a foul stench on the air, and Non realises where it is coming from when she sees Maggie Ellis rushing out the closet at the end of her garden, still in her voluminous nightgown and wearing a nightcap on her head. Though what she wants with a nightcap these hot nights is beyond anyone's guess.

Maggie Ellis stops when she catches sight of Osian, and tuts at him. 'Out in your drawers again, boy?' she says. 'And was that you screaming, or was it that old crow of yours? Well, never mind. It's your mam I want. Where is she?' She clutches her stomach and moans.

Osian pays her no attention. Non's new found resolution fades a little. Is it not enough that her husband is on his knees under the kitchen table fighting a war that has been over for more than two years? But she walks from the shade into the sunlight. 'Are you not well, Mrs Ellis?'

'Not well, Non, not well? Of course I'm not well. Look at

me.' Maggie Ellis clutches her stomach again. 'It must be something I ate. Everything's going off – the milk's sour, the butter's rancid – and the flies, well, they don't bear thinking about.' She leans over the garden wall, snagging her nightdress on the clambering rose. 'All night, Non, backwards and forwards to the closet. Do you think you could mix me a little something to stop it?'

Non suspects that Maggie's problems stem from eating too much, her gift that is no gift does not show her any illness in the woman. 'A cup of strong tea will help bind you, Mrs Ellis. No milk or sugar, mind.' She has lost count of the number of times she has told Maggie Ellis this.

'Oh, I can't abide my tea black like that, Non. No – you mix me a little something.'

'You know I've long stopped doing that.'

'I won't tell Davey, I promise you, Non. It'll be our little secret.' Maggie reaches over the roses to try to pat Non's hand where it rests on the stone wall, and Non hears her nightgown rip on the thorns. It would be so easy to mix a little something for her, but Davey has extracted a promise from her to make no more remedies. Other than her own dark drops, her lifeblood.

'Make yourself some black tea, Mrs Ellis. It's as good as anything.'

'Non, Non, we share so many secrets, don't we? And they're perfectly safe with me, don't you worry your pretty head. So one more little one won't hurt, will it?'

Non knows that Maggie Ellis has more to lose than she does from the telling of any secrets. She watches Osian who, in turn, is watching a flock of ravens wheel above him. Is he looking for Herman among them?

Maggie Ellis heaves herself off the roses leaving a shred of her nightgown hanging like a ragged white flag on one of its branches, and rubs her stomach. 'I think it's easing, you know. Maybe there won't be any need for me to take anything after all.'

'That's good,' Non says. 'Have you run out of ashes for the closet? Some marjoram on the floor would make it pleasanter in there. And a bunch of lavender to hang up.'

'I'm sure you're quite right, Non. Breathing in that terrible smell can't be doing me any good. I put plenty of ashes down. It's this weather that's to blame. Have you got any whatever-you-said to spare for the floor?'

Non has none to spare, but what is she to do? 'I'll gather some later,' she says. 'When the sun has been on it to draw out the oils.'

Maggie Ellis squints at the sky. 'The sun's not very high yet. What are you doing out here?' She glances from Non to Osian who is now busy whittling a piece of wood, and back again. 'It was him I heard screeching, wasn't it, not your old crow?'

'We haven't seen Herman for a few days,' Non says. She shields her eyes with her hand and looks up at the wheeling birds. She cannot see Herman's squared wings and flat-tipped tail. 'He flies with the ravens sometimes, but I don't think he's up there.'

Maggie Ellis nods at Osian. 'Is he really safe with that knife?'

'He's been making things out of wood since he was old enough to handle the knife. You know that, Mrs Ellis. There's no need to worry,' Non says, though she herself finds the sharpness of the knife a mite worrying at times.

'What I know,' Maggie Ellis says, wagging her finger at Non, 'what I know is that he's a great worry to dear Mrs Davies. Being odd the way he is.'

It is highly unlikely that her mother-in-law would confide in Maggie Ellis given the remarks Non has heard Mrs Davies make about Maggie. And Non would not have said that her mother-in-law was worried about Osian, or about anyone else other than herself.

'And the poor woman has had enough worries,' Maggie Ellis says. 'More than anyone should.'

Non tries to avoid thinking about Mrs Davies unless it is an absolute necessity, and when she must, she tries to avoid thinking unkind thoughts, because Mrs Davies is a sick woman.

'That old War's left its mark on us all.' Maggie Ellis beckons Non to come closer and lowers her voice. 'Poor Elsie Thomas has started having her turns again. Of course, it's the time of year, Non. But this time she's convinced herself that the body they brought back to bury in that big abbey in London is her Benjamin. Wants anyone who'll listen to write to Lloyd George for her and ask him to send Ben home. I told her not to be so silly.'

Poor Elsie, Non thinks. When the letter – no, it had not even been a letter – when the filled-out form came from the War Office, Non read it to her; Elsie could not read English. Died, it had baldly said. Elsie was still waiting for her son's body to come home, she couldn't understand that it never would, that no one came home. No one, Non thinks, not one of them, except that single unknown soldier. Not even Davey.

'I said to her,' Maggie Ellis says, 'I said, How can you have a picture of his grave with a cross on it hanging on your wall in that special frame Davey Davies made for it, and still think he's buried in that big place in London? But she's not quite the full yard is she, Non? She never was, that's where Benjamin got it from. It runs in that family, she had a cousin just the same.'

Maggie Ellis drones like the bees, but less productively. Non is too occupied with the thought that has occurred to her to pay Maggie much more attention. She has realised that Davey's waking nightmares have begun at about the same time of year as his nightmares did last year, and the year before, too, she is sure of it. As if it was somehow all tied up together, which would not be surprising since Davey and Benjamin were in the same section, though Davey said he had not been there when Ben was killed and could not tell Elsie Thomas any more about what had happened than the official form did.

'Non,' Maggie Ellis's voice cuts in on her thoughts. 'Non, I said, your Davey's all right now, though, isn't he? Back to normal?'

Non has to suppress a hysterical sob she feels rising in her throat. She sidesteps the question. 'He's busy with the Festival preparations, Mrs Ellis. Working all hours.'

'He's lucky to have the work, Non. He's a good carpenter, I'll give you that. I remember him making things from bits of wood when he was younger than your boy there.' Maggie glances at Osian again, narrowing her eyes at him and shaking her head. She would not be the first to wonder where he came from. Non no longer allows herself to wonder.

As she watches Osian's knife shaping the wood, she realises with dismay that she has completely forgotten it is his birthday today. She has been absorbed by the horror of what is happening to Davey inside the house, but it is no excuse. What kind of mother forgets to wish her child a happy birthday?

Seven years, she thinks, since Davey brought him home. Osian was a poor, mewling thing when Davey brought him to her, a newborn, long and red like a newly skinned rabbit. Davey said there was no need to know where he had come from, or who, he was now her child, as if he were somehow making up to her for the fact that she dare not bear a child of her own. Though she had not, then, felt the need for a child of her own. She had wanted to know more about the boy, but all Davey would tell her was that the young mother was dead, she had not told her family who had fathered the baby, and the boy was unwanted. But why had

Davey taken him, she had asked, suspecting that her husband knew more than he was telling her, and he had replied, For you, Non, as if that was the end of the matter. So, she had kept her questions to herself, and named the boy after her own father. To all intents and purposes Osian is hers, and to this day she does not know what to do with him.

She watches him fold his penknife, blow the dust from the wood he has been whittling, and set a tiny carving down on the wall. A perfect miniature soldier.

Maggie Ellis gasps with surprise. 'It does make you wonder where he gets it from, doesn't it?' she says.

4

Non had returned to the kitchen to find Davey sitting at the table reading his *Cambrian News* as if nothing had happened. She had sent Osian upstairs to dress himself and hastily wrapped the new shirt she had sewn for him in brown paper.

Now, they are all sitting around the table. No one else has forgotten Osian's birthday. Davey leads the singing of Happy Birthday, which Meg complains is pointless because Osian is not listening. Her father silences her with a look and retreats behind his newspaper.

'You wouldn't like it if we didn't sing to you on your birthday,' Wil says. He delves into the pocket of the jacket he has slung over the back of his chair and produces an untidily wrapped parcel that he pushes towards his brother, who takes no notice of it.

'You see?' Meg says. 'No point.' But she, too, has a small parcel that she gives Non to pass to Osian. 'I bought my favourite sweets,' she says, 'so if he can't be bothered to open it, I'll have it back.'

Non places her own parcel next to Osian's breakfast bowl. She looks at him steadily eating his porridge. 'I'll help you open your presents,' she says, and unwraps Wil's parcel so that the pouch it contains spills a handful of marbles to roll along the table. Osian stops eating to watch them bounce onto the flagstones. 'Your prize marbles, Wil,' Non says. 'Are you sure?'

Wil shrugs. 'When did I last play with them?' he says, and gets down on his hands and knees to gather them from the floor.

'Open my parcel for him, Non,' Meg says, and Non does as she is told. Osian immediately begins to sort the jelly babies into rows of different colours and puts a red one into his mouth.

'I'm afraid he likes them, Meg,' Non says.

Meg frowns and begins to complain that she is too close to the fire, she is too hot, what is the need for a fire on a day when the sun is blazing so hard yet again it is likely to set fire to the whole world. It is a marvel that all the while she scowls in complaint she looks like an angel, her golden hair a halo around her head.

'To boil the kettle for your cup of tea, Meg, to cook your oats, to heat the washing-up water for your dirty dishes.' Meg would try the patience of a saint, and Non is no saint and her patience is sometimes sorely tried. 'At least it stays cool in this part of the house in the morning. If you're too hot where you are, change places with me.'

'I don't want to sit next to him,' Meg says. She grimaces at Osian who would be oblivious to her disdain even if he were not busy eating the red jelly babies one after another.

'Osian,' Davey says. 'His name is Osian, Meg.' He turns over a page of his *Cambrian News*, folds the paper in half and leans it against the teapot.

Meg opens her mouth to answer; she always has an answer. Non breaks into the conversation before Meg can further annoy her father. It is difficult most times to know what to make conversation about. Every subject seems to lead to the War, and Non especially does not want that to happen now that Davey has started having these turns. Turns! she thinks, there must be a better name for what happens to Davey.

'Maggie Ellis next door was up and down the garden all night to the closet,' she says. Maybe Wil, clinking the marbles back into their pouch one by one, will give one of his impersonations of Maggie. Then she stops; even that could lead to dangerous territory. She puts her hand in her apron pocket to make sure that the soldier Osian carved when they were in the garden, in the space of just a few minutes, is still there and not set down where Davey can be upset by it. She marvels at Osian's skill. Her fingertips trace the tiny details and the smooth finish of what he has made. How does he know what to do to produce such a thing? She cannot recall where or when he first acquired the penknife, he seems to have always had it. She hears again Maggie Ellis asking if he was safe with it, and knows what she meant. Osian is not always predictable.

Wil has not heard her, Non realises. He is smothering a hearty yawn. 'You stayed out late with Eddie last night, Wil,' she says. 'Did he have amazing tales of his great adventures on the Seven Seas to tell you?'

Wil rubs his cheeks with vigour, as if to wake himself. 'He did, Non. The things he's done! It sounds a good life, seeing the world like that. He's been all the way across the Atlantic to Newfoundland and back with only—'

'That's enough!' Davey bangs his knife down on the table, rattling the cups on their saucers, slopping the tea over their rims. 'Eddie's no hero, Wil. His father needed him to stay at home after his brother died. Eddie should have done his duty and stayed, not gone gadding about to please himself.'

Duty! What a hard word that is for any of them, let alone a boy of fifteen. Where did it come from? It is not a word the old

Davey would have used, although he, himself, had always been dutiful. Non holds her breath as she sees the look in Wil's eyes, a compound of misery and mulishness.

'He says he's changing ships, so there's a berth going,' Wil says. 'On the David Morris. Cook and boy. Sailing out of Port in a few weeks after the repairs are done. Eddie says me being a carpenter should clinch it if I want it.'

Wil has always been the quiet one, the dependable one, too much put on his shoulders that he has carried without a word of complaint. Non is fondest of him by far; Meg is a trial every day.

'David Morris?' Meg says. 'That's a funny name for a ship.'

'I don't want to hear another word about it,' Davey says, not shouting now, his voice even and reasonable as he re-folds his paper and lays it flat on the table.

Wil is not going to stop. 'I asked Eddie if he'd vouch for me. He says he'll talk to the Master, William Griffiths – he's from Barmouth – some sort of relation to Eddie's father, cousin or something, that's how Eddie got on the ship in the first place.' He looks straight into his father's eyes as he speaks. 'His father knew all about it, he was happy for Eddie to go, to do what he wanted. He knew Eddie hated farming.'

Davey is barely listening now. He has that look in his eyes that is so often there since he came home, as if he is staring into a distance that they are unaware of, and seeing things they would not recognise even if they saw them.

'If Wil goes, can I have his bedroom? It'll be too big just for him,' Meg says, glancing at Osian. 'Osian, I mean,' she adds, giving Davey a sideways look. 'He can have my little room. He won't care. He doesn't care about anything.' She turns to Osian. 'I mean, you don't even care it's your birthday, do you?'

'Wil's not going,' Davey says.

'He's fifteen, and there is no duty to keep him here,' Non says. 'He should have some idea of what the world has to offer before he settles down.'

'I've got to get a move on,' Davey says. 'I've promised to work on the seating for the Festival this morning. I hope it'll bring better work our way, Wil, more interesting to you than making coffins, anyway.' He gulps his tea. 'And, Meg – you can help Non make up a bed for your cousin Gwydion. When's he arriving, Non?'

'He's not really my cousin, though, is he?' Meg says, before Non can answer. 'He belongs to Non's family, not ours.'

Non suspects that her mother-in-law has had much to do with Meg's education on family matters. 'He should be here before dinner time,' she says.

'He's travelled, hasn't he, Non?' Wil says. 'Gwydion?'

'Not as far as Newfoundland,' Non says. 'He was in Brittany last summer with some university friends.' She turns to Meg and adds, 'Next door to France.'

'I know that,' Meg says. 'I'd like to go to France. I already know a lot of French words – je parle français un petit peu – and Mademoiselle Green says I'm her best student and she'll lend me some French novels over the summer. And she says that if we had any relatives in France during the War we should ask them to teach us some of the French they learnt. What did you learn when you were there, Tada?'

Davey puts his palms on the table and lifts himself up out of his chair. 'Nothing of use to you,' he says to Meg. 'What can your Mademoiselle Green know of words men learnt when they were fighting?'

'Her brother was a captain in the—' Meg stops when she sees the look on her father's face.

'An officer, then,' Davey says. 'Well, that would be different, wouldn't it?'

Meg frowns down at her plate. She's not sure what to read into this, Non thinks. Non is not altogether sure herself.

Davey pushes his chair under the table. 'I know it's Saturday, Wil,' he says, 'but I could do with a hand on this job, just for the morning.'

As Davey walks away from the table, Osian stands up, his chair skittering back along the flagstones, and holds his hands up to stop his father without actually touching him. Osian plunges his hands into Non's apron pockets and, before she realises what he is trying to do, pulls out the soldier he carved and puts it on the table.

Davey's face darkens and he grabs the figure from the tablecloth and throws it into the fire where it immediately begins to smoulder. 'Cannon fodder,' he says in a conversational tone. 'Cannon fodder, little Osian. We'll have no more of them.'

No one moves as Davey heads for the door. Non surveys her children's faces. Meg looks astonished, Wil despairing, and Osian has no expression at all.

5

Wil leaves the house, wearing his workclothes, a few moments after his father's dramatic departure.

Non catches his hand. 'You follow your heart's desire, Wil,' she says.

He turns and hugs her, not something he does often; the Davieses are not a demonstrative family. 'I'll miss you, Non,' he says.

She remembers her father frequently giving her the advice she has just given Wil. Follow your heart, Rhiannon, he would tell her, it is the only way to live. And each time he would tell her the story, with only the slightest variations between one telling and the next, of how he had followed his heart's desire to carry on in the traditions of his mother's family, which in medieval times had been hailed as one of the great families in the use of herbal remedies, who could and would cure anyone, from paupers to princes, with their secret recipes. But his father had wanted him to pursue a career in the law and when he refused had cast him adrift without a penny. My own father, Rhiannon, he would cry, and then hug her so tightly that all the breath was knocked out of her. And then he would tell her the story, her favourite story, of how he had seen her mother for the first time and fallen passionately and helplessly in love with her before she had as much as uttered one word to him. She, too, he would say, was my heart's desire. So, follow your heart, my child, and everything else will follow that.

'Go,' Non now says to Wil, and he walks out into the sunshine, a man already, a man with a mind of his own, not the boy she had taken on in the blitheness of youth and the headiness of love when she was following her own heart's desire.

She turns away from the door to find Osian hovering behind her, her shadow child. 'You stay with me today, Osh,' she says. He gives her his usual blank look. 'Your big cousin Gwydion is coming to stay. You like him, remember?' After seven years it is still difficult for her to remember not to touch Osian. When he knocks against an inanimate object he hardly notices it. It is people he objects to. But she can hardly blame him for that; there are times when she finds people hard to contend with.

She sidesteps past him and into the kitchen where Meg is still sipping at a cup of tea that must surely be stone cold by now even in this heat. 'Help me clear away, Meg,' she says, and begins to stack their plates and cutlery. 'Then perhaps you can gather some raspberries for later.'

'Nain says that kind of thing is for servants to do,' Meg says. 'And she says I'm not your servant.'

Non takes a long, deep breath. Count to twenty, Non, she hears her sister counselling her. One, two, three . . . She will not become embroiled in an argument with Meg about the folly of some of Mrs Davies's teachings.

'That's all well and fine if you have servants to do the work, but we don't, so come on, Meg.'

'You have Lizzie German to help with the washing,' Meg says.

'That's different, and you know it. And she's Mrs Grunwald to you.' Non ignores Meg's huffing. 'Now, Gwydion will be here soon, and we need to get these breakfast things cleared away and his bed made up before he arrives.'

'When's his train?' It is almost a year since Meg last saw Gwydion, when she had conceived a girlish passion for him; a passion that may not have entirely vanished judging from her heightened colour.

'He wrote that he'd be here for his dinner,' Non says, 'but I'm not sure which train he'll be on. He knows his way from the station by now, Meg, so we'll have to expect him when we see him.'

She leaves Meg to finish clearing the table and wash the dishes, and goes upstairs to make the beds and empty the slops. Saturday's housework is usually done by dinner time, and she will have time to spend with Gwydion this afternoon. She pauses as her hands smooth the sheet on her bed – her bed! – it is Davey's bed, too. How she longs for the intimacy they shared before Davey joined the fighting. She lifts the bedcover from the floor and throws it across the bed where it billows before it drops into place. The War returned Davey, one of the few, and for that she is grateful, but the War seems to have returned the wrong man to her. He looks enough like Davey, he speaks enough like Davey, he even behaves enough like Davey that most people assume he has not changed. But it is all an act; this man who now lives with her is a stranger.

Sorrow overcomes her and she sits on the bed, her face cupped in her hands. The memory of his return hurts as if it happened yesterday. She remembers the tentative knock on the door and how she had opened it to find Davey standing there as if he had no right to enter his own house. She had not expected him, no one had news of when their men were coming home, they came when they came. She had gasped his name, then did not know what to say to him, what to do. Davey had walked into the house, Non retreating before him. And as if he had been practising the lines, he said, I'm glad to be home, Non, but there is something I must tell you. He had paused as if he needed prompting, given a slight start, then continued, I have to tell you that although I will look after you and the children, because that is my duty, we cannot be as we were. She remembers wanting to laugh, swallowing the hysteria that had risen in her throat. Cannot be as we were? she had said, the first words other than his name that she had uttered to the husband she had not seen for years. I am not fit to be your husband, Davey had said, I have fallen in love with another woman and been untrue to you. She remembers staring at him in disbelief. Where were there other women to meet on the battle-field? – that was the first thought that had come to her mind. Who? was all she could think to ask. A nurse, he had replied. Non had wanted to know her name, and still wishes she had never asked. Was not Angela exactly the name of the kind of woman a man might prefer to plain old Non?

She smoothes the bedcover, tugging it slightly to straighten its lines. She wishes she had cried, screamed, pleaded, said it did not matter to her. But she had not. She had possessed secrets of her own by then and had realised as soon as she saw Davey on the doorstep that she had very nearly made a mistake of her own, too, and had no right to plead. Would their lives be different now if she had behaved differently then? It is a question that has haunted her.

And so it had been. Sharing a bed because there was no other place for Davey to sleep. Sharing a house, sharing the children, sharing their lives. But not sharing a marriage any more, not sharing conversation and laughter, their hopes and dreams, their fears. She grieves for her Davey, who had loved her, and who she had loved in return, she grieves for him as if he were dead. More than if he were dead. She may have decided that she will not be defeated by the mystery of what haunts this Davey, by the puzzle of what he has become, but she has no idea how to begin to fight back, how to begin to find the Davey who loved her.

She lifts her head; her work will never be done while she sits here and mopes. She pushes herself up from the bed and finishes straightening the bedcover. From the linen cupboard on the landing she draws out sheets and pillowcases to make a bed up for Gwydion. She buries her nose in the sheets; last year's dried lavender still scents them and the cotton is crisp on her cheeks. She takes the bedding into the boys' room, and wonders, as she does every morning, how the two of them can breathe in here, never mind sleep. Wil says that Osian is afraid of some unknown beast climbing through the open window, though how Osian has told him this is something of a mystery to Non. Sometimes, she wonders if the fear is Wil's. It will be a bit of a squash for three in here, she thinks, then remembers that Wil may not be home for very much longer, and will not mind a bit of a squash anyway, Wil being Wil. She has no idea what Osian will think of it. Gwydion is rather old to be sharing with the younger boys but it was his idea to find work here during his university vacation and invite himself to stay, so he ought not to mind too much. He is probably used to sleeping in all kinds of places, student that he is. She unrolls the mattress that stays under Wil's bed when not in use and makes it up into a comfortable bed for Gwydion. She resists the strong temptation that assails her to lie down on it for five minutes – what would Mrs Davies say! – tidies Wil and Osian's beds, and decides to open the window wide, beast or no beast.

Non stands still by the window to watch Meg gathering raspberries, eating as many of them as she puts in the bowl, and
between each bite humming more tunefully than the bees working
the roses outside the boys' window. The faint and comforting
clucking of the hens reaches Non from the farthest part of the
garden as they scratch for titbits before the heat drives them to
lie almost comatose in the shade of the shrubs. The heat already
mutes the sounds of conversations from neighbouring houses and
the snatches of song finished almost before they are started because
the effort is too much. The heat lies like the hush of a Sunday
over everything.

Meg startles Non when she leaps up from the raspberry canes
as if she has been stung, a mere second before a roar comes from
the front of the house that seems to shake the walls. Fear makes
Non's heart pound: should she take some of her drops? No time.
Instead she runs down the stairs and out through the front door
to find a gaggle of children crowded around a monstrous black
motorcycle with what appears to be an airman on its back straight
from the pictures she has seen of the Sopwith Camels during the
War – though she was never able to imagine such graceless
machines flying like birds. But the War is long over, it cannot be
anything to do with the War.

The airman waves at her and leaps off the bike in one graceful
bound. He takes off his goggles and peels away his skin-tight
helmet to reveal a face that is one of those most dear to her.

'Gwydion,' she cries as she stumbles down the steps, her arms
open wide to receive him – for this family, her family, is demonstrative – not knowing whether to laugh or cry.

6

'So,' Gwydion says. 'Where is everybody?'

'We are everybody,' Meg says. 'It's only the boys who aren't here.'

'You're perfectly right, Meg, The important people are all here.' Gwydion smiles at her.

Meg's face blushes under her freckles – the freckles she is forever dabbing with buttermilk in the hope that they will vanish. But she has a point. Where would the men be without the women? Non remembers a line from a poem her father used to quote to her, *For the hand that rocks the cradle rules the World.* She balances the tray of food on the edge of the table, supporting it with one hand and handing the dishes out with the other. She says, 'Davey and Wil are at the castle making the seating for tomorrow's rehearsal for the Music Festival.'

'Ah, hobnobbing, are they?' Gwydion says. 'That's why I borrowed the bike – I thought there wouldn't even be standing room on any of the trains.'

'The real thing's not for another week and a half,' Non says. 'Do you need an excuse to borrow the bike?'

'They're building the stage, too, they're doing all the carpentry,' Meg says. 'Is that hobnobbing? I'm in Sam Post's choir. He told Nain I was the perfect little lady.'

'Don't start, Gwydion,' Non says as Gwydion opens his mouth to reply.

'But start on the food,' Meg says.

Gwydion laughs at her. 'So you are as clever as Non says.'

Meg preens, the clever young lady, then she wriggles and blushes, the girl child still.

Gwydion has a way with women Non notices anew. She remembers that it was always so. 'She's learning French,' she says. 'Fast.'

'Can you speak French, Gwydion?' Meg asks.

'Not fluently,' he says. 'Breton, Irish, but not a lot of French.'

'Tada can,' Meg says, helping herself to several slices of brawn.

Gwydion looks enquiringly at Non, and she shrugs. Who knows how much French Davey can speak or understand? He was over there long enough, he was over there for most of the War, languishing in the soil of the country. He could be expected to speak some of the language. But they will probably never know.

'And what about you, Osian?' Gwydion looks at the child they have all been ignoring from long habit. 'Parlez-vous français?'

'He doesn't know anything,' Meg says.

'What I think,' Gwydion says, 'is that Osian may surprise you all one day with what he knows.'

Meg pouts her disagreement.

And all this time Osian sits with his hands in his lap, far away from them. Or is he? Non wishes she knew how to reach him, wherever he is. He was the first to make her feel like this so that when it happened a second time, when Davey who is not Davey returned home, she recognised it, that withdrawal from her. But today is Osian's day whether he is aware of it or not.

'When you've eaten your meat and salad and bread and butter,' she says, 'we have a special cake. Because today is a celebration.'

'Because I'm here?' Gwydion asks.

'Don't be big-headed.' Meg gives the back of Gwydion's hand a light slap.

Non smiles at their exchange. 'We're celebrating Osian's seventh birthday,' she says. They all three look at Osian, but he makes no response to the sound of his name nor to their attention.

'It's not really his birthday,' all-knowing Meg says. 'It's the day Tada brought him home for Non so she could have her own baby. We don't know when his birthday is, really.'

Her own baby! Non is at a loss to understand from where the notion had come that she had wanted a baby of her own. Had she been needy without being aware of it? And Meg, poor Meg, has still not got over the invasion of this intruder into the family not much more than a year after Non had committed the same crime. 'He was a tiny baby,' she says. 'It's as close as can be to his real birthday.' It is also the date Davey had registered as the day of Osian's birth, along with the two of them as his natural parents. She thinks that must be some sort of crime, too.

'Happy Birthday, Osian.' Gwydion raises his cup of tea in a toast to the unblinking boy.

And as Meg rolls her eyes heavenward and carries on eating her bread and butter a miracle happens that makes Non catch her breath. Osian scrutinises Gwydion's raised cup, and then raises his own in return. A mirror image. It happens so quickly and quietly that it leaves Non wondering if she has dreamt it. She looks at Gwydion, and he smiles at her and nods. He has always known her thoughts.

Gwydion turns to Meg. 'You know,' he says, 'if you're as clever as Non says, when you're older you could go to university, like me.'

'Could I?' Meg stops eating. 'Could I really, Non?'

She smiles at Meg. 'You could if you wanted to, Meg, Why not?' It is costly enough to send Meg to the County School at Barmouth, but Non fervently believes in the necessity of education. Her own father had been an enthusiastic educator of his daughter. Non had not realised what an eccentric education she had received until her father died and she was sent to school. It had been an education that encouraged her to be curious about everything and to satisfy that curiosity. It had also been an education that made her aware of all the possibilities that were out in the world, most of which she discovered were out of her reach because she was a woman. But surely the War will have changed much of that? Women had done the work of men when the men were away fighting. Non had to give up her work as a teacher at the primary school when she married Davey, but the school had been desperate, she does not think it is too strong a word, desperate to take her back for the duration of the War when male teachers were in short supply. And because of those brave suffragettes, she thinks, she will even be able to vote at the next election.

'But what for?' Meg turns to Gwydion. 'Nain says education is wasted on women. Nain says, Look at Non. And she sent me back here when I said I wanted to go the County School because she didn't approve.'

Non thinks this is probably true, but she does not want the child to be troubled by it. Catherine Davies had relinquished Meg – at last – when it became apparent that she would continue her education. 'Your grandmother couldn't take care of you and your grandfather,' she says. 'We have the room here, and you are our daughter.'

Meg does not usually draw back from pointing out that she is not Non's daughter, but she is silent now. It may be that Gwydion is having a mellowing effect on her. Non looks at her nephew, and her love for him warms her. Maybe it is this feeling that makes him appear so handsome to her, so tall and dark-haired and dark-eyed, like one of the characters from the old tales her father used to tell her. But maybe he actually is tall and dark and handsome, she considers, as Meg smiles at him and blushes, yet again.

And asks, 'Are there lots of girls at the university with you? And what do they do there?'

'Not so many,' Gwydion says. 'There should be more. There's no reason why not. They're as clever as us men, and usually work a lot harder.'

The three of them laugh. Non wishes it could always be like this, free and easy, not having to consider what they say, not having to be fearful of straying into forbidden territory with a word or two if they drop their guard for a second.

'Is one of the girls your sweetheart?' Meg asks.

'Meg!' After Non's gasp there is silence. Something clutches at her heart. Is it fear? Jealousy? Surprise? She has never thought of Gwydion in this way.

Gwydion clears his throat and mumbles words Non does not catch.

Meg's eyes sparkle. 'What's her name?' she says.

'Aoife.' Gwydion says the name like a sigh, his face scarlet as the raspberries on the cake Non has waiting in the kitchen.

'That's a strange name,' Meg says. 'Is it Breton or Irish or something?'

'Irish,' Gwydion says. 'She's Irish.'

'And she's at the university in Aberystwyth?' Non has to know who this girl is who has suddenly turned Gwydion into this man, this stranger, another stranger that she cannot begin to know.

'No. Her father's a lecturer over from Dublin, just for the year.

He taught us Irish, and he had some of us round to his house for supper and the like. He's very hospitable.'

Non thinks again of the old stories her father used to tell her. Old, old stories. The Welsh and the Irish were always linked in them, as friends and foes. She thinks of the giant Brân who lived in the very place where Davey is working today, a brave and fearless leader who laid himself down across the sea to Ireland to make a bridge for his men to cross over when they went to rescue his sister Branwen from a cruel Irish king. She thinks, They are part of our history, the Irish, for better or worse, and we are part of theirs. Gwydion won't be lost to us.

'Is she pretty?' Meg says.

'She's beautiful,' Gwydion says. 'She has skin like cream, and blue eyes that can change colour like the sea, and black curly hair.'

Meg rubs the freckles over her nose. 'Are you going to marry her?' she asks, her voice suddenly shrill.

Non rises from her chair. 'That's between Gwydion and . . .' She stumbles over the name. 'Aoife,' she says, though she, too, would like to know the answer to Meg's question. 'Now, let's clear up these plates to make room for Osian's cake.'

'We're just in time, it seems,' says a voice behind her.

Davey. She turns around and smiles at him and as usual he avoids her gaze and greets Gwydion with a firm hand on his shoulder and a handshake. Man to man.

As Davey and Wil pull chairs up to the table, Non fetches the cake and places it in front of Osian. The child brings out his penknife, snaps it open and begins to mark out the top of the cake into portions.

'I'm not eating any of it,' Meg says. 'He's spoilt it now. He uses that knife to cut up all sorts of things.'

Non watches Osian's face as he concentrates on his task and suddenly she sees what Maggie Ellis avoided saying outright to her this morning. She sees that Osian, this child that Davey had brought home for her, telling her his mother had died at birth and his father was unknown, this child is carved in her husband's image.

7

The town's streets are the way Non prefers them – empty of people. They should be bustling this early on a Saturday afternoon, but the heat has driven almost everyone indoors. A lone boy rolls his hoop half-heartedly in Pentre'r Efail, coughing in the dust it raises. Non pulls her straw bonnet closer around her face against the blaze of the sun.

She has loved this little town from the moment she first saw it, its castle protected by a noisy garrison of crows, its narrow streets twisting up and down and around its hills, giving glimpses of the sea here and the mountains there, and its granite houses and cottages and garden sheds seeming to tumble one upon another so that the whole place is like a painting by a madman. She had welcomed it into her heart but it had not welcomed her, it had kept her outside of itself. But, she thinks, she is confusing the town and its centuries of history with its women here and now, the ones that still bob when she passes by, and the ones that scuttle out of sight so that they do not have to acknowledge her at all. As if I were any different from them, she had said to Lizzie German. Lizzie had replied, You are different, missus, no getting

33

away from it. And inwardly, Non knew what Lizzie said was true, it had been true wherever she had lived. She had always been an outsider.

Non walks around the sharp corner and down the hill through Tryfar. In every other house along here, she thinks, there is a woman I have helped during the War, whose intimate secrets I know. She counts them off as she passes: Nellie Evans, Lizzie Price, Gwen Morgan, Annie Jones's daughter Betty, old Mrs Williams in the chapel house, and even here, in one of the grand houses of Bronwen Terrace, the wife of Moriah's minister herself. You know things about them, missus, Lizzie German had told her, that no one else knows; it's only natural they're uncomfortable with it. And so Non stayed an outsider.

Her mind flitters to her family, and she gives herself a mental shake. She will not allow herself to think of those close to her who have distanced themselves, not even Davey. This afternoon is for Gwydion.

She pauses at the top of the long flight of steps down to the lower road. Voices float up to her like birds riding a thermal. She attempts to make out the figures she can see moving around the clubhouse – she wonders if Gwydion and Wil have arrived yet – but the air is too dense with heat for her to recognise anyone. She takes hold of the handrail and begins her descent.

'You've made Wil's day, bringing him down to the Golf Club on the motorbike so all his friends saw him sitting on the back of it.' Non smiles as she thinks of the expressions on the faces of Wil's friends. She and Gwydion had left him to enjoy his moment and followed the path across the links to the beach. Now she slips and slides down the sand dune ahead of Gwydion, pulling the brim of her straw bonnet forward so that it shades more of her face from the sun. Mrs Davies will be complaining to Davey again that she looks like a gypsy if her face browns much more. Never mind that Davey used to call her his little brown wren, that he liked her brown face and her brown limbs. But that was before. Before the War, before Angela! She swallows the lump that rises in her throat. Before she recognised Osian's shocking likeness to Davey.

'Non?' Gwydion catches her up, shuffling his feet through the soft sand. 'Does Wil do much caddying?'

'The salt will ruin your shoes,' she says. 'Why don't you take them off? And yes, Wil comes down every Saturday, morning and afternoon if he can. It's well-known, this golf course, you know, people come from all over to play, people with plenty of money. Wil can make more in a Saturday than he makes all week as an apprentice. He's got an old head on his shoulders, has Wil.'

'I'm surprised he's staying on, then, working with Davey. Couldn't he find something more permanent with the Golf Club?'

'I don't think he actually likes the caddying much,' Non says. 'Or some of the people who play here.'

Non does not know whether Davey and Wil will have talked any more about the sea-going venture. She is not sure she should mention it to Gwydion. Her father brought her up to speak her mind, to tell the truth and accept the consequences. But now . . . now she is like a scared mouse, small and brown, scurrying close along the edges of a high wall, keeping as quiet as possible. What happened? The world constantly shifts like this sand beneath her feet. What is right one day is wrong the next.

Gwydion puts his hand on her shoulder. 'I'm taking your advice,' he says and flops down on the sand to take his shoes off. She sits next to him and takes off her own shoes and stockings. The sand is scorching beneath her feet and between her toes. She and

Gwydion scramble to the top of the next dune and slither down the other side.

The heat is intense out here on the open beach. It wraps itself around her arms and legs and torso as if it were a woollen quilt, enveloping and suffocating. Along the miles of beach to either side of them the air shimmers. Figures appear in the haze like mirages, daubs of watery paint in a desert. The sea itself, monstrous on this beach in winter with its roaring, heaving waves, is becalmed, barely a ripple showing on its surface, reflecting the sky and the distant hills of Llŷn in its depth. A perfect mirror image; it is hard to tell what is real from what is not.

'I always forget how immense the sea seems,' Gwydion says. 'It's enclosed somehow at Aberystwyth. But here,' he encompasses the bay with his open arms, 'here you could almost imagine seeing Ireland on a clear day. It's not so far away, is it, Non?'

'Do you remember me telling you the story of Brân taking his warriors over the sea to Ireland to rescue Branwen?'

'Of course I do,' Gwydion says. 'I can't imagine what made Taid name Mam after her, though. She wouldn't stand for that sort of carry-on!'

Non laughs at the expression on Gwydion's face. No, Branwen would have turned the tables on anyone who tried to harm her or her children. Especially her children. King or no king. Non was always somewhat in awe of her sister, a little scared of her.

'But she has a generous heart,' she says. 'Not many would have taken in a ten-year-old like me when our father died. I think I must have been a handful, left to do as I liked by Tada. Poor Branwen.'

'I expect she enjoyed the challenge,' Gwydion says. 'But, Non – talking of names has reminded me – do you remember Owen, the herbalist you knew in Aberystwyth during the War?'

Non feels a warmth in her face that has nothing to do with the strength of the sun. She turns away from Gwydion to look out to sea, fanning herself with her hand as if it might raise a breeze to cool her. 'Of course,' she says, and is amazed at how calm her voice sounds.

'We were both at a meeting at the National Library a few weeks ago, he came up to me and asked if I knew you – don't you think that's odd? I don't think I look like you, do I? Anyway, we chatted and I mentioned I was coming up to stay. He asked to be remembered to you. He said you were well-named – Rhiannon the enchantress.'

She is too agitated to laugh at such a foolish thing. Not even Davey in his courting days had called her an enchantress.

'He said you'd tamed a bird just like your namesake. Though she tamed a flock of them, didn't she? Anyway, I didn't know you had a tame bird any more than I knew you had a tame suitor, Non.'

She knows Gwydion is teasing her, he was always a tease. But it is too close. Owen is her shameful secret; a secret that she has been able to push into the farthest reaches of her mind. No conversation is safe, she thinks, there are twists and turns you do not see until it is too late. She swallows hard and turns back to Gwydion.

'Herman,' she says, 'he meant Herman. He's not exactly tame, is he? You know, the crow chick Lizzie German's husband gave me just before the War. I named it after him. Don't you remember? He had a broken wing and I mended it. They took him away because he was German and Lizzie never saw him again. He died in one of those internment camps on the Isle of Man. Poor Herman.' She sees the confusion on Gwydion's face. 'Not the bird, the man. He was the kindest of men. But Herman the crow still comes to visit us.'

'So, can he talk? Herman?' Gwydion says.

'Of course he can.' She gives a laugh that sounds tinkling and false to her ears. 'But I'm the only one who can understand him.'

Gwydion grins down at her. He has grown so tall, but the boy is still there in the man's face. She puts her hand on his cheek.

'Non,' he says, the grin gone now, his face serious. 'I have something to tell you. And a favour to ask.'

A buzz of alarm runs through her at the gravity in his voice, her heart beats faster. Is it this that caused her to feel full of fore-boding when she woke this morning?

'That camp you just mentioned – where Lizzie German's Herman was sent? – it wasn't the only sort of camp people were sent to during the War, you know. Did you hear of the camp at Frongoch? Near Bala?'

She didn't know there had been such a place so close. She shakes her head.

'They had German prisoners of war there to begin with, but they cleared them out and the English Government brought all the Irish freedom fighters they feared over after the Easter Rising and locked them up there – nearly two thousand of them. Plonk in the middle of Wales so no one thought ill of the English for it. And we let them do it, Non.' His fist hits the open palm of his other hand.

Non has never seen him so agitated, so serious; her Gwydion made light of everything. His eyes seem to flash at her and she steps back.

'Aoife's cousin was there, that's how I came to know about it, I went there with her to see the place. He was locked away for standing up for his countrymen's rights, as if he was a common criminal. It makes me hot with shame to think about it.'

Non is ashamed that she knows nothing about this atrocity.

38

She puts out a restraining hand, but he ignores it, walking back and forth on the hard sand at the edge of the sea – the sea on which the sun will later lay down a red-gold path to Ireland – as if he were in a room, pacing.

'Aoife's father finishes at Aber this summer,' he says. 'And I'm going back to Ireland with them, Non. Aoife and I will be married and I'll help in Ireland's fight for real independence. We could take lessons from the Irish, Non. We Welsh, we're too subservient, we put up with everything that's thrown at us.'

He reminds her of his grandfather. Her memory of her father is a child's, and she sees him now, pacing up and down in their large, cold kitchen where the fire in the range always seemed to have just gone out because he had forgotten to feed it, always heated about some political or moral question or other, and all the more heated, she realises now, for being powerless to do anything about it.

'And the favour?' is all she can think of to say. Gwydion has made up his mind and nothing can sway him from his course.

At that, the man disappears and the boy returns, the boy who would always call for Non if he had fallen or if one of his sisters had stolen his toy away from him. And the boy says, 'Will you talk to Mam for me, Non? You know what she's like. Will you stand up for me?'

Time passes, the world revolves, the tide ebbs and flows. She puts her hand on his cheek once more. 'No, Gwydion,' she says. 'If you're man enough to fight battles for others, you're man enough to fight your own.'

8

Non thinks the heat will surely kill her, it will squeeze her heart until it stops beating and bursts. She has taken an extra dark drop again this morning but it is not enough. Meg complains incessantly, of the heat, of the work, of the unfairness of being a girl. Non cannot disagree with Meg; it is hot, the work is hard whatever the weather, it is unfair that it should be the women who have to do it. But she is unable to look into the future and promise Meg that one day men will be doing women's work the way women did men's work during the War. Somehow, it does not seem likely.

It is surely pleasanter in the garden, so she shoos Meg out to pick beans and pull potatoes and carrots, to gather eggs from beneath the hens if the heat has not stopped them laying altogether, to fetch the milk from the earthen store Davey has built in the shade of the garden wall to give her somewhere cool to keep the milk and the butter and the cheese. With the hem of her apron she wipes away the sweat that is stinging her eyes before taking the roast from the oven to baste it and return it to carry on cooking.

'Mint,' she says to Meg who comes through the kitchen door

with her bounty. 'We need mint for the sauce to have with the lamb.'

'It's hotter in the garden than it is in the house.' Meg pours water from the pitcher into the bowl on the small table by the door and splashes her face with it. 'At least it was cool in chapel this morning. Half the people fell asleep. Nain was snoring.' The memory makes her giggle. 'But I'd better not say it when she's here. She and Taid are coming for their dinner, are they?'

'As usual,' Non says. And when did that become usual? Was it after Billy died? Before that, Mrs Davies would never deign to eat anything that Non prepared. And she would not allow Non to send Billy any of her herbal preparations to alleviate the symptoms of his illness. Non was never fond of Billy, there was something about him that made her flesh creep, but he was her husband's brother, and that was that, it seemed. He worked so hard, Billy, at avoiding being recruited, faked illnesses and conditions with his mother's connivance that she, Non, knew he did not have, only to die ingloriously of influenza after the War was over. In Manchester. No one knew what he was doing in Manchester. Non had not been brought up a believer but she sometimes thought that Billy had suffered a divine retribution of some sort. Now, she hopes Mrs Davies had given up the strange idea she had conceived that Billy's name should be on the town's war memorial as a casualty of the influenza brought back by the returning soldiers.

'Mint,' Meg says, thrusting a bunch of it at her. 'And I'm not doing anything else.'

Non inhales the scent of the mint. 'Oh, Meg,' she says, 'just smell the coolness coming from it.'

'Nothing is cool,' Meg says. 'Absolutely nothing. We'll all roast to death before we get to eat the roast.'

She is pleased with that, Non thinks, as Meg forgets her threat to do nothing and takes the tablecloth and cutlery through into the dining room. She hears her open the window though there is no breath of air to be had to blow through the room.

Meg returns briefly into the heat of the kitchen. 'And,' she says, 'the stink from Maggie Ellis's closet is dreadful. She says it's your fault, you forgot to pick whatever it was you promised her to put in there yesterday.'

'How can you expect us to eat hot food in this heat, Rhiannon?' Mrs Davies seems hotter than anyone else, if such a thing is possible. It does not improve her temper.

'Mother,' Davey says, 'you'd complain just as much if we'd given you cold food for your Sunday dinner.'

Non is grateful that he allies himself with her. It is always a battle with Catherine Davies. She would prefer to remain neutral; she is not sure what particular cause this battle is being fought over. Some kind of supremacy, no doubt. Is that not what all battles are about?

Catherine Davies fans herself with her napkin. Non thinks, Bite your tongue, hold your breath and count to twenty. The sickness that only she can see eating at Catherine Davies must affect the way the woman thinks and behaves. Surely? And her mother-in-law has suffered, Maggie Ellis was right. Billy was the child she adored. To the neglect of her other three children, admittedly, but still . . . And now old William Davies, who had been Non's ally through all the dark days of the War, is slipping away from them into a world of his own. When did that begin? Was that, too, a result of Billy's death? William Davies loved his children equally, except he maybe loved Billy a little less. Non is sure he would have liked to have seen more of his daughters. Perhaps when this great heat has run its course and the days and nights have become bearable again, she will write to her sisters-in-law, Bess and Katie, far away in the south, to see if they can have a family gathering. Davey would like that. The old Davey would have liked that, she corrects herself.

'And how long are you intending to stay, young man?' Mrs Davies turns to Gwydion as she speaks.

'Until Non and Davey throw me out,' he replies, with a smile. But Gwydion's charm leaves Mrs Davies unmoved, exactly as it did when he last met her.

'That contraption of yours made a commotion when it arrived. It disturbed us all.' Mrs Davies purses her lips into what Wil calls her cat's-bottom mouth. Non buries her mouth in her napkin at the thought.

'I borrowed it from my professor,' Gwydion says, but Mrs Davies continues to be unimpressed.

'Davey tells me . . .' She dabs delicately at her mouth with her napkin as if she is about to impart something that might soil her lips. 'Yes, he tells me that you are going to be doing some sort of work for this . . . person that lives in Wern Fawr.' She leans towards Gwydion slightly and lowers her voice. 'He is a socialist, you know. Would throw out Lloyd George like that.' She flicks her fingers at Gwydion.

'So would I,' Gwydion says. 'But I'm only going to catalogue Davison's library for him, unfortunately, not help him plot the overthrow of the Government.'

Catherine Davies gasps and rears back from him. 'You're not one of these socialists, are you?' She fans herself vigorously.

'No,' he replies. 'If anything, I'm a nationalist. I don't think we should have an English Government leading us into wars and other mischief that have nothing to do with us.'

A look of utter horror appears on Catherine Davies's face. She

43

turns to her son. 'Davey?' she says, and waits for an explanation.

Wil jumps in. 'Tada's a socialist, too, Nain, didn't you know? He and Ianto Hughes are setting up a Labour Party branch right here in town.'

Catherine Davies recoups. 'Nonsense,' she says, and carries on eating her dinner, or her luncheon as she had explained to Non she preferred to call it, using the English word.

The lull does not last long. Davey lays down his knife and fork and leans towards his mother across the table. 'Well, no, Mother,' he says. 'Not nonsense. Though I'm not sure I'd call Davison a socialist. Anarchist, maybe?'

His mother stares at him. She chews her mouthful of food rapidly and swallows it with a gulp. 'Anarchist?' She looks around the table. 'Aren't they Bolsheviks? Is he a Bolshevik?' She begins to fan herself again, her napkin dipping into the gravy on her plate and splattering the tablecloth with brown specks. 'They kill their betters, the Bolsheviks. I'll never feel safe again, never. A Bolshevik!'

'He's not a Bolshevik, Mrs Davies.' Gwydion makes the mistake of laughing at her.

Catherine Davies narrows her eyes at him. 'I don't want him mentioned in my presence, whatever he is – or isn't.'

'Listen, Mother.' Davey looks at everyone around the table, as if he is addressing them all.

Non puts down her own knife and fork; she can't keep up the pretence of eating. What is Davey doing?

'The world is changing. It has changed,' Davey says. 'Working people aren't going to put up with the sorts of conditions they had before the War. We have to . . . to band together, and look after each other.'

'No one knows better than I that the world is changing. I, who

44

have lost so, so much.' The napkin comes into play again as Catherine Davies dabs her eyes with it.

Gwydion turns slightly in his chair so that he faces Davey. Osian is seated between them. Over the boy's head Gwydion says, 'You think the workers in England care about the workers in Wales, Davey?'

'They've more in common with us than with their own upper classes, Gwydion. I saw that over in France. Think about it.'

'Well, you have the advantage, Davey. You were there. But those aren't the stories I've heard. What about the bigotry? What about the name-calling? What about not being able to write home in Welsh?'

Davey shrugs. 'That was ignorance, not malice, Gwydion.'

Gwydion shakes his head. 'The English have bled us dry, Davey. And you think they're going to stop? Hah!' He hits the table with the flat of his hand, causing everyone except Osian to jump. Osian is intent on his food and oblivious to the argument raging above his head.

'Can I have the rest of these potatoes if no one else wants them, Non?' Wil, too, has been eating steadily. 'And some more meat?'

Non nods at him. She looks at Meg who is sitting with folded arms, her plate clean and pushed to the side. She gives her a little conspiratorial shrug but Meg ignores her.

'It's time we took our fate into our own hands, Davey. The Irish are doing it. So should we.'

'It won't work for them,' Davey says. 'And it wouldn't work for us. What would we gain?'

'Freedom?' Gwydion says. 'Self-respect?'

'They're just words,' Davey says. 'They don't mean anything. Solidarity between working men of all nations, Gwydion – can't you see the strength it would give us?' He turns around in his chair to the bureau behind him and rummages inside the top until he brings out a fat notebook, which he waves at Gwydion.

'You're saying that working men aren't as greedy as their employers,' Gwydion says, ignoring the book being shown him. 'There's always going to be someone who wants more than his fair share.'

Old William Davies rouses himself out of whatever alternative world he occupies and bangs on the table with his knife. 'Hear, hear,' he calls, but there is no telling who or what he is agreeing with.

Gwydion picks up his fork from the table and wags it at Davey as he orders his thoughts, and Davey jabs his forefinger at one of the pages in his notebook and shouts, 'Clause Four, Gwydion. Clause Four. It says it all. Listen . . .' He begins to read, in English, from his notebook. 'To secure for the workers by hand or by brain – see, it means you, too, Gwydion – the full fruits of their industry and the most equitable distribution . . .'

As Davey reads on panic surges through Non. How will this end? Fisticuffs? She gulps down a hysterical giggle. She wants to join in the argument, she wants to shout at them to be quiet, she wants to push Catherine Davies off the chair where she sits like a martyr, she wants to smack Meg for her insolent stare. When Davey pauses, she says, 'Is anyone going to have some pudding?'

9

After an afternoon spent under the shade of the butterfly tree in the garden Non has recovered. Supper is cold lamb and bread and butter, and salad leaves for those who want them, and they all seem lost in their own thoughts during the meal. When she leans over Davey to clear away his supper plate the strong smell of his father's pipe tobacco rises from his hair and clothes and makes her cough. Though William Davies forgets many things, he never forgets his pipe of tobacco after his meals.

She takes the plates, and the salad leaves that had wilted before they could eat them, across to the sink. The kettle is already tinkling on the fire in the range and she takes the poker to the coals to bring it to a boil. She may let the fire die down then; they can do without their late evening cup of tea in the interests of cooling down a little.

Davey had come home exhausted from helping his mother fill in her census return, exhausted in a way he rarely became after even the hardest physical work. When he arrived at his parents' house, it was to find that his mother had locked his father in the small room in the roof all afternoon. Old William Davies was distressed by the heat and lack of water and had cried when Davey released him, telling him he wanted to go home, that his mother would be worried about him. Catherine Davies could not see that she had been wrong to lock her husband away. She had told her son, He is nothing but a nuisance. Then, when Davey sat with her to fill the census return, she insisted that Billy's name should be on it because he was still there with her in spirit. His refusal to include Billy left his mother in a greater sulk than the one she had fallen into at dinner time. Davey had forged his father's signature as the head of the household. He told Non that he was thankful they no longer had to fill in a column about the mental health of any person on the form. He wouldn't have known what to write about either of his parents.

All day Non has been glad to think that the people she loves best are with her for this occasion; that the census will be completed to show that her family is all together on this one night in 1921, that it will be written down and made true so that generations into the future her descendants will see that it was so, and no one can ever deny it. Now she begins to be concerned that the picture it will present may not be the absolute truth.

She carries their cups and saucers into the parlour, a room they tend to use only for special occasions, for which Non is sorry because it is a well designed and pleasant room, looking out to the north and the peaks of Eryri. Plumes of smoke snake into the sky from the distant foothills; they have heard tales of spontaneous fires occurring on the hillsides where the grass and gorse has withered and dried under the relentless glare of the sun.

And here is her family sitting waiting for her, for their after-supper cup of tea, and for this once-in-a-decade event to begin. Meg is excited, Non can hear it in her high voice and giggles. Davey will be irritated by her girlish silliness before the evening is out. He has already laid the form on the writing table behind the sofa, filled the inkwell, and has two pens lying in wait on a pristine sheet of blotting paper. Gwydion is attempting to read the form over his shoulder and, from the expression on his face, failing.

'Strictly confidential,' Davey says, pointing to the words printed boldly at the top of the sheet.

Non is not sure whether he is joking or not. As she goes back to the kitchen to make the tea she remembers how full of jokes and laughter he used to be, and her heart leaps at this sign that maybe the old Davey is still there, somewhere. In the same instant she remembers his treachery, and her heart steadies.

She returns with the tray bearing the teapot, the sugar bowl and a jug of milk she hopes has not noticeably soured, and deposits it on the table next to Davey. 'You can pour, Meg.'

Meg busies herself, and Non sits and waits for Davey to begin.

'We've got to get this right first time,' he says. 'No blots, no crossings-out that suggest we're incapable of it.' He picks up a pen and dips it in the ink. 'The example they've given shows that I have to put my name first, then yours, Non, then you children in order of your age, then Gwydion last because he's a visitor.'

'I don't suppose it matters as long as they have the information,' Gwydion says. 'Does it?'

The pen shakes in Davey's hand and a drop of ink falls on the table. 'Quick, a cloth!' he cries.

Non fetches a cloth and mops up the ink. The tremor in Davey's hand is something as new as the attacks that send him under the table to fight his war all over again. Why have his nightmares turned into something so physical? Surely he had done his duty, more than his duty even; he had been made a corporal, he had been mentioned in despatches. Why does he have to bear it all again? She wishes she knew if any of the other men who returned suffer in this way, but no one talks of the War: they all want to forget it, to leave it safely in the past where it belongs. She wonders how many others find it erupting into their present.

'Non, you fill in the form.' Davey has moved to sit on her chair while she was returning the cloth to the kitchen. 'Your writing is much clearer than mine. I'll dictate what you have to write, so I can sign the form knowing they are my words on it.'

Non sits and takes up the pen and looks expectantly at Davey. He avoids her gaze.

'First, David William Davies,' he says. 'We'll do a whole column then go on to the next one, Non, rather than travel across. I think that will be easier. They need to know so much.'

Non scratches away with the pen, dips it in the ink, scratches some more.

'It doesn't hold much ink, that nib,' Davey says. 'Try the other pen.'

She could do this in quarter the time, left alone to do so. She waits for Davey to tell her what next to write.

'Rhiannon Davies,' he says. 'What am I doing? Just write our names in age order, Non . . . but leave Gwydion till last.'

Obediently, Non writes their names in the first column. There we are, she thinks, together for posterity on this piece of paper, that much is true – we are all here physically in this parlour on this sultry evening in June.

'Next column,' Davey says. 'Head, Wife, Son, Daughter—' He stops and looks at Osian. 'Son.'

'You can't say that,' Meg says. 'He's not your son, is he? That would make him my brother, and he's not actually, is he?'

'Surely you can say son if he's your adopted son?' Gwydion says.

Non and Davey have never admitted to anyone that they have

registered Osian as their natural son. Osian sits to Davey's left, unconcerned by all that is happening around him, his face and the way his hair grows so like Davey's that Non cannot believe she has never noticed it before.

'Son.' Wil's voice is strong and sure. 'He is your son, Tada. What else would you put?'

Before anyone can argue about it, Non writes *Son* against Osian's name, and wonders exactly what Wil can have meant by stating so strongly that Davey is Osian's father, whether he meant more than she would have seen in his words only yesterday morning. She puts *Visitor* against Gwydion's name and blots the column to dry the ink before moving on to the next one.

Here, their ages are required. 'Meg, we need years and months for this. You're very good at your numbers, so will you work them out for me?' Meg does the sums and Non fills the column, asking Meg to take Osian's birthdate as the day he came to them, the day that she and Davey had given to the registrar as his birthdate. And who is to say it was not?

Meg sighs theatrically at her request. 'His birthday was only yesterday, Non. An idiot could work it out. Seven years and one day.'

Non quickly runs down the sex column, nothing to argue about here, she thinks. Four males and two females. How unlike her own family, all those dead girls, come and gone before they ever appeared on a census return.

'What next, Non?' Wil is beginning to fidget. 'I'm meeting Eddie in a while, I can't be late.'

'Marriage or orphanhood,' Non reads. 'If you're over fifteen you have to be single, married, widowed or . . . divorced.'

'Divorced!' Meg is animated. 'Do we know anyone who's divorced? It's very . . . racy, you know. Fancy putting it on that form.'

Racy! Where has Meg come across a word like that?

'Hold your tongue, Meg,' Davey says. 'You get carried away about matters where you're too ignorant to have an opinion.'

Meg sulks, her expression exactly like her grandmother's. So, that is where she gets it from, this whole tedious sulking thing. Non does not recall anyone ever saying Meg's mother was a sulker. She shrugs slightly at the photograph of Grace hanging over the fireplace. Her angelic beauty belies the tales Non heard about her before she was married to Grace's widower.

'I have to put you down as single now that you're over fifteen,' she says to Wil who blushes scarlet at the very thought.

And then, while Meg and Gwydion are laughing at Wil's red face, she slips in *Mother Dead* against Meg's name, and *Both Alive* against Osian's, according to the instructions at the head of the column. It is enough to confuse utterly any descendants.

'Shall I put Harlech down as the birthplace for all the children?' she asks Davey.

He begins to nod then pauses for a heartbeat as his eyes flicker towards Osian. 'Harlech,' he agrees. There is doubt that Osian was born here, then. Where did he come from? She wonders if there is a penalty for giving the wrong information on the form, it must say so somewhere. She leafs through the papers that have come with it. Here it is, signed by the Registrar-General – a fine of £10. And the moral enormity of giving false information that will carry on down the generations for as long as the paper does not turn to dust! She is not at all sure about this. And yet, here is Osian, and as far as the authorities are concerned he is their natural son. And it may not have been a complete lie, she thinks. Although, contrarily, she wishes it were.

She returns to the form. 'Everyone at school has to have whole-time next to their names here,' she says, 'so, that's you, Meg, and you, Osian. What does it say about university education, Davey? What do I write next to Gwydion's name?'

Davey's concentration is intense. Is he, too, thinking of Osian's parentage?

'Whole-time,' he says. 'I don't think we have to count the work he does in his holidays.'

'I rather like the idea of being put down for posterity as an archivist or researcher,' Gwydion says.

'Is that what you're being at Wern Fawr?' Meg pulls her chair closer to his.

'Well, no, just sorting out the man's books, Meg. But it sounds grand, doesn't it?' Gwydion puts his arm around Meg and gives her a casual hug until she pushes him away, her face as scarlet as Wil's. 'Anyway, I may not be going back to university after the summer.'

Not studying for his doctorate as his parents expect? No wonder he's afraid of telling his mother about his plans.

Then Davey slaps his hand on his thigh and says, 'Whole-time. We're doing this census for this exact time here on the nineteenth of June and never mind what you were doing a week ago or what you think you'll be doing after the summer. Whole-time. Write it down, Non.'

Non scratches the words on the form. A photograph is a picture of a few moments captured by the camera when they dare not move, but this census is capturing a picture in words where they have jumped about like . . . like fleas. Does that mean it will be blurred? She does not want to hand down a blurred photograph.

And what will be happening in another ten years' time when it is done again? Where will they all be? It is hard to remember where they all were ten years ago. Davey married to Grace with no idea that she would soon be dead. Wil started at school and Meg playing with her dolls at Grace's knee. No thought of Osian on anyone's mind. Gwydion just about to start at the County School with his future stretching before him, a clever and graceful boy already. And she, a student teacher in lodgings, already at nineteen, it seemed, meant for a single life, looking after other people's children. No children for her or she would be dead. And it is true that the descendants she imagines will not be flesh of her flesh.

'Next column, Non,' Davey says. 'It's easy, look, carpenter for me, housewife for you, apprentice carpenter for Wil.'

Dip, scratch, dip, scratch. Non fills the form with her bold handwriting. Her father insisted on absolute clarity when she wrote first the Latin names, then the Welsh, on the labels for the herbs and concoctions and decoctions and ointments and pills that he made, for fear of anyone mistakenly taking or applying the wrong and dangerous remedy.

'Then put Albert's name down in the next column as my employer and Wil's, then the workshop address in the last column.'

'But Albert's never there, you say he lets you do what you like,' Meg says.

'He still employs me, he pays my wages,' Davey says. 'He still puts food in your mouth and clothes on your back.'

'It's your hard work that does that,' Non says as she blots the ink.

'Is that it? Is it finished now?' Wil stands up. 'I've got to see Eddie, Tada. I promised.'

'Two more columns,' Non says, 'but you can go, Wil. One's to say which language we speak – Welsh or English or both – and the other's putting an X by all you children's ages here. I don't know why it has to be done again when it's already on the form. Ah, well. See you later, Wil. Try not to wake Osian and Gwydion if you're very late.'

Wil vanishes from the parlour and a moment later they see and hear him leaping down the front steps and running down the hill.

'Oh – to be footloose and fancy free,' Gwydion says, making a face at Meg that makes her giggle.

Non gives the form to Davey for his signature. The tremor has vanished from his hand and he signs it neatly.

He would have made such a performance of it, the old Davey. He would have had them all laughing at him. The last thing Non wants is still to be like this in ten years' time. She has to find what is troubling him. It is something more than that wretched nurse, that Angela, she is sure of it. How would she go about finding someone who served with him in the War? Would the War Office tell her who his comrades were? Maybe she can concoct a story, pretend he is ill and needs to see his old army friends. She does not know where to begin. And she has no idea where it would all end. But anything would be better than this. Wouldn't it?

10

She recalls what she had thought last night, anything would be better than this. Is it a memory from last night that has brought on Davey's attack this morning? She has not seen the start of one of his attacks; she cannot fathom what might bring one upon him. She remembers the way his hand trembled and swallows her tears. Tears are of no use to Davey or her.

She settles on her chair. By now, she has discovered the best vantage point for seeing Davey without being in his line of sight. She glances at the clock. Five past six, and the sun is already hastening over the back end of the garden. There is no coolness even at night, no dew to soften the edges of the heat. The clucking the hens make sounds cross already; they have become so bad-tempered that they will peck her hand at the least provocation. Only two or three of them are still laying; she will have fewer eggs than usual to give to Lizzie German today.

Herman waddles in through the door, skirts around Davey without looking at him, and flutters up onto the back of Non's chair. He pulls gently at her hair with his beak, cawing softly now and then. She puts up her hand to stroke his head; she has missed him over the last few days and is glad of his company. He is almost the same age as Osian; she wonders if this is old for a crow. She remembers the tiny bundle of feathers Herman Grunwald had brought for her, jostled, he had said, out of the nest by his brothers and sisters as they fledged. The skills her father had taught her enabled her to mend the chick's broken wing. Sometimes she thinks she lavished more care and attention on the crow than she had on Osian. Herman was the one who spent time with Osian, huddling up to him in his cradle or in his perambulator – much to the horror of the town's women who peeked under the hood to catch a glimpse of the new and mysterious baby. Non had soon stopped wheeling the perambulator through the town and instead had taken the boy and the bird for walks along the roads and tracks that led up to the farms in the hills.

Davey is lying completely still under the table, except for a slight twitch in his shoulders and the tensing of his forefinger on the trigger of his imaginary rifle. Is this what it was like for him in the trenches? Did he have to lie as still as death in the mud, in the rain, in the snow, in the heat, in the stench? She has no idea what it was like.

No one had any idea what it would be like. Seven weeks after Davey brought Osian to her, four weeks after Herman Grunwald presented her with the crow, Britain had declared war on Germany. Some of the town's younger men, mere boys, had rushed to join up immediately, sensing a big adventure waiting for them. Everyone said it would be all over and done with by Christmas, the enemy routed, the proper order restored. We'll show them, the young men had promised, cheerfully and confidently, as they waved their goodbyes. Non wipes away a stray tear from her cheek. The War had gone on and on. Lloyd George had encouraged reluctant Welshmen who felt the quarrel was not theirs to realise it was their duty to fight. And Davey had always been dutiful, she thinks, always dutiful. It won't be for long, Non, he had said as he held her close to him that last night before he left, I'll soon be home. She had tried her hardest to be brave with him, for him, but already the lists of the dead were daily growing longer in the *Liverpool Echo* that the early evening train delivered without fail.

Herman is becoming impatient with her. He pecks more vigorously at her scalp, so that she moves her head away from him sharply. He caws his disapproval, and flaps his wings. Davey gathers himself into a crouch, shoulders his rifle and peers out through the fringe of the tablecloth. His head bobs like a kestrel's as he searches for his prey, his eyes beady with concentration, his mouth contorting with unspoken words. Herman flutters from the chairback and lands on the floor in front of Davey who jerks backwards then strikes out with his arm and sends Herman bowling across the flagstones. Davey, Non thinks, who would not harm a soul. She jumps from her chair to go to Herman but he stands up and ruffles his feathers, his beak pointing upwards in umbrage, and trundles out through the back door. Non does not know whether to laugh or cry.

Behind her, Davey mutters. Then he screams, 'Down, Ben, keep your head down', and dives to the floor. It is to do with Ben every time, Non thinks, that much I know, but I feel as if I am circling the meaning without finding my way any nearer to its core.

Davey's eyes are closed and he seems to have fallen asleep. She is never there at the start of his attacks but she is never there at the end either; she does not know what his reaction is to finding himself lying under the table. Does it not puzzle him? It is not something she can ask him while the chill of that look is so fresh in her heart. She walks out through the back door, following Herman's affronted footsteps, and along the path to the far end of the garden and her bad-tempered hens.

11

On Wednesday, when they arrive outside a small terraced house in one of Portmadoc's back streets at that awkward time just before dinner, Non's first thought is, Whatever am I doing here? The house has a large number thirty painted on the door but the street's nameplate is overgrown with ivy and impossible to read. It is a wonder they have arrived here at all. Catherine Davies took them in all directions to throw anyone who might be watching off the scent because she was so worried that someone would find out that she was in Port to consult a medium. In a séance. It is hard to believe that such a creature exists in Port, it is such a practical sort of place, full of shops and businesses and ships of all shapes and sizes coming and going in the harbour. Non wonders how Mrs Davies found out about the event, it is hardly the kind of service that is advertised in the *Cambrian News*. Go with her, Davey had said yesterday, she cannot go on her own, God knows what might happen to her. Go with her and keep an eye on her.

She knows that Catherine Davies's illness may be affecting what she thinks and says, so she had, dutifully – there is that word again – trotted down with her mother-in-law to catch the mid-morning train to Port, only to find on the way that Catherine was pretending that the visit to the medium was for the sake of poor Elsie Thomas, and that she had persuaded Elsie that she would find out exactly what happened to her Benjamin if she went along. So, when they reached the station, there was Elsie, sweltering in her best dress made of winter-weight black wool, waiting for them.

Their first knock on the door of Number Thirty has produced no result.

'Knock harder, Rhiannon,' Catherine Davies says. She prods Non with her parasol, black in respect to Billy. 'I wrote a week ago – we are expected.'

Expected! So this has been arranged, letters through the post back and forth, time taken. This has been on the knitting needles for some time. Non knocks sharply on the door. She does not know anything good about mediums nor these meetings they hold with the dead, these séances. She knows they are all the rage among the well-to-do and the gullible and the heartbroken people left behind without hope by the victims of the War, people who find it difficult to believe their husbands and sons and brothers are dead when they have no bodies to bury and grieve over. She knows they take advantage of desperate people like Elsie.

The door creaks open. The hinges need a drop of oil – Davey would not have let them get into that state – but Non supposes it is intended to add to the atmosphere. A tiny girl dressed from head to foot in a white filmy costume, as if she has just arrived from the land of the fairy people, gestures them to enter without saying a word. Non wonders if she has the same problem as Osian, but the child allows Elsie Thomas to pat her on the head without screeching the way Osian would have done. The door creaks again as it is closed behind them, and Non finds herself standing much too close to her mother-in-law and an Elsie pungent with sweat

60

inside a narrow hallway lit only by daylight filtering through the fanlight and a mottled mirror which reflects it. She is disconcerted to find that she has no reflection in the mirror, though she can see both Catherine Davies and Elsie, who are behind her – but then she glimpses herself with relief when she moves after the child who now seems to have vanished into the bowels of what had promised to be an ordinary terraced house. It is unsettling; the muggy, fusty smell of a house left unaired for a long time is stifling. Non's heartbeat is erratic today as it is. She is aware of it. No one should be aware of her heart beating, she thinks, it makes one feel too mortal. The days when she is not aware of the beat of her heart are Non's good days.

A door to their left swings open, silently this time, and a disembodied voice cries out. 'Enter,' it says in English, though the accent is so strange here in this house in Port's back streets that Non cannot immediately place it.

Catherine Davies pushes her to enter the room first. Non stumbles into a dark void before her eyes become accustomed to the even dimmer light in this room. She can hear the squeak of Elsie Thomas's asthmatic breath at her shoulder. She must make her some oil of thyme, surely Davey can't object to that. And some herbs would freshen this room considerably; fresh air would be even better.

'Welcome,' the sonorous voice says. 'You are Mrs Davies?'

Non is about to agree in amazement that she is indeed Mrs Davies when it occurs to her that she is not the Mrs Davies the medium, if this is the medium, is expecting. She stands aside to let Catherine Davies move forward.

'I am Mrs Davies,' stresses her mother-in-law as if Non has no claim to the name at all. 'It is I who wrote to you on behalf of my dear friend here who lost her only son in the cruel fields of

61

Flanders and would like to know that he did not suffer.'

Non is ashamed of the words that enter her mind to describe her mother-in-law.

'I want him come home,' Elsie says in her broken English. 'Is all I want.'

'Please,' the woman says, 'be seated around this table with me.'

Non can barely see the table. She takes hold of Elsie's hand and leads her to sit so that she, Non, is between Elsie and the medium. Catherine Davies is left to take the remaining chair.

'I am Madame Leblanc,' the medium says. 'And I am so very familiar with the fields of Flanders and those dear departed who lie beneath them.'

Madame Leblanc! What is a Frenchwoman doing in Port? Has she sailed in on one of the ships?

Mrs Davies is having trouble with her chair, though Elsie is seated with her hands clasped together in front of her on the table and her eyes closed looking for all the world as if she is an old hand at this. Non smiles at the thought of the instructions Elsie was given by Catherine Davies during the train journey detailing exactly how she ought to behave once they reached the house.

'Move your chair nearer to Non's, Elsie,' Catherine Davies says, pushing Elsie in Non's direction.

Elsie does as she is told, as always, and Mrs Davies yanks her chair from beneath the table and manages to sit down. Her bulk must make life difficult for her, especially in this weather. Non can feel sweat running in rivulets down the nape of her neck and between her breasts, but there is little she can do about it. Her heart seems to be drumming beneath her ribcage.

'Please hold the hand of the person next to you. We must form a closed circle. And please – do not speak.' Madame Leblanc's accent is more pronounced now. She makes fluttering gestures with her hands, and calls out 'Esmé, ma chérie.' The child appears; she draws a curtain of muslin over the doorway, then vanishes into the darkness behind Elsie Thomas.

'My spirit guide will join our circle to open the door for us into the world beyond. But she will not show herself.'

Elsie tightens her fingers on Non's hand. Non is furious with Catherine Davies for using Elsie this way and with herself for going along with it once she realised what was happening. They sit in silence for what seems an interminable time. She should get up from her chair and stop the nonsense now, but she doesn't. What am I afraid of, she wonders, or am I just so heavy with tiredness that I can't make the effort?

Madame stirs and announces that someone is there with them. Non experiences a frisson of fear and feels her own fingers tightening on those of Elsie and the medium.

'Billy,' Catherine Davies cries, and Non can hear the longing in her voice. 'Oh, Billy, speak to me.'

'No, not Billy,' Madame says. 'Please . . . quiet . . .' Her breathing becomes slow and heavy. 'But a B, yes – young – a boy. A child, yet not a child? Who are you?'

Ben Bach? Surely not. This is nonsense, it must be nonsense. Has the room become colder? Non shivers.

'It's Benjamin,' Catherine Davies says, 'it's Ben, Elsie. Talk to him. Ask him if my Billy's there.'

Elsie's breathing becomes squeakier. Does she understand what is going on here?

'Ben Bach,' she says, her breath wheezing from her lungs.

Madame slumps in her chair, sliding down on the seat, her chin tucked into her chest. Non thinks, She is a good actress, she is behaving just as I would expect a medium to behave. Will there be a spirit made of smoke appearing in a moment? Madame jerks

63

Non and Catherine towards her as she draws her hands in to her chest.

In the gloom Non sees Elsie's moonface turn towards her and she squeezes her hand as reassuringly as she can given that she herself does not know what is happening. Elsie squeezes back. Elsie is not as silly as Catherine Davies, whatever Maggie Ellis may think.

Non's mouth turns dry when Madame lifts her head, her eyes staring, the whites gleaming in the dark room, her mouth open wide. Non's heart thuds in her breast and she hears Elsie struggle to catch her breath as harsh noises come from Madame's mouth, and then a voice, not Madame's voice with its French accent, but a boy's voice calling in Welsh, 'Mam, Mam. Where am I, Mam?'

Elsie struggles to stand up. 'Ben,' she calls. 'Ben Bach, you stay where you are.'

Catherine Davies slips sideways off her chair, falling on the floor like a sack of potatoes. Esmé appears from the darkness at the edges of the room and lights a lamp. As she rises to help her mother-in-law, Non scrabbles in her bag for the oil of thyme she always carries in case Osian has one of his rare breathless attacks, pulls out the stopper and hands the bottle to Elsie to sniff, then turns to Catherine Davies to see the child wave a singeing feather under her nose in an attempt to revive her. Just as Non begins to fear that it is something worse than a faint, Catherine starts to cough and moan.

How on earth is she going to get the pair of them home? She does not know anyone in Port, she will have to hire a cart to get them to the station, she will need help to lift Catherine Davies. And what else? At least Elsie's breathing has eased with the thyme. She has not counted on Catherine Davies's sense of humiliation and shame. As her mother-in-law comes out of her swoon, coughing and spluttering at the smell and smoke from the feather, she looks at Non and says hoarsely, 'Not a word of this to anyone, Rhiannon. Is that clear?'

And during all this, Non realises, Madame has not stirred from her chair where she sits looking as astounded as Non feels at her powers to contact the dead.

12

Every single morning this last week she has sat in the same chair to watch Davey. And she has learnt nothing. Every morning he has re-enacted the same incident, watching and waiting, finding the strain intolerable to judge from the twitching of his shoulders and the way his finger squeezed ever tighter on his rifle's trigger, until an attack on his position seemed to take place and he would fall flat onto the flagstones, yelling at Ben to do the same.

Always Ben, Non thinks. She shivers slightly, gooseflesh rising on her arms despite the heat, at the memory of Wednesday's debacle at the séance. Catherine Davies would not speak of it on the way home and Elsie would not stop speaking of it. Non does not want to think of it, it was nonsense, she is sure, and yet . . . and yet . . .

This morning, the large mound of dirty washing in the basket by the door, which she sorted out last night ready for Lizzie German, is what is drawing Davey's attention. She wonders what it is he sees there in the innocuous pile of bedding and clothing. She feels too tired to even think of the day's work ahead of her; she has had to increase the intake of her tincture by several drops. Her eyes close. Just for a moment, she thinks. There is no point in wishing the War had never happened, but she does wish it fervently sometimes. She wishes that when she opens her eyes she will find it has all been a terrible dream. But no, here is Davey beneath the table in the throes of his own terrible dream.

It had been a strange time for them all who were left behind, as if they had gone to sleep one night and found themselves over-taken by a nightmare from which they could not wake. Many families found it difficult to manage without their menfolk – though Non knows of two women who were glad of the respite from the beatings their husbands regularly administered – but Non supposes she was one of the luckier ones. She was lucky that the school wanted her back, having lost so many of its male teachers to the War. She was lucky that Lizzie German was able to look after Osian for her. By then, Lizzie's Herman had been taken away, and Lizzie was struggling on her own to bring up three small grand-children whose parents had both died of tuberculosis. Lizzie had been glad of the money Non paid her. And I was lucky, Non thinks, to have old William Davies as an ally. He had protected her from the worst of Catherine Davies's machinations, and he had kept Billy out of her way. She was lucky, too, that she had all the skills with herbs her father taught her – unused for years, but easily recalled and practised again. Her remedies were popular, women came to her rather than to Dr Jones or Williams the Pharmacist – she does not suppose she was very popular with those two. She wonders, now, if it was one of them who complained to Davey – almost the moment he returned – about her activities, and persuaded him to stop her helping anyone.

They managed, she thinks, somehow most of the women managed, everyone helping one another. How they all waited for the postman to come on his rounds – in those days it had been one-legged old Peg. Someone would always have news, though the postal service from the battlefields was erratic. There would be nothing from Davey for weeks and then a bundle of half a dozen letters and cards would arrive. He was not the best of letter-writers, but she had expected a little love to appear in his words. Maybe it was because for months he had to write in English to her, and the writing appeared stilted and formal, like that of a stranger. She would have been glad even of those, she thinks, when his letters became less and less frequent and more and more distant.

A sound startles her from her reverie. Herman is rapping on the window pane with his beak. She has had to leave the window and door closed in the early mornings since Herman's display last week. Now, the bird's noise disturbs Davey who crawls to the side of the table nearest to the door and sits in a huddle, staring at the wash basket. He lays his imaginary rifle carefully on the ground at his side and cups both his hands over his eyes. Non edges forward on her seat; she has not seen him do this before. Davey lets his hands drop to his sides, a helpless gesture, and begins to rock slightly back and forth, his eyes closed.

Was that when the worm had entered the bud, when she thought Davey no longer cared even to write to her? She would not have known if he were alive or dead, she thinks, if it had not been for the occasional mention of his name in other men's letters home. She had felt the cruelty of that keenly. But as she watches him rock and rock she knows that she had had no notion of what he had been enduring. Who could think of home and the people they loved when they were experiencing the kinds of horrors that Davey was suffering here every morning? She wishes she had known, but she had not.

And because she had not, she had tried not to think of him. She had tried to assuage her loneliness and longing in ways other than looking ahead to how wonderful it would be when Davey came home again. She had begun to encourage attention from Owen, flirting shamelessly with him. She squirms on her chair at the embarrassment of it, a married woman behaving like a young girl looking for a husband. She knows she was not the only woman to behave in that way – some of the remedies she was asked to provide were proof of that – but that is no excuse, and neither is the knowledge that though she was foolish she did nothing improper. Her association with Owen never went that far. It had been too easy to allow the monthly visit to Aberystwyth and Owen with her supplies of herbs for the War effort to become more frequent. She had liked Owen from the start, he was a knowledge-able herbalist, and interested in her stories about her father and his work. She had lent him her father's herbal, and he had been impressed by it. She remembers now that she had felt a little sorry for him, too, there had been a sadness about him that moved her. He had been spared from the War because of his club foot, but he told Non that his family were Quakers and that he would have objected to fighting, anyway. I would have become an ambulance driver or a stretcher-bearer, he had told her. But he had not had the choice. Unlike Davey, she thinks now, Davey had to choose to leave all he loved to go and do his duty. She has not seen or been in contact with Owen since Davey returned, she had pushed away every thought of him – her guilty secret – until Gwydion spoke of meeting him. She should have been more gracious towards Owen, she thinks, he had never been anything other than kind to her. But she no longer remembers how she felt about Owen. Her feelings have been confused since the day Davey confessed his infidelity, and now there is Osian's likeness to Davey to add to the confusion. She bows her head and closes her eyes. Maybe she should—

A sudden noise startles her into opening her eyes. Davey is crawling out from beneath the table. She holds her breath for fear of disturbing him. He stands up straight, as if he is in a military parade, settles his rifle on his shoulder, aims it at the basket of dirty washing, squeezes the trigger and staggers back with the recoil, so that Non thinks he will fall over her in her chair. But Davey folds up and sinks to the ground in a heap, banging his forehead on the flagstones. Non leaps from her chair and crouches beside him. His eyes are shut, and his collapse continues slowly until he lies there, fast asleep. He will not want me here when he wakes, Non thinks. She takes a cushion from the fireside chair and lifts his head to slip the cushion beneath it.

She opens the back door, lifts out a flapping Herman with her foot as he tries to rush past her into the kitchen, turns around and begins to drag out over the threshold the basket of washing that set in motion whatever memory it was that Davey played out this morning. What was he doing, she wonders as she lugs the basket towards the area where she and Lizzie German wash the clothing every Monday. The way Davey stood and aimed his gun with such concentration had reminded her of something, and it comes to her now that Davey had settled his rifle on his shoulder and aimed and fired it just as she had seen the farmer do when he shot his mad horse all those years ago.

13

Lizzie heaves the wooden tub onto the table for Non to scrub the collars and cuffs in it. Non marvels at Lizzie: the woman is thin as a piece of string, and where her strength comes from is a mystery. She could not, she knows, manage without Lizzie German. And Lizzie is glad of the money she earns and the produce Non gives her from her garden every Monday, Lizzie's own garden being so meagre. Non used to provide salves and decoctions to keep Lizzie's grandchildren healthy; now she supplies the means and instructions for Lizzie to make her own.

'I must remember to check the pockets in everything this week, Lizzie.'

Non is still mortified at having last week handed Lizzie a shirt to pound in the big tub which had a bill meticulously made out by Davey, still in its crisp envelope, in the breast pocket. She delves into every shirt's pocket before rubbing the collar and cuffs with the bar of yellow soap and scrubbing them against the corrugations of the washboard. Lizzie takes each shirt from her, drops it into the big tub from which steam rises lazily into the still morning air, and pounds it with the dolly.

'Look,' Non says. 'In his apron pocket this time.' She waves the envelope at Lizzie and pushes it into her own apron pocket. She gives the front of Davey's apron a quick rub on the washboard and passes it to Lizzie, to add to the big tub's load.

Non is already sweltering and tired though it is barely mid-morning. Davey had left the kitchen by the time she had returned indoors from dragging the wash basket outside into the garden, and he and Wil have long left for the workshop. Gwydion has made his no doubt leisurely way down the hill to Wern Fawr and the library where his work is done, and Meg had to race, as usual, to catch the train to school, complaining as she went. And it is slow, warm work all the way to Barmouth, Non knows, each halt and station with children waiting to board, and then the long walk from the station to the school.

The first time Non had to attend school was when she was living with Branwen. A little orphan! She remembers kicking the first person she heard calling her that. She had not been exaggerating when she told Gwydion that Branwen had taken in a child who had been left to run wild. When she went to school she found she knew more than the schoolteacher about some subjects and nothing at all about others, which did not make for happy schooldays. She had to spend her days learning tasks she hated: cooking and mending, scrubbing collars and cuffs, and starching loose collars the proper way so that they rubbed the neck of the wearer raw.

The County School had been an improvement; the whole day was not spent on housekeeping tasks. But what she had learnt there was not to question, not to be curious, to learn by rote: the opposite of everything her father had taught her. When she matriculated – by a miracle, Branwen had said – she became a student teacher, thinking she would have the freedom to teach her pupils the way her father had taught her. By the time she was nineteen she had learnt that there was no place in the world for her father's daughter.

And now here she is, doing the cleaning, the washing, the scrubbing, the cooking, the mending in an endless cycle. Because she followed her heart's desire. She thought that she had found her place in the world at Davey's side, but she is no longer sure of that. Will she ever have the need or the time again for the many things her father taught her?

With the back of her hand she sweeps back the strands of hair that are sticking to the sweat on her forehead, leaving a trail of soapsuds, and catches sight of Osian watching the bubbles that rise from the tub where Lizzie is still pounding with more energy than Non ever experiences. He studies the bubbles where his world is captured in rainbow colours, as if he is trying to work out how to climb inside one of them, the way he clambers into his own little world inside the coffins in Davey's workshop. Lizzie's dolly beats like a drumstick against the bottom and sides of the wooden tub. Non is certain the wood at the bottom is thinning more rapidly than it should; Lizzie does not know her own strength. She watches the bubbles with Osian as they float up into the air and tremble before vanishing with a pop. The vanishing makes her think of Wil.

'Won't be doing Wil's workclothes much longer is what I hear, missus,' Lizzie says.

Non is often surprised by Lizzie's prescience. She has more clairvoyance in her little finger than that Madame Leblanc had in her whole body. But she has to smile when she thinks again of the journey back from Port, with Catherine Davies in a deep sulk because the spirits had snubbed her when she had taken so much trouble to arrange the whole thing, and Elsie overjoyed that Ben Bach was with her again, repeating over and over that he would not leave now that she had told him to stay where he was. Non thinks, Never again. But she wonders about Madame, who was as shocked as any of them with what happened. The fright might make her give it all up, this fooling of gullible people.

'He's a good lad, young Wil. Quiet, like his father, but he won't take no nonsense. He'll make his way just fine, don't you fret. O' course, Meg takes after her mother.'

'I never met Grace. I remember her being talked about when she died,' Non says. She hands Lizzie a pair of Davey's trousers after making sure there is nothing in the pockets. 'What was she really like, Lizzie?'

'Pretty,' Lizzie says, 'to look at.'

Non thinks of the photograph of Grace hanging above the mantelpiece, the photographer's name embossed on its corner – *H Owen, Barmouth*. Grace had never lived in this house, but Non had felt obliged to have her photograph there so that her children would not forget her; though Meg was too young when her mother died to have any memories and Wil's memories are of being smacked for no apparent reason. Grace had been pretty, fair-haired and fine-boned, and so young. 'I know,' Non says, more sharply than she means to, 'I've seen her photograph.'

'Ah, but her character don't show in a picture, do it?' Lizzie says. 'Bit too much like your mother-in-law for my liking. A troublemaker.'

'Like Mrs Davies?' Non is surprised. She has not heard this about Grace from anyone. 'Grace wasn't family, was she?'

'No, but she were more like Mrs Davies than Bess and Katie ever were. Odd, isn't it? Anything else to go in here, missus?' Lizzie stops heaving the dolly up and down and leans back to ease her spine. 'Yes, Mrs Davies met her match there. It were quite funny to watch them sometimes.'

Another photograph that does not tell the truth, Non thinks. It shows someone angelic, soft and tender, who needs to be cosseted and looked after, unlike Non herself with her straight brown hair and brown skin and the dark brown eyes that Branwen used to complain looked right through people and made them feel queer. Davey's little wren. What did he call Grace, a more rarefied bird altogether?

'Right,' Lizzie says. 'Time to put this lot through the mangle.' One at a time she draws the clothes out and hands them to Non who places them between the rollers and holds them there while Lizzie turns the handle, bending with it and pulling it up round again.

The ease with which she does the work is beautiful to watch. 'I'm sure I could do that bit, you know, Lizzie,' Non says. The work does not seem so onerous, though she is aware that the heat makes her heart beat faster and she has had to increase the number of drops she takes of her tincture again. But she does feel so tired despite the help she receives from Lizzie.

'Harder work than you think, missus,' Lizzie says. 'Just you keep pulling them out t'other side and put them in the rinsing tub.'

They work silently until Lizzie says, 'Them séances, missus, I went to one once. Thought I could talk to my Herman. Load o' nonsense.'

Non pulls a shirt from between the rollers and drops it into the rinsing water. 'I didn't know that,' she says. 'You've heard about me going with Mrs Davies and Elsie Thomas to that medium in Port last week, then?'

'Elsie can't keep anything to herself, can she?' Lizzie begins to stir the clothes in the rinsing tub with a stout stick. 'I'd have thought old Mrs Davies'd know that. No good doing anything with Elsie if you want it kept quiet.' She gives her harsh cackle of a laugh, which reminds Non strongly of her own Herman.

'I think she was too anxious to contact Billy to think about anything else,' Non says. 'I don't know how I got her home, Lizzie. She took to her bed the minute we got back and hasn't got out of it since.'

'Not well, is she, though,' Lizzie says.

Non thinks, So I'm not the only one who can see that. What else does Lizzie see? 'Well, losing Billy hasn't helped,' she says.

'She weren't well before that,' Lizzie says. 'As you know, missus.' She gives her stick a final twirl through the water and drags the mangle round to make it easier to reach from the rinsing tub, and then she and Non begin the process of lifting and wringing the rinsed clothes and dropping them into the second tub of rinsing water.

'I know,' Non says. 'It's hard to remember it sometimes, though, Lizzie. And she never has got over Billy's death.'

'I don't mean to be unkind,' Lizzie says. 'But you know, missus, not many people were that sorry to see the back of Billy. Sly and troublesome from the minute he were born, that boy. He were the one took after his mother, not them girls, or your Davey, bless his kind heart.' She plunges the clothes in and out of the cold water. Her hands are raw-red and swollen, their permanent state, despite the soothing ointments Non has shown her how to make for them.

With old William Davies's help Non had managed to avoid Billy as much as possible throughout the long years of the War. She still cannot explain, even to herself, why she had disliked him, except that something about him repulsed her.

'Mrs Davies wants his name to go on the war memorial,' she says.

Lizzie stops her work and looks at Non. 'What?'

'She reasons that the influenza came over from the trenches in

France with the returning soldiers and so Billy is a victim of the War, too.'

'I expect she blames your Davey,' Lizzie says, turning back to the rinsing without waiting for an answer.

'I think you know her better than I do, Lizzie.'

'Known her a long, long time,' Lizzie says. 'Here, give me a hand with these now. We'll soon have them through the mangle and spread out to dry.' She stands upright and looks to the sky. 'No danger of rain today.' She gives her crow-like cackle. 'So, she didn't get to talk to Billy at this séance thing?'

'What a nonsense it was, Lizzie, all that way in the heat, and what for?'

'People want to know, don't they, missus? War Office isn't much use. All them lost boys out there. Stands to reason their mothers and wives and sisters want to know what happened to them, don't it?'

'Yes, I know that, Lizzie, I understand that, but the woman was so obviously a fake. How can people be so foolish?' Belatedly, Non remembers that Lizzie has just told her that she went to a medium to make contact with Herman. The information about how he had died in the internment camp had been just as vague as some of the information that had come back about missing and dead soldiers. At least Davey is alive. Confusion fills her mind like a cloud as she thinks of Davey. She does not know what to think, what to believe. The only thing she is sure of is that she must do something, take some action to help him. If nothing else, she thinks, it is her duty. Her duty!

'I don't know, though.' Lizzie shakes her head as she cranks the handle on the mangle, and Non pulls the shirts out the other side, then the aprons, and shakes them out as well as she can and spreads them on the clothesline to bake in the sun. She sighs at the thought of the ironing they will take. Oh, what she would give for just a puff of wind.

'What about that voice that came out of her at the end, then?' Lizzie bursts out. 'Elsie told me it were her Ben Bach for sure.'

Non hears the voice again and sees the look of shock on Madame's face. She thinks, I don't know what that was about. She pulls the last apron from between the rollers and shakes it out.

Lizzie begins to wipe the rollers dry, picking stray bits of lint from them. 'Ben Bach used to shout like that you know, missus, when he were little. Where am I, Mam, he'd go, used to make the other boys laugh. And old Elsie – well, young Elsie then – she used to run out the back door shouting, You stay where you are, Ben Bach, I'll find you. Poor Elsie, she should never've had him, but there you are. No one ever knew who his father was, don't think Elsie knew.' Lizzie gives the mangle a final wipe and sighs. 'Heart of gold, though, and she lived for that boy. Poor Elsie. At least she's content now that he's there, wherever it is, waiting for her to find him.'

14

It is too hot to build up the fire but Non has to do so this morning to heat the smoothing irons. The pile of clothing is back in the basket after yesterday's wash – clean and dry now, and waiting to be ironed. She does not feel up to the work, she is tired – from the heat, from rising so early morning after morning with Davey, from the sheer effort of watching him suffer. Today he had gone through exactly the same scene as he had yesterday: crawled from under the table, stood up ramrod straight, and aimed and shot at someone or something. Whatever Davey was doing, she thinks, was not done in the heat of battle, it was too deliberate. And surely if he had been aiming at a rabbit or bird for the pot, or even at a horse, he would not be re-living it in this way. She does not understand, but she does know that the experience is exhausting Davey. He had left for work ashen-faced and so grim with tension that she wished he could go back to his bed and sleep for a day.

She shovels coals onto the fire and takes off her coarse apron, giving it a shake as she turns to hang it from the back of the door. The rustle in its pocket reminds her of the bill she stuffed into it yesterday, and she takes the envelope out to put it aside for Davey. She glances at it to see who it is for and sees that it is addressed to Davey, at the workshop. The handwriting is delicate, done with a fine nib and pale ink, the tops and tails of the letters curving and curling. She thinks, Someone has an artistic clerk to send out their bills. Then she notices the postmark. She looks at the envelope for a long time, the fire and her ironing forgotten. Should she see what it is? An envelope postmarked London may hold a clue. And she will be looking for Davey's sake. She takes out the single sheet of paper inside the neatly cut envelope and reads the words written on it in the beautiful and obviously feminine writing. She knows the name at the end of the letter too well. Angela.

She lays the letter face down on the table and stares out into the garden through the open door. The hens cluck disconsolately, the bees drone, Herman stands on the threshold with his head on one side and watches her with his bright brown eyes for a while, then flies away. She picks up the sheet of paper and re-reads what is written on it. It has not changed. Davey had told her he had betrayed her with this nurse, this Angela. But the letter says not. In no uncertain terms. She reads the letter once more. I never believed it, she thinks, I never believed Davey could do such a thing. The room revolves around her, faster and faster. She bends forward with her head between her knees until she feels steady. The letter has scrunched in her hand; she smoothes it flat. It must be true, she thinks, it feels true. But . . . Davey has made us live for more than two years as if he had done this thing. Why? Why did he invent such a story? It has made us so unhappy. And yet again, she remembers, there is Osian . . .

The dying fire sighs in the grate and galvanises her into action. She shovels more coal on the embers and blows them alight with the bellows. She sets her smoothing irons to heat. The letter has turned everything on its head, but the ironing has to be done. So, she scatters drops of water onto the dry and wrinkled shirts and aprons and trousers and handkerchiefs and blouses and skirts and underclothes from the previous day's wash and rolls them tight for the dampness to spread through them evenly. Then she takes her first iron from the fire and cleans it and begins to iron the damp articles – on which the words of Angela's letter seem to be imprinted – until they are free of their wrinkles and creases, then hangs them on the pulley above the range to air. When her iron becomes too cool she swaps it for the hot one waiting on the range, and by the time Osian comes home from school she has ironed all that needs ironing. She is tired, hot, hungry, and still puzzled – she is no nearer the answer to the mystery that the letter presents than she was when she began the ironing.

She prepares bread and cheese for herself and Osian to eat. 'We'll go to meet Tada and Wil from the workshop,' she tells him. Osian likes being in the workshop amid the sawdust and the scents of the wood – though it is difficult to tell for sure – and she longs to ask Davey about the letter.

'We've come to visit you, Osian and I, and to walk you home,' Non says as she walks in through the workshop door. Osian immediately vanishes into one of the coffins lining the back wall. Davey stops what he is doing and looks towards her, not at her but at something through and beyond her.

'Wil's gone down to the station to meet an order off the five o'clock train,' he says. 'And I'm very busy, Non, can't stop. Did you hear old Evan Williams died? Got to get the coffin made today, in oak, none of the ones at the back will do. Pity the family didn't care about him as much when he was alive. Funeral tomorrow, because of the weather.'

'No, I didn't hear,' Non says. 'But I've been ironing all day. I haven't seen anyone to talk to.'

'They found him first thing,' Davey says. 'Been dead since Sunday night they think. Flies busy already. State he's in we can't leave the coffin open.'

Non knows the man's daughter, knows things about Evan Williams that Davey won't know; knows he was unkind, a bully, violent sometimes, not a man his daughter willingly went to visit. Maybe she wants to make sure he is well nailed down in a sturdy oak coffin.

The letter rustles in her skirt pocket as she turns around to look out of the door. She has read the words so many times that they whirl in her mind. And she has written down the return address in case Davey wants the letter back.

She had hoped Wil would take Osian off with him to the back of the workshop somewhere, as he usually did when they went there, and keep a watch over him so that she could talk to Davey.

But Wil is not here and Davey is too busy.

'What can we do to help?' she asks.

'I don't need help,' Davey says. 'I just need to finish this coffin. Take the boy home. He'll only hurt himself or damage something without Wil here to look after him. You know how he is.'

Osian is clumsy in many ways, and yet, watching the intensity with which he examines the different kinds of wood stacked in the workshop, Non knows that he will be at home and safe here amid the aromatic shavings and dusty air. She runs her hand along a piece of wood Davey has shaped and sanded and laid aside while he makes the coffin for old Evan Williams. It is warm and smooth as flesh, a living thing that leaves a sweetness on her hand for her to inhale. Is this what Osian senses, a life in the wood that he awakens with his whittling knife and his dexterity?

'This is lovely, Davey. What is it for?'

Davey has his back to her, sanding one side of the coffin. The muscles clump in his shoulders. He is as overwound as a stilled clock. He did not use to be like this before the War. He has to hold himself tight to keep everything, whatever everything is, inside him. She thinks, He inherits that kind of control from Catherine Davies. But he never used to exercise it.

'A cabinet to go into the library at Wern Fawr when your nephew's finished sorting Davison's books for him.'

'What wood is it?'

'Cherry. He had it brought here 'specially for me to work it. First time I've made anything with cherry. See what a fine colour it is, that brown, and how different the grain is compared to the pine and oak?' Davey, too, strokes the wood, he lifts the piece to breathe in the scent of it. His shoulders relax. 'It'll polish to perfection, this.' His love of his work cannot be disguised. She wishes he did not have to spend so much of his time making coffins, but he is employed by Albert Edwards, Carpenter & Undertaker, and has to do what is needed when it is needed.

Osian has come out of his hiding place to wander the length of the workbench, stroking and sniffing at the coffin until Davey fetches a small block of light-coloured wood from the woodstore and gives it to him.

'See what you can make out of that,' he says. 'It cuts like cheese, that wood.'

Osian turns the block around, smoothing it with his hands, rubbing it on his cheek, licking it and studying the change of its colour.

'What wood's that? It's got no grain at all.' Non peers at the block.

'Lime. It's lime.' Davey is impatient. He really does not want

83

them here. But he is not happy in whatever false world he has made for himself, either.

Osian has scurried back into one of the upright coffins and taken his knife from his pocket. He will not hurt himself, this is one thing he is not clumsy doing, this working with wood.

'We'll be off then, Davey,' Non says. 'But you should have some rest or you'll be ill. I'll make supper ready early tonight so that you can have a longer evening.'

She will speak to him then, when he is rested. She will ask him about Angela. About Osian. About all the things that have remained hidden.

'I'm off to a meeting tonight, straight from work,' Davey says. 'If we're to have a proper Labour Party branch here, we have to get on with it. It'll be election time before we know it. We have to be organised.'

'Is it only for men, this meeting?'

'Well, you can't vote, can you?' Davey says. 'Not until you're thirty.'

'I can take an interest,' Non says. 'Nancy Graves is a socialist, you know. She's too young to vote but it didn't stop her being interested. We talked a lot about it when little Mary Pugh who helped her with the baby and the cleaning and cooking was poorly and I took her some herbs and—'

'Socialist, is she?' Davey interrupts. 'D'you think she has any idea what it's about, socialism? With all that money her family's got? And that husband of hers with his poetry?'

'Well, he fought in the War like everyone else,' Non says, having a fondness for poetry.

'You'd think, wouldn't you—' Davey bangs his hand down on the workbench, sending a cloud of sawdust into the air. 'All his fuss about this place – his family here all these years – and when some of the local boys went to complain about conditions and ask him to stand up for them he sent them off with a flea in their ear. Someone told them he made fun of them after, made fun of the way they spoke. They never asked his help again—' His shoulders slump. 'You've no idea, Non!'

How did they get here? What wrong turn did the conversation take?

Davey notices the sawdust settling on the wood he was sanding when she came in and dusts it away, tense and furious again.

Non looks round for Osian. 'Come on,' she says. 'We'd better be getting home. Meg will be back soon, and Wil, and I expect they'll both be starving, as usual. Bring your new piece of wood with you.'

She really does have to do something. And now she has a way to do it. *Dear Angela . . .* She rehearses the letter she will write. *My name is Rhiannon Davies. I hope you do not mind that I am writing to you like this, but . . .*

15

She had not expected to be on the train to Port again so soon. She looks at Wil seated opposite her, his hair flattened to his head with his father's haircream each side of his parting, wearing the Sunday clothes that she had pressed yesterday for the occasion. Leaving home and going to sea! But at least he will be coming home with her today, she will be the first to know whether the Master has taken him on, which she is certain he will do because Wil is such an excellent young man, sturdy and sensible beyond his age, anyone can see that and hear it when he speaks to them. And an outstanding reference from Albert Edwards in his pocket.

And in her own pocket a missive of a different kind altogether, but one that may change her life every bit as much as Wil's may soon change. She fingers the envelope. She thinks, Don't be foolish, it is still there.

She had kept her letter short in the end. Yesterday morning, when everyone else had left the house, she sat at the kitchen table with pen and paper and poured out her story onto the pages, so many of them, and when she finished she pushed them all into the fire and started again. She had written, *Dear Angela, I am Davey Davies's wife. I would like to meet you and talk to you about what happened to Davey during the War. He is such a changed man. I can come to London if you would be willing to see me. Yours sincerely, Rhiannon Davies*, and blotted the words after every line so that they would not smudge.

She took the greatest care with her handwriting, but though it was bold and clear and beautiful for its purpose, it was no match for the lovely hand in the letter to Davey, however hard she tried to curve and curl the letters. She puzzled for some time, while the unattended fire died back and the breakfast debris remained around her, about how to ask Angela to reply. The postmen knew everyone's business if it came through the post; one of them might mention it to Davey if she received a letter from London.

After she re-lit the fire and carried out her morning chores, she sat to sew a button on Wil's best shirt for the following day, and it occurred to her that she could re-use one of the envelopes in her sewing box in which her dressmaking patterns had come from London. She chose the tidiest of them, which housed a shirt pattern, removed the old stamp and replaced it with two penny ha'penny ones just in case one was not sufficient for such a large envelope, wrote at the bottom of her letter to Angela, *P.S. I enclose an envelope with stamps on it for your reply*, and folded it all up together into a smaller envelope onto which she wrote the address at the top of Angela's letter to Davey. This way, she thought, she should be able to receive a reply from Angela without arousing any curiosity whatsoever in anyone. No one paid attention to clothes patterns; that was women's work.

Now, as she listens to the train wheels singing their way over the rails, she thinks, I have become good at subterfuge, all that work with the herbs in the War, and Owen – I must put things to rest with Owen – and now this, which will probably lead to more subterfuge. It occurs to her again that she is, though in different ways, as changed from the Non that married Davey as Davey is from the man she had married. She wonders if Davey has remarked the change in her. She realises that Wil has spoken to her and she has not heard what he said.

This is an important day for him and time to stop thinking about her own troubles. 'Sorry, Wil,' she says. 'I was far away. What did you say?'

'It was only, did Osian show you this little carving he gave me?' Wil holds out his cupped hand in which rests a carved head and shoulders. 'I think he thought I was going away today and not coming back. I did try to tell him but he just gave me his blank look. You know.'

Non peers at the carving and with a jolt of recognition realises that she is seeing herself. She takes it from Wil's palm. Osian has made it from the block of lime that Davey gave him. As she studies the head her own fierce eyes stare back at her – with no sign of the timidity she sometimes catches in them when she sees herself in the looking glass – the slight frown of concentration between them etched here for ever.

'How does he do it, Non?' Wil says. 'Just look, it's absolutely perfect, he's got you just right – and, you know, it's not just how you look, is it?' He takes the head back from her and draws his forefinger down her carved face. 'It's how you are, somehow.'

'He's a bit of an enigma, little Osian, that's for sure,' Non says. 'You know, you were only a year older than he is now when he came to us. He seems such a baby in many ways compared with the way you were. And yet he produces a thing like this. And there was that soldier he carved that upset you father. That was perfect, too.'

'I didn't get a look at that,' Wil says. 'He's got dozens of crows he's done – all Herman, I suppose – under his bed. I've never seen him make anything like this before.' He turns the head around in his hands.

'So you think this is the essence of Non Davies?' She makes a melancholy face at him. 'It scares me.'

Wil laughs at her and stuffs the carving into his jacket pocket. 'Maybe I can find him a good picture of a ship, and he could make a carving of that. It's funny to think he's never seen a ship, Non.'

'It's a bit hard to take him anywhere when he won't let you hold on to him,' Non says. 'Imagine me with him in Barmouth or Port harbour trying to stop him falling into the water and him screaming his head off because I'm touching him!'

Wil smiles at her, and she can see from his smile that he understands the difficulties she has with Osian. They are both silent as the train pulls into the station at Talsarnau with much screeching and juddering. Steam hisses from under the engine and coils along the platform past their open window, causing them to clamp their hands over their mouths and noses, and try not to breathe. Wil jumps from his seat and yanks at the leather window strap but the window stubbornly refuses to close. As the train sets off again he flops back into his seat, patting his hair where it has become ruffled by the battle with the window. She imagines him out on the ocean, the wind blowing his hair into tufts just like the ones he is trying to flatten.

She wants to smooth his hair for him, the way she used to when he was much younger. 'Why the sea, Wil? Why not farming or just staying with your father, or any other thing? You can't even swim.'

'I will come back and see you all, you know, Non. Especially you. I'll miss you more than anyone.' Wil blushes at his own words.

'Oh, Wil,' Non says, 'you know I could never have managed to keep going all those years when your father was away if it wasn't for you. You and your grandfather.' It seems to her now that she must have placed a terrible burden on such a young boy.

'You looked after me, Non,' Wil says, 'and you didn't have to. You could have left me to live with Nain, same as Meg.' He grimaces at Non who laughs at his expression.

'I still don't understand why you picked the sea,' she says.

'To see the world,' Wil says. 'No, well, I don't really know, either, Non, but there was a job going and it sounded exciting – hard work, you know, but different to anything else I know about. And I've often wondered how people go on in other places, other countries . . .'

'I hope you won't be sea-sick,' she says. Or homesick, she thinks. 'And I can't imagine you cooking,' she adds, though she is sure he will do that as competently as he turns his hand to anything else.

'I haven't got the job yet, Non! I'll find out a bit more today,' he says. 'I don't think it's cooking like you do, from what Eddie said. Anyway, I think I have to do lots of other things, too. I don't mind what I do, really, so long as they take me on.'

The trouble is, she thinks, I cannot bear to think about it, I cannot bear the thought of losing Wil, too. 'Does Eddie know when the ship's actually leaving?' she asks.

'When the repairs are done, he said, but he wasn't sure how long they'd take. A week or two he thought. Maybe they'll tell me today. If they give me the job.'

'They are sure to give you the job, Wil.' She had not meant to sound so melancholy.

'Don't worry, Non.' Wil leans forward in his seat and takes hold of her hand in an uncharacteristic gesture. 'There's something else I want to talk to you about,' he says, not looking at her.

He is blushing, as if he is embarrassed. What can he have to say?

'I don't know how to say it, really, Non,' he says. 'But I've seen the way you look at Osian and Tada lately, one to the other, when you think no one can see, and all that stuff with the census, and I can guess what you're thinking.'

Non tries to pull her hand away, but Wil's grip is too tight. Has she been as obvious as that?

Wil leans closer and looks up at her face. 'Eddie told me something about Uncle Billy he thought I should know,' he says.

'Billy?' Non does not know what he is talking about.

'Maybe boys talk about these things more than girls,' he says. 'But Eddie said that Uncle Billy got himself into trouble more than once . . . well, I should say he got girls into trouble.'

'Girls?' She sounds like an echo. She thinks of all the young women she helped during the War who had got into that kind of trouble when their husbands or sweethearts were away fighting. Loneliness was a terrible thing. She knew all about that. But they were women, not girls.

'He liked them really young,' Wil says. 'You know, Meg's age and even younger. I don't suppose they knew they were expecting till it was too late to do anything about it. Well, you know . . .' Wil's face is scarlet.

Non tries to take her hand from Wil's again; he is clinging to her so hard it hurts. This must be much more embarrassing to him than it is for her. Has Wil somehow got to know about the kind of help she gave women during the War? Does he think she helped one of these girls? She is not ashamed of the work she did:

she has kept it quiet for the women's sake. But Davey had been furious when he found out – and, now that she has had time to consider it, she is sure it was Williams the Pharmacist who was to blame, not Dr Jones – and made her promise to stop treating anyone for anything immediately. No more killing, Non, he had said. Killing! She never gave a woman anything harmful after the quickening. But Davey had not been in a state of mind to be argued with.

'And,' Wil says, 'Eddie said that Nain has been paying out money on the quiet for the keep of Uncle Billy's bastards – sorry, Non – for years.'

Non is speechless. She had never liked Billy; she should have realised why. How is it that Maggie Ellis has never brought it up? Or Lizzie? Is it because they feel sorry for Catherine Davies? Or because they don't know?

'How does Eddie know all this, Wil?'

'He knew one of the girls. She lived the other side of Port somewhere. He said all the girls were out that way, that Billy didn't dirty his own doorstep. But, Non,' Wil is still struggling to explain, 'I expect that's why Tada has to keep helping Nain out with the money since Billy died.'

Non knew Davey was helping out but she had not asked why. It had seemed a generous thing to do after Billy died, that was all.

'Anyway, sorry, Non, but I thought you ought to know that Osian is probably one of Billy's and that's why he looks like Tada, like the family really. You've seen how Tada looks just like that old picture of Taid, haven't you?'

She is stunned that she has not made the connection. She had been too quick to judge Davey. But she had doubted him because she could see no other answer to Osian's likeness to him. And

Davey had prepared her mind for the thought by telling her that . . . that story about Angela. She blinks back tears. To think of Davey shouldering these burdens on his own. If only she had known. But, she thinks, I did ask him and he would not tell me. And he was so forbidding about it and I was such a new wife. She had been following her sister's adamant instructions on how a wife should behave. She must, Branwen had said, take notice of what her husband said, and do as he told her even when she disagreed with him; that was how wives were expected to behave. She should have known better than to listen to Branwen, but she had so very much wanted to be a good wife.

'Is that why Meg came home to us?' she asks.

'I wouldn't be surprised,' Wil says. 'I expect Nain didn't want trouble a lot more than she wanted to keep Meg. Anyway, they're all safe now, aren't they, all the girls? He's dead. No one was very upset about it, didn't you notice?'

'Well, yes,' Non says. She thinks back to Lizzie saying much the same thing. 'The funeral was rather small. I thought it was because it was just after the War, you know, and everyone was so sad and despondent.'

The train is slowing; here they are at Port station, the braking engine filling their compartment with steam and smoke and specks of soot. She coughs, and smiles at Wil as she loosens her hand from his grip. He blushes again when he realises he is still holding on to her.

'Shall I walk to the harbour with you?' she asks.

'Would you like to see the schooner? The David Morris?'

'I think I would, you know, Wil. And then I'll be able to picture you on the deck sailing the oceans of the world, or in the galley cooking up delicious breakfasts and dinners and suppers for the crew.'

Wil leaps out of the carriage before the train has completely stopped. 'Come on then,' he says, striding ahead of her along the platform and grinning at her over his shoulder.

16

The schooner lies in the distance from where Non and Wil enter the harbour; it shimmers in the warm air as if it is a reflection of itself in water, seeming too small and frail a vessel to go sailing across the vast oceans of the world. She wants to hold Wil back, to keep him safe, but watches as he runs off from her, with a quick backward wave, to weave in and out, round and about the wooden crates, the coils of rope, the small hills of shattered slate, damaged before they were loaded, no doubt, until he, too, looks small and frail in the distance.

Non has arranged to meet him under the town-hall clock in an hour, and promised him a pure white ice cream in a glass dish in Mr Paganuzzi's new ice cream parlour, as if he were a child still. A treat, a celebration, she thinks, because he is sure to be given the job. And a treat for her in celebration if she is able to do what she really must within the next hour.

She holds her parasol to shield her head and shoulders from the burning sun. She cannot remember a summer so torrid, she cannot remember being so vastly tired all day, every day, so that each single act or thought requires twice the effort it should take.

Her father used to comment from year to year about the changes in the seasons, one spring was never like another spring, and every summer brought more heat, unless it brought more rain. Good for some of my herbs, he used to say on each occasion, but not for others. He had been an old father to her, the last of his children, older than many of the grandfathers she knew; she remembers that he was often tired, and she thinks now that she must have been a worry, even a burden for him. She cannot use the excuse of age for her own tiredness. Is it the heat? Or is it the death her father told her was always at her shoulder creeping ever closer?

She half sits on a low wall in the shade of the tall house behind it. Such magnificent houses here in Port; there used to be money made from the slates shipped out from here and the many other goods brought in before the slate trade began to decline. The War had hastened the decline. The War had changed everything; she does not think that is an exaggeration. Everything. She tries to steady the rhythm of her breathing, to calm her heartbeat.

She furls her parasol – not the smartest parasol she had seen on her walk from the train to the harbour with Wil, but not the shabbiest, either. I am putting off what must be done, she thinks. She pulls her bag onto her lap, unclasps it and rummages inside, fingering her purse, the bottle of thyme oil for Osian's breath, an emergency bottle of Sal Volatile that she had decided to carry with her after the debacle at Number Thirty. The small box she seeks has sunk to the bottom, caught in the folds of her bag's lining. She frees it and draws it out, admiring the grain of the green leather with which it is made as she unhooks the brass clasp to open the lid. Inside, minute writing on the white lining says *John Dalby, Jeweller & Goldsmith, New Bond Street, London*; she knows it by heart. Although Non sits in deep shade, the light is strong enough to make the diamond on the ring scintillate at the opening of the lid, as if the sun and the air in this street are all it has been awaiting to bring it to life. The ring waits in its silken nest. Her mother's betrothal ring.

Her father's story of how he had come to buy the ring never tired her. She believed his every word although she now recalls that the detail of the story changed slightly with every telling. Like all the best stories until they are written down; it is the writing down that stops them in their tracks, she thinks. Osian Rhys told her how he had courted her shy and beautiful mother, whose father had a different occupation in every version but was always rich, and had eventually persuaded her to marry him. Here he would sigh in rapture. Amor vincit omnia, Rhiannon, he would say, love conquers all. He told her that he had been in London, the greatest city in England, presenting a paper on his recent voyage of discovery to distant lands where he had come across all manner of new plants and herbs and been taught, and learnt quickly, the ways and means in which they were beneficial to a vast variety of diseases, especially, and here he would pat her on the hand or knee, especially diseases of the heart, and how impressed the Fellows at the Royal Society had been, and how they had made a collection to finance a further voyage, and how he had walked out of the spacious hall and through the grand doors and along the streets where he had been blinded, yes Rhiannon, he would say, blinded by this light that came from the window of a small shop on a street corner, a jeweller's shop as he saw when he shielded his eyes from the blinding light. Here he would pause, spellbound by the memory of what he had seen. Then, he would give himself a little shake, like a dog, and tell her that the light, the incandescence, came from the most beautiful stone, the most stupendously lovely diamond he had ever seen, held aloft like a beacon in the shop window by the most delicate and exquisite silver setting on a fragile ring of pure gold. He had vowed that if it was the last thing he ever did, he would buy it for her mother, because it was obvious that it had been, and here he would give Non's hand or knee a squeeze, that it had been made for her, meant for her, she was fated to wear it. And so, he had entered the jeweller's shop which sparkled and shone like a cave full of treasure, and the jeweller had brought from the window the very ring that Non now holds. The rainbow of light from it eclipsed the other treasures, and – here Osian Rhys would grip Non's hand or knee so tightly that it was all she could do not to cry out, and say slowly – and its price was exactly the amount of money that had been collected for me at the Royal Society, Rhiannon. Down to the very last guinea.

And, now, she is going to part with it. Her most treasured possession. She had decided yesterday when she wrote to Angela that she needed to be certain she could finance a visit to London, for which she would need money for the train fare, for other travel in London, for lodging, for food, and for who knew what else. She had also decided that it is a visit she will make whatever Angela replies; Non is sure that it is in London she will find out the truth that will help Davey. He has not mentioned Angela's letter; she is not sure what this signifies, but she has decided that she needs to know more before she asks him about it. Wil's revelation about Billy has removed any lingering doubts about what she plans to do. She takes a deep, long breath to calm herself. She makes a final farewell to the ring and closes the lid on it, swings the brass hook up and around to latch it, and drops the tiny box back into her bag.

She knows where to go. She had noticed the shop with its three golden balls when she was in Port with Catherine Davies and Elsie, and wondered about it. She fastens her bag, unfurls her parasol, pushes herself up from the wall with an effort, and sets off once more.

This town is big compared to her own, and teeming with people talking at the top of their voices; with children – why are they not at school? – running and shouting; with beggars – beggars! – at street corners; with men dressed almost in rags knocking at doors here and there, so many tramps, she thinks; with dogs of all shapes and colours and sizes, fighting and barking and whining; with horses pulling carts with rickety wheels; with new-fangled motor cars and delivery vans chugging their way along the road, raising clouds of dust in their wake; with the mournful hoots of a train in the station; with distant cries and thumps and crashes from the harbour. Between the jostling and the noise and the heat she feels quite faint and is glad to see the name of the street she seeks across the road from her. She thinks, London is going to be a hundred times, no, a thousand times worse than this. Her heart almost fails her at the thought. She quickly furls her parasol and uses it as a walking stick to lean on to cross the street and to fend off the two dogs that swirl around her, yapping at each other, as she crosses.

Apart from its golden balls the outside of the shop is plain and shows no indication of what may lie inside it; but she knows what kind of establishment this is. She has a memory of going with her father to just such a place in Liverpool; she had been fascinated then by the variety of goods laid out in the window – watches, chains, ornaments, clocks, and hanging behind them articles of clothing, coats and hats, even one top hat, and rows of boots. Her throat closes up at the memory of them all, the trade in human misery they represented, but she swallows hard, holds herself upright and pushes open the door.

A bell jangles somewhere in the curtained area behind the

counter. The violence of the noise makes her start. She takes another deep and calming breath and sits on the round-bottomed chair beside the counter. When a man appears from behind the curtain she composedly takes the box with the ring in it from her bag and hands it to him. He glances sharply at her, then opens the box. He cannot disguise the gasp he gives, which he quickly turns into a cough. He produces a device from his pocket like a miniature telescope and puts it to his eye and examines the ring from all angles. The light from the diamond seems to Non to blaze in his face. He sets the ring back in its box. He reads the writing on the white silk, examining it closely. He places the box on the counter between them. He purses his little cherub lips and smoothes back his blond hair unnecessarily. He names a price.

'It's worth a great deal more than that,' Non says, but she has made a rough calculation of the sum she may need, based more on guesswork than knowledge, and the sum he names, she thinks, will be more than enough. And it will be less money to find when she wants to buy back the ring, it will gather less interest. She will not think now about where the money is to come from to redeem it.

He shrugs, holds his hands open as if to say, Take it or leave it.

'I'll take what you offer.' She lifts the tiny box from its place on the counter, hands it to him and accepts the pile of coins he gives her in return, and the receipt, which she places even more carefully than the money into her purse. Thirty pieces of silver. She knows the story, even if she is not a believer.

The light out of doors is blinding, the sun at its height, its rays powerful, the shadows cast by the buildings stunted and solid. She glances up at the town-hall clock in its elegant tower. She thought she had spent a lifetime in that shop and it was no time at all. The same two dogs are circling each other and whining in the street, and the old carthorse pulling the brewery dray is still standing outside the *The Australia*, listing slightly and munching on its oats or whatever food its owner put in its nosebag. And my life is completely changed, she thinks.

There is one more thing to do, now that she knows she has the means to go to London. She fingers the letter in her skirt pocket; the envelope is becoming just a little creased, just a little furred at its corners.

She crosses the road, her parasol held high, sidesteps a pile of dog droppings in her way and mounts the steps to the Post Office. There is little chance, she thinks, feeling as if she has taken on the role of a Catherine Davies, there is little chance of anyone I know seeing me here, posting this letter, and wondering what I am doing, why I am not posting it at home. When she hears her name called she turns quickly from the letterbox, hiding the enve- lope behind her bag, to see Wil running down the street from the direction of the harbour, leaping up and punching the air. She quickly turns to the letterbox and slides the letter into the voracious mouth, before turning back and waving, gaily, at Wil.

She smoothes her hand down the side of her skirt, down over the empty pocket. Now for their celebration.

17

Non is pouring the breakfast tea and trying to work out what the earliest would be when she might reasonably expect a reply from Angela. She thinks that if the reply comes too quickly, by return, it would say that Angela does not want to see her. And why should she, after all? No, she needs Angela to have considered her request and thought about what they might discuss and maybe how she can help before putting pen to paper in reply. I posted it yesterday, she thinks, pausing in the pouring of the tea until Gwydion says, 'Non?' and she carries on pouring. Angela should get it today, or maybe tomorrow, say tomorrow, Saturday, so that would give her the weekend to think it over, then she would post her reply on Monday, so I would get it by . . . well, say next Wednesday. Nearly a week, then. She will have to put it out of her head, in the meantime, and think about all she needs to do here to be able to go away suddenly for a few days. She has no idea, yet, how she will manage the going-away.

The letterbox in the front door rattles open and shut, which makes her spatter golden tea into all the saucers when she starts at the noise. Don't be foolish, she tells herself, Angela will only get my letter today at the earliest, it cannot possibly be a reply. Unless Angela is psychic like Madame Leblanc.

Meg scrambles from her chair, all notions of being a young lady forgotten in the race to find out what the postman has delivered to them. Non hears her scrabbling at the mat by the front door, then there is a silence, and then her feet can be heard slowly shuffling along the passageway back to the kitchen.

'Nothing too exciting, then?' Gwydion says.

'It's for you,' she says, holding the envelope and staring at it. 'From Ireland. And it's taken for ever to get here, just look at the date-stamp.'

'Well, give it to him, then,' her father says.

With a scowl on her face and a quick sweep of her arm Meg sends the letter spinning across the table to land in the bread and jam on Gwydion's plate.

'Meg!' Non can see that something has upset Meg, but cannot let such behaviour go unremarked. 'Say sorry to Gwydion for being so careless with his letter.'

Gwydion is shaking crumbs from the envelope and wiping smears of jam off with a lick of his finger. 'Don't worry, Non, it's what's on the inside that's important,' he says.

'Open it, then,' Meg says. 'Who is it from? Is it from her?' She invests the final word with a sneer.

'That's enough of that behaviour,' Davey says. 'Sit down and drink your tea, Meg.'

'You're jealous.' Wil laughs at Meg. 'As if Gwydion would have you for a sweetheart. You're too young, and too cross and too silly. And you've got freckles.'

Non gives him a disapproving glance and he has the grace to look sheepish. He is on tenterhooks. He belongs neither with them any more nor on the ship yet. Poor Wil. He ought to be able to enjoy the feeling of pleasure at being given the job he wanted so much without feeling guilty about mentioning it in front of his father. Davey had taken the news in his stride yesterday when Wil told him and shaken Wil's hand and clapped him on the back and wished him well, and told the rest that they were celebrating that evening. But . . . Non thinks, and sighs. It had not been exactly the kind of celebration Wil might have wished for. They all went to sit outside the castle to hear the oratorio that was the highlight of the day's Music Festival. Davey felt proprietorial because he and Wil had done all the carpentry for the stages and the seating. Non remembered her father speaking to a visiting colleague about hearing an open-air performance of Mendelssohn's *St Paul* in Germany; for some reason it had ended in an argument she was never likely to forget, because it left her father with a bloodied nose. She wondered if she would discover what it was about the music that had caused such strong feelings, but she did not, unless it was the subject matter – religion always seemed to arouse people to extremes. Meg was inside the grounds all evening, helping, as a result of being a member of Sam Post's choir, which had performed earlier in the day – maybe the excitement and late night are the cause of her bad temper today. Osian watched flights of birds patterning the sky against the colours of the setting sun. Wil left after half an hour to play billiards at the Institute. It had not been an entirely successful celebration.

'If you just think about it . . .' Gwydion is waving the letter at Meg. 'Aoife is still in Aberystwyth, not returned to Ireland yet.'

Meg looks down at her lap and seems to find a loose thread in her apron pocket that requires her complete attention.

'This,' Gwydion says, and flaps the pages enough to create a breeze, 'this is from my friend Idwal who went to Ireland about three months ago.' He looks at Non. 'He went to see what the situation really was like out there. I'm not so stupid that I take everything anyone says to me, however much I admire them, without checking things out for myself, Non. But Idwal says Aoife's father is perfectly right in what he's told us. That he's been quite restrained, in fact.' He sits back in his chair with his arms folded, the letter dangling from between a finger and thumb. 'Things are moving on fast. Idwal says there'll be a truce soon.' He turns to the start of the letter to look at the date. 'And look, he wrote this before de Valera met with Lloyd George in London. There's got to be a truce now.' He waves the letter in Davey's direction. 'So, what have you got to say to that, Davey Davies? A free Ireland!'

'Sounds to me as if you're all hotheads, the lot of you,' Davey says. 'It'll lead to nothing but more trouble.' He rises from his chair as he speaks and disappears through the back door before Gwydion can reply.

Gwydion pushes the letter into his trouser pocket.

'Aren't you going to read it to us?' Meg asks. 'We always read our letters out loud.'

But not our sewing patterns, Non thinks.

'News to me,' Wil mutters. 'What letters?'

'Later,' Gwydion says, ambiguously. 'I'll be late if I'm not off out soon. And I've just remembered, Non. Davison asked me to take some things to the post for him after work yesterday, and when I got there it was shut, and they're too big for the letterbox. So please, Non, dear, sweet, pretty Non, will you take them along for me later?'

Non laughs. 'Anyone would think you'd been to Ireland already and kissed the Blarney Stone,' she says. She remembers an Irish friend of her father's visiting him, and saying to her, Sure, and hasn't old Osian here been courting the Blarney Stone. And then having to explain to her what he meant and tell her the entire story of the stone. He must have wished he had never mentioned it.

'What's that?' Meg asks.

Non takes a deep breath to tell Meg the story she had been told, and at the same time Wil pushes back his chair and says, 'Was Tada going to the workshop, just now? Have I got time to drink my tea, Non?'

'Plenty, I don't think he was going off to work,' she says, 'and you, Osian, come on, try to eat some bread and butter at least. And eat the crusts, too – I don't want to find any more hidden under the edges of your plate when I clear the table.'

'Well, he'll be able to eat meat with his bread and butter for breakfast every day if he carries on like this!' Davey's voice precedes him into the kitchen. He is so loud and jolly that Non is alarmed. Loud and jolly is as unlike the old Davey as morose and far away. Davey never used to pretend anything, and now he is all pretence. Sitting here at the table, she is overcome by such a yearning for her lost husband that it is all she can do not to burst into tears.

They all, except Osian, watch Davey carry a package into the kitchen. Meg raises her eyebrows and feigns a lack of interest but Non can see that she is as eager as anyone else to see what her father has brought in.

Davey sets the package on the centre of the table and pushes the breakfast crockery aside. Slowly he peels back the wrappings to reveal a – Non is at a loss to know what to call it – a carving? a statue? a sculpture? It is a young girl seated on a rock with the sea frothing about her feet. The water looks so real that Non almost expects a wave to break and splash onto the table. The girl gazes down at her hands folded in her lap, and her face, that is both centuries old and years young, bears a look of loss and longing that is heartbreaking to see.

Gwydion is the first to break the entranced silence. 'It's you, Meg,' he says.

Meg looks more closely at the carving, and obviously, from her expression, is struggling to decide whether to be pleased or not.

'Did you carve it, Osh?' Wil asks his little brother who sits at the table, taking no notice of what is happening around him, chewing at a piece of crust as if it were a leather shoelace.

'He certainly did,' Davey says. 'And while we may know it's our Meg, your employer, Gwydion, has taken it into his head that it's Branwen, mourning the loss of her son and homesick for Wales. He wants to buy it to give as a gift to that pal of his, that American, the one in Cae Besi.'

'That American is a famous – a very famous – photographer,' Gwydion says. 'He did that book of photographs from round here last year. Alvin Langdon Coburn. I've already met him at Wern Fawr. You must know who he is, Davey.'

Davey shrugs at him. 'Oh, I know who he is, he's another of these—'

'Shhhh.' Non puts a finger out to touch the carving, to stroke it gently. Osian has brought the wood to life again, and through the wood the girl lives and suffers, the sea ebbs and flows. 'Is this made from the same wood as the piece you gave him in the work-shop, the lime?' she asks Davey.

He nods. 'And Davison is offering to pay Osian more money for this than he is going to pay Albert for the cabinet and all the other work Wil and I have done for him put together. And he wants to know if he can carve more.'

'But that's wonderful,' Gwydion says. 'That's a great talent you have, Osian.' He puts a hand out to touch the carving, his face full of wonder.

Osian munches on his crust. Has he no idea of what he has

achieved, has he no idea of what this is all about? But Gwydion is right, Osian does have a great talent, a talent that can be put to practical use. A way for him to earn a living when he is older. Non glances at Davey, wondering if he, too, can see what this means for their child.

'See,' Gwydion says, 'I was right, wasn't I, when I said he'd show us he knew more than we thought? Who else of us can do something this amazing? He's immortalised you, Meg.'

'What does that mean?' Meg is not yet persuaded of the value of this lump of wood in her image.

'It means he's made sure you'll live for ever,' Gwydion says.

'Live for ever?' Meg sounds dismayed. 'I'm not sure I want to live for ever. And get really old. Ugh! And I don't think it looks a bit like me.'

18

She had heard Davey rise from their bed this morning and the tread of his feet on the stairs, always light, as he went down. She heard him moving about in the kitchen, glugging water from the jug into a cup or glass to drink. Then she heard nothing for a while, and because she was so tired after yesterday's events she dozed, thinking that today Davey was not going to have one of his attacks, until a muffled cry made her sit straight up in bed. Then there was silence again, but she quickly mixed and swallowed her draught, rose and dressed and went down to the kitchen. And found Davey under the table.

Her instinct was to flee into the garden; she thought she could not bear to watch him suffer any more. But instead, she had half-opened the back door to let some air into the stifling atmosphere of the kitchen and sat on the chair from which she could see Davey.

And while he lies flat on the stone floor, his mind in a far country, she stares past the door out into the garden where the heat of the sun is already releasing the pungent oils in the herbs and plants so that the air is redolent of summer. This early in the morning the birds are still singing, not yet hushed by the weight of the day, and the drone of the bees is so constant as to make her think they must labour all night as well as through the day. How can it stay so . . . ordinary just through that door when this horror is happening in here? She hopes a reply will come from Angela very soon. She is sure to find a way to go to London without anyone knowing. It means more subterfuge, but she will do anything to rescue Davey. She can hear her sister's voice cautioning her against being headstrong, counselling her to count to twenty, but her father's voice urges her on, Follow your heart's desire, Rhiannon.

She wonders, as she did when Davey used to shout out during his nightmares and wake her, whether it is something someone says or does, or does not do, whether certain words or actions prey on his mind and remind him of whatever it is he re-lives time and time again. Yesterday, for instance – does what happened yesterday have any bearing on Davey's behaviour this morning?

The day had begun with more promise than usual. Davey had seemed genuinely proud of Osian's burgeoning talent, if at the same time he seemed to feel that the skill and the effort he and Wil always put into their work were diminished by it. And Meg had been persuaded, by the time she left for school, that it might be something rather special that Osian had done for her which she was longing to boast about to her friends. It had all left Non to go about her housework with a lighter heart, but by dinner time the day had been turned on its head. Catherine Davies had run – run! – to the house, clutching her heart, or at least – and here Non had uncharitable thoughts again – clutching at where her heart would be if she had one, and lamenting that William Davies had climbed out of the dining room window – At his age, Rhiannon, how could I have known he would do such a thing? –

and escaped. An appropriate word, because Catherine Davies had locked him in while she had a little nap, having been up most of the night trying to make contact with Billy in heaven, a place where she was unlikely to reach him.

Non had left off fanning her mother-in-law in the parlour's best chair and raced to the workshop where she met Maggie Ellis's niece who had been passing over the railway line on her way up to town when she saw William Davies on the station platform, and had called into the workshop on her way up the hill to tell Davey that old William Davies had not recognised her, but asked if she knew whether the Pwllheli train was due any time soon. She said she had left him in the care of the stationmaster, so there was no hurry, Mr Humphreys would not let him board the train. Davey had left Non and Wil in charge of the workshop and run down the hill to the station where his father was waiting to catch the train that would take him home to his mother who would have his supper ready for him and be worrying about him. And who had been dead for more years than Non had been alive.

William Davies had been returned to his wife who had berated him for his lack of consideration for her. Davey had given up trying to explain to her that his father could not help his behaviour, and gone back to his work.

How different that Davey was to this one, thinks Non, looking down at the stranger under her table. But it is obvious that he cannot help his behaviour any more than old William Davies can help his; for who would ever choose to suffer like this? It is as if he is fixed in this one place in his mind, this one occasion. She finds this scene he plays out more frightening than when he called out to Ben Bach. In this scene he makes no sound, all his actions are quiet and stealthy, a deadly intent inherent in them. In his mind, she thinks, he is still in France, fighting – it is as if his mind has been injured as well as his ankle. Is it possible to repair damage done to the mind? She cannot recall her father teaching her that particular skill.

She shivers as she listens to the sounds of the house, creaking in complaint at the already hot air both inside and outside its walls, and is comforted by knowing that none of the children or Gwydion are yet stirring. Maybe this can be over again before they are about; poor Meg certainly needs the rest, a sleep to calm her, because yesterday's upsets had not ended with William Davies's safe return.

Catherine Davies had arrived unannounced as they were finishing supper to say that she had to have Meg return to live with her to help her look after William Davies. Meg had turned instantly to Non, her eyes brimming with tears, and whispered that she did not want to return to her grandmother's house, did not want to give up her education and the prospect of going to university like Gwydion. Non was not sure whether to laugh or cry, then Wil, dear, dependable and sensible Wil, said that it would be illegal to take Meg from school, and he did not want to see his grandmother incarcerated, too, a barb that missed its target, and that he would stay with his grandparents each night until he went to sea, in case help should be needed. He pointed out to his grandmother, who was still insisting on Meg's company, that he would be far more useful than a mere girl – he could run after William Davies if necessary and was not afraid of the dark. Meg ceased her sniffling to say that she was not afraid of the dark and could run as fast as anyone until Non kicked her, none too gently, on the ankle, and she realised it was not quite the right thing to say. Non hoped that William Davies would sleep better, too, knowing his grandson was there to look after him.

She shifts on her chair. She can think of nothing in yesterday's events that would take Davey back to where he is now. She hopes again that a reply will come soon from Angela. In her mind she reads through Angela's letter to Davey, and it occurs to her now that the date of the letter coincided with the start of Davey's attacks. She closes her eyes, she can see the date, written in that flowing hand, as clearly as if she were reading the page – *Monday, June 13th, 1921.* Davey would have received the letter on Tuesday, the day before his first attack. It was what Angela had told him that started the change.

She will not wait for him to come out from under the table this morning, she has seen what he does, she does not want to see it again. She slips out through the door and stands in the shade, leaning against the door frame. Herman struts past, pretending not to see her; he has been in a huff since she has shut the door against him in the early mornings, and now will not enter the house at all. She hears dragging noises behind her as Davey crawls from under the table to act out his aiming and shooting. She walks further into the garden; she will not turn around to watch him. She shudders when she thinks of the farmer shooting his horse. He had aimed right between its eyes. The horse had not died immediately, it had kicked out as if it were trying to gallop away before collapsing into a twitching heap of flesh and bone.

Is that what Davey is remembering? Shooting an enemy deliberately and stealthily, the way the farmer shot his horse? Surely not. Davey would not do such a thing, he would not harm anybody. She does not want to think differently.

19

It is barely breakfast time and she is exhausted. Is it what is happening to Davey? Is it the humidity? Her heart? Should she take more of her drops in the morning? Start to take some in the evening? She slumps in her chair.

'What is it, Non?' Gwydion stops behind her as he makes his way to his place at the table and puts his hand on her shoulder.

'It's this heat,' she says. 'And I was up very early because I couldn't sleep.' A glance at Davey as she says this elicits no response. She is unsure again whether it is a pretence that he does not remember these attacks he has, or if he truly does not remember.

Gwydion pats her shoulder and leans down to kiss her cheek. 'You do feel a bit warm,' he says. 'Shall I get you a drink of cool water instead of your tea?'

'I'm fine, Gwydion. Really. Sit down and have your breakfast. It's bread and jam and tea. It's simply too hot to even hold bread by the fire to toast.'

'There's no bilberry jam left, only old blackberry full of seeds that stick between your teeth,' Meg says.

'My favourite,' Gwydion says. 'Smile at me,' he commands Meg and when she grimaces at him showing her teeth, he says, 'Not a single seed in sight, Meg!'

Non feels as if she has stepped back a little from the table, as if she is watching her family from afar. It is not an unpleasant sensation, this dreaminess. She is able to listen to Meg's complaint about the jam without needing to respond. Meg has been remarkably quiet since her panic at the thought of having to return to live with her grandmother. Maybe it has made her realise that living with Non is not as bad as she has persuaded herself it is. Though Meg will probably never acknowledge it to anyone.

The conversation ebbs and flows around Non, rather like the sea, she thinks, a background to the things that really matter, though she feels so lethargic that she cannot quite summon these things to mind, either.

'You're not listening, Non,' Meg says. 'I said, is Wil coming home for his breakfast?'

'Your grandmother might feed him,' she says. 'But if she doesn't, I'm sure he'll be here any minute now.'

'He's sort of gone away already, hasn't he?' Meg says. 'So, when he goes to sea we might not really notice.'

'How would you feel, Meg, if we said that about you?' Gwydion says. 'That we wouldn't notice if you weren't here?'

Meg turns scarlet and tears start in her eyes. 'I don't mean it nastily,' she says, rubbing her eyes with the back of her hand. 'I only meant . . . maybe it will be easier not to miss him when he goes if he's gone a bit already. That's all I meant.' She turns to Gwydion. 'I shan't miss you when you go. I don't care if you go to Aberystwyth or Ireland or . . . or anywhere else!'

Gwydion laughs. 'Sorry, Meg,' he says, 'I asked for that, didn't I? But I'll miss you when I have to go away.'

Meg begins assiduously to spread the blackberry jam and its seeds on her bread, right up to the crusts and into every curve and corner.

Non watches Davey's face during Meg and Gwydion's argument. He is not listening to them, his mind is elsewhere. When she had walked out into the garden earlier, leaving Davey in the throes of an attack, she had despaired of finding a way to help him, and her trip to London seemed as impossible as . . . as going to the moon. She thought of the heat hanging over the huge city, she had read in the *Daily Herald* about people dying there in the heat. And the crush of thousands of people, their noise filling her ears, the height of the buildings leaning over her – a thousand times worse than Port, she reminded herself. She didn't know how she would do it, this task she had set herself. And she is fearful – she, the child who had never feared anything! – she is fearful that she might not find the answer to the mystery of her lost Davey, and she is beginning to be fearful of what the answer might be.

Her ramblings are interrupted by Wil's arrival and the announcement that he is starving and that he had to stay up half the night waiting for Billy to get in touch with his grandmother and that he has also brought a letter just this minute pushed into his hand by Jackie Post outside the house. 'For Gwydion,' he says.

'You have all the post,' Meg says.

'But you don't write to anyone so who's going to write to you?' Wil says as he spreads butter, then jam, on what looks like half a loaf of bread.

Non hopes that the *David Morris* is well stocked when it sails. Wil can eat enough for six men by himself.

'Yes, I do.' Meg sounds so smug and pleased with herself that Wil and Gwydion pause with their bread and jam part way to their mouths and look at her.

'Who?' Wil says. 'Go on – who do you write to?'

Meg plays with her bread. 'I write,' she says, and looks round at them all with her nose in the air, 'to my French penfriend.' She gazes in satisfaction at their faces. 'Mademoiselle Green found French penfriends for all of us who wanted one. I have to write in French and she, my penfriend, has to write back in English.'

'She won't be getting much of a letter then.' Wil returns to his food.

'What's her name?' Non breaks in quickly to avoid another confrontation at the table.

'Jean,' Meg says. 'Jean Laurent.'

'Jean?' Wil says. 'That doesn't sound very foreign.'

'But, Meg,' Gwydion says, 'that's a boy's name in French. You say it Jean – a bit like Siôn. See? It's French for John, like Siôn is Welsh for John.'

'A boy?' A look of panic spreads across Meg's face. 'A boy – are you sure? Oh, no – I told her – him – oh, it can't be a boy. Why would a boy be called Jean? Why would Mademoiselle give me a boy?'

'Perhaps she didn't know it was a boy's name, either,' Wil says through a mouthful of bread and jam. Throughout his schooling, Wil had never had a high opinion of his teachers. Except for Non, he would say. And she had taught him for only a short time before she had to leave to marry his father.

Meg mutters to herself as if she is recalling her letter word by French word, looking more worried by the minute.

Gwydion lifts his letter from the table. 'From my mother,' he says, looking at the writing on the envelope. 'Do you want to know what she has to say, Meg?'

Meg scowls at him. 'No.'

Gwydion shrugs and rips open the envelope with his buttery

knife and scans his letter. 'Nothing special,' he says. 'Arianrhod's keeping well despite the heat. And Mam's sent you a note, Non. Here—' He passes the folded sheet with her name underlined on it across the table to Non.

Non has been expecting Branwen to write to her. Arianrhod's first baby is due mid-August, and Branwen will be expecting her to help with her herbal preparations. She has not mentioned this to Davey yet, but hopes that help for family is not banned. Non unfolds the note. Her sister has obviously written in haste and Non has trouble deciphering some of the words, but it seems that Arianrhod has not been quite as well as Branwen has told Gwydion, this being women's business, and Branwen is worried that with only six weeks to go until the birth the baby is still feet down in the womb and she fears a breech birth. As Non stares at the note, a notion occurs to her that she can use this as an excuse to go to London without having to tell anyone where she is going. She can take a ticket to Aberystwyth, as if she were visiting Arianrhod, then go on to London with a ticket from there. Maybe it is not such an impossible task, after all.

Davey is watching her but averts his eyes when she returns his look. He pushes back his chair. 'Osian can come with me to the workshop this morning,' he says. 'I've got work to do on that cabinet if I'm to finish it on time. I got held up with Evan Williams's coffin. And I've got some wood for Osian to choose from to make his next carving.'

'What did Mam want?' Gwydion nods at the note Non still holds in her hand.

Non looks at Davey. 'She needs some preparations,' she says. 'She needs raspberry leaves urgently, she says all the bushes in their garden have had their leaves stripped to a skeleton by yellow-tail moth caterpillars.' She cannot quite believe she is telling her husband these lies and is astonished at herself for thinking of them so easily. 'I'll have to take some down there,' she says.

Davey doesn't reply. He stands up and slowly pushes his chair in under the table.

Why is he looking at her so strangely? Does he know she is lying? The room becomes a blur, she cannot tell who is sitting where, she cannot see what is on the table, she is floating on air. In the distance she hears voices, frantic but muted.

'Non, Non.'

She hears Davey's voice above all others. This is the Davey she married, all those long years ago. She is lifted and held, she smells Davey's soap, feels the roughness of his work shirt against her face, hears the beat of his heart in his breast as he carries her up the stairs and lays her on their bed.

20

All afternoon, Maggie Ellis has been in and out of her house, in and out of her closet, back and forth along her garden. Non will not give her the opportunity to speak. She has too much on her mind to spend time listening to Maggie's lamentations about her bowels or whatever it is that is troubling her this day, and has avoided looking over the wall in Maggie's direction, has kept to her own work, intent on her own preoccupations.

Non is still not entirely recovered from her indisposition on Saturday. She had spent the remainder of the day and a large part of Sunday in bed, and Lizzie had helped her by doing the washing by herself yesterday, and spending this morning ironing it all. Her illness had caused a fiasco. On Saturday, Davey had put Meg, who had made a surprisingly competent and kind nurse, in charge of looking after her while he was at the workshop. But trouble had arrived when Catherine Davies discovered that Non was in bed and would not be making dinner for her and William Davies on Sunday. She had marched into the house. Non had heard her steps reach the stairs with military precision then falter a little as she pulled herself up the treads. Non had turned coward and drawn the bedcover up over her face and lain there as if she were dead. But it made no difference. Catherine Davies berated her for her dereliction of duty until she became hysterical and had to be led away home by Wil, fortuitously arrived from helping his father at the workshop.

Nowadays, Non only has to look at her mother-in-law to be reminded of the sickness eating away at Catherine Davies's faculties. Non became aware of it during the War, long before Billy died – it was not the shock of Billy's death that had brought it into being. Non has never believed, as her father told her some did, that a malevolent spirit is responsible for such sicknesses. But there are times when she wonders if maybe, just maybe, this is so in her mother-in-law's case. It is impossible to know how much of Catherine Davies's behaviour comes from her own selfish nature and how much from the equally selfish illness that is devouring her.

Now and then, doubts about her gift creep in at the edges of Non's mind. Her father had been so proud that she had this facility for what he termed diagnosis. And it is true that when she sees an infirmity, a sickness, there is invariably something there, just as, invariably, sooner or later, the sickness kills its host. When Non came to realise this, her gift became her burden. She could not understand why her father was so proud of her ability to diagnose illnesses for which there were no cures. He had said, One day Rhiannon, we may discover the cures; think what a blessing your great gift will be then. Non had learnt young not to tell anyone about her unwanted ability. And it is, she realises, yet another thing that she has kept from Davey.

Seeing is not the exact word for what she does; it is more an awareness of a disturbance inside a body rather than an ability to see into the head or stomach or leg and look at a tumour or ulcer or break in a bone. But she has discovered in the last few years that she cannot diagnose illnesses of the mind and she is thankful for this small mercy; she knows something is amiss with old William Davies, she suspects something is amiss with Davey, she fears something is always going to be amiss with Osian, but their minds are an undecipherable scribble to her. Whatever mysterious infirmities have caused them to withdraw from the world remain a mystery to her.

She shifts her position slightly. She does not think she is about to float on air again, but there is still a lethargy, a tiredness, a sense of unreality about her that she cannot quite shake off. She has collected as many raspberry leaves as the plants can stand to lose and packed them in a basket, though she thinks she may as well spread them out to dry, as they will not stay fresh to carry to Arianrhod in such heat as this. Of course, the leaves are not strictly necessary, the yellowtail moth attack having been a lie. She stretches her back and neck muscles, and pulls the fold of the sun bonnet down over her nape, to avoid any chance of sunstroke, and carefully digs out a henbane plant to transplant into a pot to take with her. She is sure the baby will turn of its own accord, that Branwen is worrying without cause, but if the birth is a breech the henbane, meticulously administered, will send Arianrhod into a waking sleep to help her through the ordeal.

All the while she works she is conscious of the letter she has tucked away in her skirt pocket. Angela's reply has arrived. Boring old pattern, Meg had sung out as she tossed the envelope to Non across the breakfast table. Non's heart had galloped at the sight of it until she thought it would leap from her breast. She could not wait for everyone to leave for work and school but this morning every one of them seemed to have had a reason for loitering. Gwydion had been the last to go, later even than Osian, because his employer had not needed him until later in the morning. Non's hands were trembling by the time she had sat at the table in the quiet kitchen, run a knife under the flap of the brown envelope and drawn out a slip of paper on which Angela had written, beautifully, an exceedingly brief note. *Do come*, it had said, *but I am not sure how I can help you. Let me know the time your train arrives, and I will meet you.* Non had read it over and over, hoping for a meaning other than the obvious. But what Angela wrote was what she meant. Non will not allow herself to be cast down by the brevity of the letter nor by Angela's comment that she is not sure how she can help. She pats her pocket to make sure the letter is still there, and feels a flash of delight that her simple trick with the envelope had worked so well. But the most difficult part is yet to come.

She has decided that tomorrow she will travel to Aberystwyth with the herbs. But instead of staying there for a few days to help Branwen and Arianrhod make preparations for the birth, as she has told Davey she will be doing, she will take the train from Aberystwyth to London the following day, meet Angela, and be back home before anyone has time to miss her. Her family and neighbours will think she is in Aberystwyth, and Branwen will think she has returned home. It is so simple. But devious, all the lying and the pretence. She is sure it will be worth it, that she will discover the truth from Angela, the truth that she is convinced will set Davey free from his turns, his waking nightmares, his dark visions – she is still not sure what to call them. It is like a fairy tale, the kind her father used to tell her, where Davey has had a wicked spell cast upon him, and she is setting out on a quest to find the one thing that will break the enchantment.

She becomes aware of Maggie Ellis again, a hovering presence behind the low wall that separates their gardens. From the corner of her eye she can see Maggie's hands plucking at the roses that ramble along the wall. She sighs, stands up and turns around fully to face Maggie and stops with her mouth agape when she sees Maggie's hat, a monstrous creation that looks uncannily like a large parasol perched on Maggie's head with veils dipping down at intervals from the spokes.

'You're very busy, Non,' Maggie says, and with a toss of her head sends all the veils fluttering. Non wishes Wil was here to see the hat.

'I am,' Non says. 'I'm off tomorrow to stay with my sister in Aberystwyth. My niece is expecting her first soon and there are one or two little problems to smooth out.' As soon as the words have left her lips she knows she should not have uttered them.

Maggie Ellis's hat quivers. 'Davey says it's all right for you to mix your preparations, now, does he?'

'This is different, Mrs Ellis. I'm just gathering these leaves and plants for my sister to use, they're just a little relaxant for the birth, nothing more.'

Maggie carries on as if Non has not spoken. 'Well, it's such a coincidence, Non, you see – this is exactly what I wanted to have a word with you about.' She leans over the roses, crushing them so that their petals scent the still air. 'Now, my sister Mary's youngest, she needs help, too – of a similar kind, if you take my meaning, Non. You know, something like the help you gave Annie Jones's daughter during the War – before her father came home on leave and found out what she'd been up to.'

Betty Jones had been one of the youngest Non had helped, the only one who might be called a girl still, at fourteen. Non thinks of Wil's revelations about Billy, and wonders. Betty had been raped, and Annie had brought her to Non, just in case, she had said, and Non had been thankful that she could help the girl.

Annie had said her husband would have killed his daughter if he found out, even though it was not the girl's fault. The decoction Non had mixed for her had been successful as far as she knew, or had not actually been needed.

'But, Mrs Ellis, I really can't do that any more. You know that.'

'I know, Non. But we are neighbours, aren't we, close neighbours? And what are neighbours for? Why, I don't suppose anyone else in the world knows about Annie's daughter except you . . . and me.'

From the distance, muted by the heat, Non can hear other people's lives going on, a snatch of song, conversation, laughter. No one has a right to take these things away from people. Maggie Ellis has no right to threaten to take away Betty's happiness. The girl is now married and expecting her first child, and has a smile on her face whenever Non sees her. And Non has no right to say what she is about to say to Maggie Ellis, but needs must. 'I've been meaning to ask you, Mrs Ellis, if you've had a recurrence of that . . . little problem you told me Mr Ellis passed on to you when he came back from Manchester that time. It's not easily curable with herbal preparations, you know, you may need to visit Dr Jones to get something a bit stronger.' Non is speaking in a conversational tone, and has not raised her voice, but Maggie Ellis starts to bob up and down behind the garden wall, her ridiculous hat making her look as if she is about to take flight.

'Shhh, Non, shhh. That was in complete confidence. You promised, Non. And I'm absolutely fine and so is Mr Ellis. And he never bothers me now. There's no need to mention it again.'

Non stares back at her. She feels a little guilty at the agitation she is causing. But, she reminds herself, Betty's treatment had also been in complete confidence. Except that confidentiality had been difficult – impossible – with Maggie Ellis twitching her curtain every time anyone came to ask for help.

'You see, Non, I promised Mary I'd ask you,' Maggie Ellis says, holding one imploring hand out over the rambling rose to Non, and clutching her bosom with the other. 'She's frantic about the silly girl. Got herself sweet-talked by some door-to-door salesman – did you ever hear of such a thing? – and it turns out he's got a wife and family Bangor way. I said I'd ask.' She looks sorrowfully at Non. 'I wouldn't say anything to anyone about Annie's daughter. Oh . . .' and she clutches her bosom with both hands, 'oh, you didn't really think that, Non?'

Non takes the cloth that covers the raspberry leaves and gathers some of the mugwort that has grown again abundantly despite Davey's attempts at eradicating it, and wraps it in the cloth and gives the bundle to Maggie Ellis. 'Tell your sister to boil these and have her daughter drink the water,' she says. 'That's all I can do for you.'

Maggie Ellis takes the bundle gingerly, as if it contains something distasteful. 'But, Non, can't you do that—' she begins. When she sees Non's face she scurries away, her hat bobbing and swaying until it becomes entangled with the purple flowers of the potato vine around her back door as she pushes her way into her house.

21

She is in a foreign country. And yet it doesn't look so very different from her own country. She had made an irreversible move into this other world when she stepped onto the platform at Whitchurch to take the train to Crewe, and thence to London.

In physical terms her journey from Aberystwyth had been uneventful. Her seat was comfortable enough, the heat not too unbearable with both windows let down to draw some sort of breeze through, even if it did carry smuts and smells from the engine's steam and smoke with it. Other passengers joined her and left her, and the stations at which the train stopped became countless. But she sat by the window with *Jane Eyre* open, and unread, on her lap; neither did the changing scenery catch her interest: her mind was too full of what she hoped to find in London.

She had felt a slight frisson of anxiety as the train drew into Abermule and she remembered the photographs of the terrible accident there earlier in the year, which she had seen in the *Cambrian News*, but no one else seemed to be thinking of the tragedy as they chattered and laughed their way past. Her compartment had a whole family in it at that point travelling to

Welshpool, a boisterous all-boy family apart from one small and dainty girl with a huge bow of white ribbon in her hair and who, Non could see, was not going to live long. She had turned away from them all in her distress and gazed sightlessly through the window as the train rattled and swayed its way along the tracks.

When she changed trains at Crewe, the thing she noticed most, apart from the larger engine drawing the train and the plusher compartment in which she sat, was the language. Everyone spoke English, no one spoke Welsh.

She was seven when her father had taken her with him on a trip to Liverpool where he was visiting a colleague recently arrived back from a voyage to some distant country – she never understood where – with plants he thought might interest her father. It had astounded her to hear all the children she saw in the city playing and singing and speaking in English. Though her father had taught her to read the language, she stumbled over speaking it, and most of the children she knew at home spoke little English and read even less, despite being punished at school for speaking Welsh. It is because we are in England, Rhiannon, her father had patiently explained to her, it is a different country with a different language.

Her father had been used to receiving many visitors from around the globe, visitors who had usually spent time aboard a ship to reach him. Until she travelled to Liverpool Non had always assumed she would have to cross the sea to visit a country where a language other than her own was spoken. She wonders, now, what those visitors had made of their home and their language; maybe they were not particularly aware of their surroundings, for they lived a life of the mind. But to her, today, it is strange not to hear a single word spoken in her own language. A foreign country. What will she find there?

She is glad to have brought a basket of food with her from her sister's house. She had invented an excuse, saying that she might stop in Machynlleth to walk around and catch a later train to continue her journey. It is a little worrying, the ease with which she lies. She delves into the basket for a chunk of the bread she packed and a piece of cheese she wrapped in damp muslin to keep it from sweating in the heat. The train she is on now is much hotter than the one she changed from, the little country train; she feels a pang of longing for it. These compartments are crammed with people, she had difficulty finding a place to sit, until a young man, still in uniform, gave up his window seat for her. People are even sitting in the corridors, she has seen them squatting on their bags and cases. She wonders why the railway company does not provide another carriage.

She is ravenous the moment she begins to eat the bread and cheese; breakfast at Branwen's house was a long time ago. She does not possess a watch, but she thinks she must be over halfway by now, so that is, say, four and a half hours or so after the train set off at half-past nine. It must be about two o'clock by now. The sun is still high in the sky, beating relentlessly down on the metal roofs of the carriages, but at least not blazing in through the window, which she really does not think she could bear. No one has spoken to her since the train left Crewe, not even a Good afternoon, though she has smiled and nodded at the other occupants of the carriage as they arrive and leave. She worries that perhaps the English are not a friendly people. What if Angela is not friendly, not forthcoming? But her letter had been friendly enough, short and to the point, to be sure, but friendly.

It is with some dismay she notices that the clothes she wears are not as fashionable as those that most of the younger women who are travelling wear. So much of their legs showing; she would be the talk of the town if she dressed like that. But the freedom of not having to wear skirts down to her ankles appeals to her; she may shorten her skirts just a little when she returns home. She looks surreptitiously at two women about her age sitting diagonally across from her and sighs. It is not just skirt length – it is shoes, it is collars, and more than anything, it is hairstyle. She hopes she will not appear to be old-fashioned, she would not like Angela to think she is old-fashioned in her ways and her thinking just because of her clothes.

She is being frivolous when she has matters to consider that are too serious for frivolity. She does not need to take Angela's letter from her bag, she knows the words in it off by heart. And she had sent, this morning before catching the train, a telegram from the Post Office at Aberystwyth to let Angela know the time the train would pull into Euston. It was the only way to announce her imminent arrival. Everything needed doing in such a hurry, the time at her disposal was rapidly vanishing, and her sister and niece would soon genuinely need her help at the birth.

She sips lemonade from the bottle her sister has pressed upon her, her sister who thought she was returning home until she was needed again. The drink is refreshing and the sweetness will give her back some of the energy the journey is dissipating. Non pushes away the feelings of guilt that assail her. She will not allow herself to think of what may be happening to Davey in the early mornings when she is not there. She is deceiving him and everyone else for a very good reason. She is not sure how she will explain to him what, she hopes, she is about to find out from a conversation with Angela, but she will have plenty of time to think about that on her journey home.

The wheels sing over the rails in their familiar way. Non is glad of the window seat. At least now and then she is able to press her forehead against the coolness of the glass and watch the fields, the villages, the towns flash past, but they flash past so much more quickly than she is used to that it is difficult to capture their images. It makes her dizzy and she has to look away again. The carriage passes into shade as dark as the inside of a tunnel and then into sunshine so piercing that it makes her eyes ache. She closes them, she is already weary. The heat does not suit her, the press of people does not suit her. At home, everyone she knows has been complaining of the relentless heat. Will it ever cease?

She has no idea what she expects Angela to be able to tell her. She is placing all her hopes on Angela, and that is probably wrong. It may be that Angela will not be able to help, that she meant precisely what she said in her letter. Non is suddenly not at all sure how well Angela knows Davey. She had nursed him for a long time according to the story Davey had told Non, but that might be as untrue as his story of an affair with Angela. The last line of Angela's letter to Davey had been, *You must stop this nonsense; it is insulting to me.* Non is not comfortable with leaving so much to chance but cannot see what else she can do. She has to feel her way through this, much as blind old Aggie Hughes who lives next door to Lizzie German, has to feel her way around her house. Is she foolish to be doing this at all? It occurs to her that other people may not go to these extremes. Branwen would accuse her of being headstrong. She is uncomfortably aware that she is taking herself away from all she knows to journey towards something – a place? a people? a revelation? – that is utterly unknown to her.

The train has slowed its journeying. She watches buildings glide by, growing taller and blacker, and suddenly the train enters a cavernous building with a roof made of glass and grime through which light struggles to enter; it is some kind of netherworld, full of smoke and steam, clatter and hissing and whistling, and over it all human voices clamour and call. Euston. She presses back into her seat as the other passengers stand up and walk into the corridor or take bags down from the overhead netting. She hears the cries of the guard as the train slows to a halt and people scramble and spill out of the train doors, pushing past one another. Non gathers her handbag and carpet bag together and makes her way down the step, over the gap full of rising steam, onto the station platform.

People race past and away from her. How will she know Angela? A surge of panic makes her heart beat so fast she becomes breathless. She had better wait until most people have gone so that she can see who else is on the platform. And so she does. It does not take many minutes. Out of the misty smoke and steam a figure comes towards her. Non is puzzled by the familiarity of the form and face she sees. And then she realises, and she gasps, 'Grace!'

22

Angela's room is cosy. Poky would be an unkind word for it, though it is a smaller home than any Non has ever seen. But it is . . . modern, she supposes. She is having difficulty in reconciling the two ideas of pokiness and modernity; they seem to be the antithesis of one another. Angela herself is negotiating for the use of the landlady's spare bedroom for two nights, having ascertained that Non is able to pay for it.

Non is still perturbed by Angela's likeness to Grace. As Angela had raced her away from Euston, walking faster than Non was used to, under a gigantic archway with gates of black and gold and immense pillars, along streets crowded with people and traffic, through swirling dust from wheels and hooves, beneath the looming presence of houses blackened by soot and smoke that seemed taller than the castle at home, until they stopped at this shabby house in William Road, Non had sneaked glances at her profile. What can it mean, this likeness?

She puts her carpet bag and handbag on the floor and surveys the room more closely. Angela had opened the sash window wide the moment they came in, but it has made little difference to the temperature. The small table with two kitchen chairs tucked under it by the window holds what looks like a Bible. She does not like to pick it up and leaf through it, her usual response to any kind of book she comes across; it seems ill-mannered here. There is an armchair with a blanket thrown over it next to the fireplace. And in the fireplace a contraption that takes the place of a fire, possibly, though she cannot see how it will work. Along the wall opposite the window is a narrow bed, with cushions on it that are intended to make it look like a couch, but do not really disguise its true nature. And at the foot of the bed is an alcove with a curtain drawn across it; maybe a wardrobe, or shelves. There is nowhere to wash or cook, though Angela had mentioned that she has only the one room. Rents are outrageous, she had said. There is not much comfort here, Non thinks, seeing her own home in her mind's eye, not for the body or the soul. Though some might count the Bible.

Angela returns with good news. 'The room is yours,' she says, 'for two nights, which you'll probably need. Give me your bag and I'll take it along and put it in there.' And with that she vanishes again.

Her energy exhausts Non. Angela had been working until she came to meet her. And a nurse must be on her feet all day, running about. Non wishes her own heart—, but here she stops herself. Her father had taught her that to wish for the impossible was a waste of energy and effort, whether mental or physical. She puts her hand out to rest on the back of the armchair, to take her weight, to stop her from sliding to the floor.

'Sit down before you drop.' Angela has bounced back into the room.

Like a jack-in-the-box, Non thinks. 'Thank you,' she says. And she is truly grateful to sink into the one armchair, which is more comfortable than it looks, before she disgraces herself by fainting away as she had done at home.

'I'll put the kettle on,' Angela says, and she whips open the curtain at the foot of the bed to reveal a tiny kitchen. There is a small sink with a tap – running water! – and a narrow shelf along the wall next to it that seems to serve as a table, with a wide cupboard fastened to the wall above it.

'You must be gasping for a cup of tea. I know I am.' Angela has an oil stove of some kind, which she lights before balancing the kettle on top of it. 'I can make toast and a poached egg if that's all right for you. Eggs are one of the few things I can get plenty of. A friend of mine at the hospital comes from a country family and they send her so much food every week she can't eat it all herself.' Angela pauses. 'Well, that's what she says, anyway. I think I could eat as much as anyone wanted to send me!'

Non is not hungry. But she says, 'Thank you. That would be lovely.'

Angela rushes past her and kneels down to fiddle with the contraption in the fireplace. She applies a match to it to make it spring instantly into flames. As she jumps to her feet, she looks at Non's face. 'Gas fire,' she says. 'It's much too hot to have it on but we have to toast the bread. Will you do that?'

How easy, Non thinks. She supposes the fire can be put out just as quickly as soon as she has toasted the bread.

The kettle whistles on the stove and is replaced by a pan of water for poaching the eggs while Angela makes a pot of tea.

The ease with which the meal is produced is a revelation to Non. A stove like Angela's would save her lighting the range these hot days just to boil the kettle. She wonders where she could buy one to take home with her. Then she wonders why she is letting her mind wander to inconsequential matters when she needs to concentrate on what she wants to find out from Angela.

They sit opposite one another at the small window table. It reminds Non of a little bamboo table in her father's house that he kept next to his armchair, and which was always piled high with books and papers. Angela had reverently removed the Bible and placed it on the bed. A believer, then. Angela eats her food quickly and neatly but Non struggles with the egg on toast, she is so very tired, though she could drink the whole potful of tea by herself.

'I'm sorry,' Angela says after sniffing at the milk jug, 'I think the milk's soured. It's hopeless in this weather. Well, we'll just have to have our tea black.'

Black tea. Non hopes Maggie Ellis is not nosing about too much at home, making trouble when she is not there to head her off. Some wars are never over.

Angela chatters as she eats, and Non is glad not to have to talk. She tells Non about her work at the University College Hospital, how her ward specialises in the treatment of heart conditions. Non is astonished to hear of so many soldiers developing heart problems in the War, and how brave those men are coming back in for treatment, some of them over and over, for other injuries they received during the War that will not heal. 'But at least they're alive,' Angela says, 'and where there's life there's hope, wouldn't you say?' She enthuses about the doctors and surgeons and their skill in restoring the men to a semblance of normality, but is less enthusiastic about the hospital matron. 'Rules with a rod of iron,' she says. 'But I suppose everything runs like clockwork because of her.' And then her face lights up and she tells Non about a friend from before the War who works there as a doctor. 'He worked in the casualty-clearing hospitals all through the War,' she says. 'He's brilliant. Dedicated.'

Non looks up from pushing her poached egg around her plate. 'Oh, are you courting?' she asks, and instantly wishes she could bite out her tongue.

Angela has gone still. 'No,' she says. 'My fiancé was killed. He wasn't a soldier, he was a priest, went out to give comfort, he said. He didn't get any himself. That's why I went to nurse in the battlefields, like a lot of the other girls, to feel a bit nearer to him, to find out what happened. He was never found, you see.'

'I'm sorry,' Non says, giving up altogether on the egg and toast and pushing her plate away. 'But you sounded . . . well . . . fond of your friend.'

'He's my friend because he was Edward's friend – they both began with medicine, but Edward said he was more interested in people's souls, he thought they were more important.' Angela gives a little shrug, as if to say she is not so sure herself.

Not reverently, then: perhaps the Bible was Edward's. Non glances towards it on the bed, as if it might tell her something that will get her out of this embarrassment.

'Some girls are able to . . . forget, I suppose,' Angela says, 'or put it behind them. I can't. It's as if it happened yesterday. And those girls, you know, there isn't anyone for them, is there? Why, I've even seen advertisements in magazines for husbands. Imagine!' She shakes her head. 'How desperate they must be to find someone, anyone. But I could never replace Edward. Never.'

Non looks around the poky room. Why is Angela telling her all this? She does not know her. But she supposes she wants to ask Angela questions that are just as intimate. Suddenly Non is desperate to be home. What possessed her to think she could come here and somehow find the one thing that would make everything all right? What she has is more all right than what many people have, it seems. She lifts her teacup and gulps down her tears of longing with the lukewarm tea, then sets the cup back in its saucer. 'You're helping a lot of people at the hospital,' she says. 'That must give you satisfaction.' What a tawdry word to use, she thinks, when what we all want is happiness, fulfilment, ecstasy.

Angela nods her head. 'Yes, oh, yes,' she says. 'All those poor young men, in and out of the hospital even now. But some find it so hard to help themselves, you know, they just won't try. At least your husband came home in one piece.'

Non wonders if she can hear accusation there. 'His ankle bothers him at times,' she says. She pauses, wondering whether to carry on. It is what I came for, she reminds herself. 'But it seems to be the memories that trouble him, Angela – it's as if his mind has been wounded. That was what I wanted to talk to you about.'

'I'm not sure I know what you mean.' Angela jumps up from her chair and begins to stack their plates and cups and saucers with more clatter than is necessary.

'I think you do, because I saw your last letter to Davey—'

'That was my only letter to Davey,' Angela says, rattling the cutlery into a bundle on one of the plates. 'I don't understand what made him think that we . . . well . . . you know. As if I would do such a thing. I treated him the way I treated everyone else. I mean, I know lots of the men got crushes on the nurses, because, you know, they're so glad to be out of the fighting and somewhere a bit civilised, and I suppose seeing a girl reminds them of their wives and sisters and so on, but . . . well, Davey was never actually like that, even, which is why I remember him.'

'Let me tell you what he told me,' Non says. 'When he came home Davey was changed from the Davey who went away. I know all that fighting would probably change anybody – but I couldn't understand why he was changed towards me. He said that he'd been unfaithful to me, and because of that he wasn't fit to be my husband any more. It wasn't like Davey to do such a thing. I could hardly believe it. But he insisted he had, and I don't know why.' Non is becoming ever more concerned about why Davey should have told her such a story.

'Well, I'm sure I don't know why,' Angela says.

She is standing sideways to Non at the table and her likeness to Grace in profile is uncanny. Non does not know what to make of it and it unnerves her so that her reply is sharper than she intends. 'I'm not blaming you for anything, Angela. I'm asking for your help. I know this never happened, but I don't understand why Davey said it did. He seems really to believe what he told me.'

Angela purses her lips and stops clattering the dishes about. 'He wrote me a lot of letters,' she says, 'but I only got them recently, sent on in a bundle from my old address – I don't know where he got that. We never gave out our addresses, you know. And they were all about this . . . this liaison we were supposed to have had, so I just wrote back right away and told him it was a nonsense and to stop it. I can't imagine why he believed it. Maybe he dreamt it or something, d'you think?'

'I don't know,' Non says. 'But tell me what he was like when you treated him in France.'

Angela draws her chair from under the table and sits down again. 'He came to us twice at the clearing station, but only for a few days both times,' she says. 'But, like I said, he wasn't like so many of the others. I remember him because he was quiet and respectful, but very sweet, you know. Yes, that's the word, a very sweet man. I told him about losing Edward that first time he was in and he seemed to understand just how I felt. That's why those letters were so odd.'

'Twice?' Non says. 'I know he was in hospital for weeks with his ankle injury, because he wrote regularly then, to me and to his parents. I didn't realise he was hospitalised later, too. What was that for?'

'I've been trying to remember all this since I heard from you,' Angela says. 'But, you know, I can't recall much detail. He would have gone on from us to the hospital that first time. Clearing stations were exactly that – we either sent the men on for more treatment or sent them back if they were fit enough after two or three days.' She leans her elbow on the table and tucks her chin into her hand. 'The second time he came in was when his section had been hit, and most of them had been injured, one or two rather badly, and they'd lost quite a few men. It was a shambles. I remember they brought bodies as well as the injured to us. He was quite dazed by it, withdrawn, but, you know, we saw a lot of that – the thousand-yard stare we called it – when they looked right through you. I remember him writing a letter to be sent to you if he . . . well, you know. He was awfully anxious about that, he wrote the letter over and over, as if he'd forgotten he'd already done it. He gave a letter to anyone who'd take it, to send on to you. That was very sweet, too, you know, but sad, terribly sad. There was one chap I remember because his name was Edward – though he was nothing like my Edward – well, he was in a very bad way himself, he made a big fuss about looking after the letter . . .' Angela pauses and slowly shakes her head at . . . what? The madness of it all? Her memories of it? What might have been?

Non feels a scream rise to her throat at this glimpse of what Davey had to endure. She clamps her hand over her mouth to stop the scream escaping.

'But, you know . . .' Angela uncups her chin from her palm. 'They had to pull themselves together and go back. And I'm sure your husband's injuries were minor because I don't think he was there more than a couple of days that second time. He must have been patched up and sent back. And the next I heard of him was this bundle of letters I mentioned. And that was a funny thing, too, you know – every letter was sort of the same and he never seemed to notice that he wasn't getting any letters back from me.' She looks at Non with a little moue of helplessness. 'I don't know what else to say.'

'And I don't know what to ask,' Non says. 'Maybe something happened to him during the attack, but I don't know what it would have been to cause him to invent this story.' She stares at the table for a moment. She has learnt more than she expected but the revelations she had hoped for have not materialised. 'Maybe I should go to bed, Angela, and be up early to catch the train home tomorrow. That's where I should be – at home.'

'I had a thought about tomorrow,' Angela says. 'I think it might be a good idea for you to come with me in the morning and meet some of my patients.'

Angela may look like Grace, Non thinks, but she sounds just like Branwen when she had arranged some visit or chore for me. But as she is about to refuse, a thought occurs to her that makes her heart leap. 'Do you think any of them would have known Davey?' she says. Even as she asks she realises that it would be unlikely.

'It might give you an idea of what it was like at the Front. What kind of terrible injuries some men would have suffered.' Angela looks straight at her.

Non considers this challenge. It would be a miracle, but if there is a chance, a slight chance, the minutest chance, that she might meet someone who knew Davey, she should go. 'Thank you. I'll do that, Angela. Will it be all right with your matron, do you think?'

'She's always glad to have people visit the men to chat to them or read to them,' Angela says, 'so we'll pretend that's what you're doing.'

More subterfuge, thinks Non. One of these times I shall forget who I am or what I am meant to be doing and put my foot in it. But it is a good idea. She smiles at Angela. She still looks like Grace. Is that why she had made such an impression on Davey? Do not dwell on it, she tells herself.

'I've got a seven o'clock start,' Angela says. 'I'll give you an early call. Good thing I asked old Mrs Wishart if you could have the room for two nights.'

'Shall I help you wash up?' Non asks. 'And may I have a cup of water? I have some drops I have to take in water before bed and in the morning.' She rummages in her bag and draws out the bottle. Your lifeblood, Rhiannon, she hears her father say.

Angela squints at the bottle. 'What are they for?' she asks.

'Oh, my heart condition – that's why I'm so exhausted – my heart beats too fast and too erratically. My father said I was born with it. These are made from a very old recipe he used—' She gasps as Angela whisks the bottle from her hand.

Angela pulls the stopper out of the bottle and sniffs at it. 'Good Lord, what is it?' Her face puckers up at the smell.

'May Lily – Lily of the Valley,' Non says. 'It's not too bad if I swallow it quickly.'

Angela sniffs again at the open bottle. 'What a stink! Treatment has moved on since the Middle Ages, you know. What happens if you don't take this . . . stuff?' She pushes the stopper back into place.

Middle Ages! Non snatches her bottle of lifeblood from Angela and tucks it into her skirt pocket. 'Father said it kept death at bay,' she says. 'So I suppose I would die.' She takes her plate and cup and saucer over to the little sink and rinses them under the tap. She fills the cup with water, picks up her handbag from the floor and says to Angela who is watching her, 'Will you show me my room, please?'

'Don't mind me,' Angela says. 'But . . . there may be more modern remedies, you know. Is your father a doctor?'

'He was a herbalist, a famous one,' Non says. 'He showed me how to make these drops because he knew I would have to take them all my life. He died when I was ten.'

'Hmmm . . .' Angela says. She taps her foot on the floor, studying Non. 'I've had another thought about tomorrow. My friend, Edward's friend, the one I told you about, he's one of the cardiac specialists. I'm sure he'd be interested in taking a look at you.'

Taking a look at me! Non thinks. Angela's thoughts on her behalf are too reminiscent of Branwen's attempts to make her conform to some standard of which she is unaware.

'I'll call you in plenty of time to have a piece of toast and cup of tea before setting off. Can't have you passing out on me on the way there.' Angela smiles at her.

'Thank you,' Non says, although she is not sure what it is she is thanking Angela for. Just go to bed, she tells herself.

'And don't worry,' Angela says. 'You know, Davey showed me your photograph when he was in the clearing station with his ankle injury. That's how I recognised you at Euston. You haven't changed. He carried it in the pocket over his heart. He said he thought you'd put a spell on him.'

23

The smell sickens Non as she and Angela enter the hospital. Disinfectant, and underlying it another pervasive, elusive smell that she cannot quite catch long enough to recognise; sweet, but definitely unpleasant. She decides to breathe through her mouth.

The walk here has tired her; she is stumbling as she follows Angela up the ornate stairs. She has never before been in a hospital, she has never been in a building this big. Angela had told her the hospital was large, and fairly new – built just after the turn of the century – so Non had not expected to see a place straight out of another of her father's fairy tales, with turrets and pointed roofs where only fluttering pennants were missing, and tiny windows through which maidens might lower their long hair for their suitors to climb, and walls built of rosy brick that had not yet attracted much grime from the smoke and smogs of London. Is it any wonder that at times she thinks she lives in a dream?

She had been awake off and on during the night, falling into periods of drowsing after being wide awake, her mind active, trying to work all that Angela had told her into some kind of sensible explanation of what was wrong with Davey, and trying not to dwell on what he had told Angela about her. I have put a spell on him, she had thought. In the small hours it was difficult to forget that it was only a few days since Gwydion told her that Owen had said she was an enchantress; she knew she had to speak to Owen, to tidy away that part of her past. But she could not think about him when she was here, in London, trying to find help for Davey. And all the time what she really wanted was to go home. She did not want to make the visit Angela had promised for the morning. But she felt obliged to Angela, who had been generous to her, and there was always a possibility that she might learn something.

She waits for Angela to change into her uniform, glad to lean against the wall of the corridor for a while, to catch her breath, to steady her heart. After Angela joins her, looking austere in her uniform despite the beauty of her face, they both enter a long ward, its two rows of iron beds reflected in the glossy linoleum beneath them as if they are standing in water. A long, well-polished table in the middle of the room has two nurses sitting at it. They wear the same stiff headdress as Angela, and are so busy writing they do not even look up from their work. A bouquet of flowers in a tall glass vase in the centre of the table is already wilting, leaves and flowers bowing down over the sides of the vase until they are almost touching the table.

But it is the occupants of the beds, or of the chairs beside them, who catch Non's attention. Every bed or chair holds someone lying or sitting and looking towards the door to the ward where she stands with Angela. She had not expected to see so many bandaged limbs and heads in a ward that deals with diseases of the heart. What on earth is she doing here? This has nothing to do with Davey. Why has Angela brought her? She turns to her.

'Smile,' Angela says. 'Walk around, talk to the patients, be pleasant, ask them if they want you to read to them. Make your-self useful. But, whatever else you do, don't forget to smile. Keep it light, keep it bright – that's our motto here.'

All at once Non hates Angela. More than she hates Catherine Davies. It surges through her like a tide, the hatred. She forces herself to smile and walks forward.

Angela claps her hands for attention. 'I've a visitor for you today, chaps. Non Davies is staying with me and I've brought her along for an hour or two. Anyone who has a letter they want read to them, or written, or just wants a chat with a pretty face – here's your chance.'

Cheers greet her announcement, but Non notices that not all the patients join in. She resolves to talk with some of the men who are not cheering. This is the kind of place that is a hell for her, with her gift – which Angela would dismiss as something from the Middle Ages again. Though Non would cut out her tongue before she would mention it to anyone, let alone Angela.

She walks down one side of the ward. She has already lost sight of who was cheering and who was not. Most of the men have a newspaper or book they are actually reading for themselves, she sees, and look up from their reading to nod and smile at her as she walks past. So who was Angela thinking of when she mentioned reading letters? She walks past a bed where a man with a ban-daged stump instead of his right arm is writing awkwardly in a notebook with his left hand. But he is managing to do it, she thinks.

At the next bed she stops. Her heart contracts. A young man who looks no older than Gwydion sits staring at the row of beds opposite, his face expressionless. He could be one of Osian's carv-ings. She wants to put her hand out to see if she can feel warmth and life in him. She smiles, but he does not respond.

The man with the missing arm says, 'He's blind. From the gas.'

So young, thinks Non, so young. She blinks back the tears that start in her eyes, and moves to the side of the bed.

'Oi, Johnny, where's yer manners?' the one-armed man calls out. 'Pretty lady standing here by yer bed!'

Johnny moves his head as if searching for her.

'I'm here, beside your bed,' she says.

He turns towards her at the sound of her voice and smiles. How can he smile so sweetly after what has happened to him?

'I'm Johnny,' he says, putting his hand out in her direction.

'And I'm Non,' she replies, holding his hand. 'Shall I sit for a while with you?'

'You're not from round here,' Johnny says. 'I like the way you talk. We had a Welsh bloke with us when this happened to me.' He points at his eyes. 'He talked just like you, all soft, like. Jones, his name was. He led me out.'

Non sits in the chair at his bedside, still holding his hand. 'Where are you from, Johnny?'

'Northampton way before the War,' he says. 'Don't know any more. Nowhere, really.'

'Maybe you'll be able to go back when you're better,' Non says.

'No. No point in going back to the shoe factory if I can't see to do the lasting. And me family's got enough to worry about without worrying about me.'

'Oh, Johnny, I'm sure they wouldn't think about it like that.'

He remains silent. She looks searchingly at him. She is glad that she can see no physical illness in him – whatever is wrong with his heart must be curable – but his mind is a scribble to her, like Osian's or Davey's.

'What do the doctors here say?' she says. 'What do they think they can do for your sight?'

Johnny pulls his hand from her grasp. 'They say there's nothing wrong with me eyes,' he says. 'They say it's all in me head. They say I can see if I want to.'

Non is horrified to see tears running down his face. She looks around for Angela. The one-armed man is watching, as if he is curious to see what she does.

'But I do want to see, and I just can't. I can't. They don't know what it were like, them doctors.' Johnny is convulsed with his crying now.

One of the nurses at the central table looks up from her work, comes over to Non and motions her to leave the bedside. Non whispers goodbye to Johnny who is wracked by sobs and curled up like a foetus on his bed.

'Happens all the time, poor bugger,' the one-armed man says. 'Bet it don't do his dicky heart no good.'

Non tries to smile at him, but fails, and carries on walking until she is at the far end of the ward, then she takes a deep breath and turns around and walks down the other side.

A man with his eyes bandaged calls out to her. 'Missus, is that you going past?'

She walks to the side of his bed. 'What can I do for you?' she asks.

The man in the next bed laughs, and says something Non does not catch.

'Don't you take no notice of him, missus,' the man who called to her says. "E's ignorant. I got a letter yesterday, missus, and nobody's 'ad time to read it to me.' He scrabbles about on the surface of his bedside cupboard until he finds an envelope and waves it in her direction. "Ere it is. Will you read it, missus?'

Non opens the letter and looks at the signature. 'It's from Edith,' she says.

'The wife,' the man says.

Non scans the letter. How unkind . . . how can his wife write to him like this when he is helpless in here? She cannot read this letter out to him. Especially if he, too, has a dicky heart.

'Go on, then,' the man says, settling down against his pillows as if he is about to listen to a story.

Non reads aloud, 'Dear Fred.'

'That's me,' he says, nodding and smiling.

Non begins to improvise. 'Dear Fred, how are you? We are all well here and looking forward to having you home. We think about you. Love from Edith.'

Fred sits bolt upright. 'Edith said that?' he says. 'It don't sound like Edith. Something must be wrong. Drat, I'll be fretting till the next un comes now.' He kneads the letter Non has pushed back into his hand, as if he might read it through his fingertips.

'I'm sorry, Fred,' she says.

'Not your fault, missus,' he says, still worrying at the letter.

Non pats his hand and walks away, back into the central aisle and as quickly as she can towards the ward doors. She does not want to be here, she wants to go home.

Ahead of her is Angela, coming back into the ward. Angela nods to indicate a bed near the door where a man lies flat on his back staring up at the ceiling. She mimes that she wants Non to talk to him.

Non does not want to do this. She shakes her head at Angela but Angela nods vigorously at her and indicates that she should smile. Non grits her teeth until they squeak in her mouth. She stands alongside the man's bed and smiles down at him. 'Hello, I'm Non,' she says. 'Is there anything I can do for you? Shall I read to you?' She indicates the books sitting in a pile on the bedside table.

He shakes his head. A smell seeps from under the bedclothes that cover him. It is the sickening sweetness Non could smell under the disinfectant when she first came into the hospital.

'You can't do anything for me unless you can make miracles happen,' he says. 'Can you do that . . . Non?'

'No miracles, I'm afraid,' Non says. If she could, she would have performed them by now and she would not be in this terrible, stinking place. She is instantly ashamed of her thoughts.

'Wishing you were a hundred miles away?' the man asks. 'Sorry about the stink, by the way. That's the gangrene. Eating away at my leg. The docs have to keep chopping bits off it.'

Non can see that nothing will save this man. She swallows hard to keep from retching.

'Go away,' he says. 'You do-gooders are useless. And I know what you Taffs are like. Lying, devious, thieving bastards the lot of you. Bad as gypsies, you are.'

Every last bit of sympathy leaves Non as if it has been punched out of her. She wants to hurt this man back, but she turns away from him and leaves. Past the last two beds on the ward, ignoring their occupants, and out through the double doors. And then she has to stop because she does not know where to go from here.

Angela catches up with her. 'You see,' she says. 'Davey doesn't have it so bad, does he? He's home and he's not injured.'

Non feels the blood drain from her face. She has never felt so angry, not even with Catherine Davies at her worst. 'Davey has no injury that you can see,' she says. 'But his mind has been wounded, I'm sure of it.'

Angela shrugs. 'Well,' she says, 'I don't know what anyone can do about that except Davey himself. He'll have to pull himself together. Like young Johnny down there – he'd be able to see fine if he stopped his nonsense.'

Surely there must be doctors who can cure damaged minds as well as doctors for damaged hearts here in this enormous hospital; surely there must be people who are concerned about what this War has done to soldiers' minds as well as to their bodies? Surely Angela's Edward would not have thought the way Angela does? Non cannot understand why Angela is not aware of the agony of mind that is the consequence of the War for men like Davey and young Johnny. Is it possible that Angela has hardened herself so that she can survive day after day as a nurse? Non knows very well what a slippery notion the mind is to deal with; it is not like an arm or a leg, or even a heart.

'But look,' Angela says, as if Non is not furious, as if Non must agree with her, as if there is nothing more to be said about the subject, 'I've arranged for you to see my friend. He agrees with me that there's something very odd about this heart thing of yours. Go straight there now, he's free. Down that corridor, down the stairs on the left, turn right and it's the second door on the left. His name's on it.' And she rushes away back into her ward.

24

Non's heart is beating faster than she thinks is possible. She cannot read the plate on the door that Angela directed her to find, because her eyesight has blurred as it often does when she is angry or agitated, and anyway she cannot remember Angela ever saying his name, it was My friend or Edward's friend. But she has followed the directions to the letter so this must be the correct door. She raises her fist and raps on it.

A commotion on the other side of the door causes her to step back a little, but when it is opened she is greeted by a tall young man who instantly makes her think of Gwydion's description of Aoife: bright blue eyes, pale skin, copious black curly hair. He is not her idea of what a doctor should look like, but he is wearing a long white coat and she recognises the stethoscope around his neck from her memory of the one her father possessed.

'Yes? Yes?' He moves impatiently from one foot to the other, as if he were dancing. Non sees he has one brown shoe and one black shoe on his feet. Why has no one told him?

'I'm Angela's . . . Angela sent me,' Non says. She won't claim to be Angela's friend. 'Rhiannon Davies.' She holds her hand out to shake his.

'Come in, come in,' the young man she hopes is Angela's friend says. He holds on to her hand and draws her into the room, which looks like a trap for the unwary. She flinches away from a skeleton twitching on a hook on the back of the door.

'Don't mind him, he's been dead a long time.'

Is that the skeleton of a real person? Should it not be in a grave? Non is not sure about this second plan of Angela's any more than she was about the first. This young man does not have the gravitas she associates with the medical profession. Not that she has had much experience of the profession, having only once visited a doctor in her life, dragged to see him by Branwen, an experience never spoken of again by either of them, and never repeated.

'I'm Seb O'Neill,' the young man says, still holding on to her hand and now pumping it up and down in greeting.

'Sebon?' she says, feeling a nervous giggle bubbling up her throat.

'Seb,' he says, 'easier than Sebastian.'

She cannot help it, the giggle becomes a laugh, and she feels slightly hysterical, as if none of this is quite real. 'Sebon,' she says. 'It means soap in Welsh.'

'Soap?' He looks at her, frowning, for a moment, then gives a brilliant smile. 'Well, I do try to wash out disease, scrub it away, I suppose. Soap!'

Non does not think this is an auspicious start once her nervous laughter has ebbed away, leaving her more nervous than before.

'Sit down here,' Seb says, indicating a chair in front of what must be his desk. 'Now, how do you say your name, again?'

'Davies,' Non says. 'Oh . . . Rhiannon . . . but most people call me Non.'

'Non.' He sits behind the desk, pushes aside a stack of journals that leave a trail of dust and leans over towards her. 'Angela only had time to explain to me very quickly what the problem is. She was most concerned. She says you're taking some drops your father makes up for you for a heart condition you have. A herbal remedy. Is that right?'

'My father died when I was young,' Non says. 'But he'd shown me how to make the remedy, so I make it myself.'

'What does your local doctor say?'

'I've never had to see him for anything,' Non says, heartily glad, as always, that she has not, though Dr Jones is well and fondly spoken of by those who do see him.

'Have you the drops with you?' Seb holds his hand out for them.

Non is reluctant to hand her vial over to him; it is somehow a betrayal of her father and his years of work, all that he had done in a lifetime, and a betrayal of trust. But she does not know how to refuse the open hand stretched out to her across the desk. She takes the vial from her bag and lays it in his palm.

He unstoppers it and sniffs cautiously at the contents. 'What is it?' he asks.

'May Lily – Lily of the Valley some call it. It's a distillation of the flowers. It has the same effect as foxglove only not so strong. I may have to use foxglove soon, I don't think this is as powerful as I need it to be.'

He does not reply. He stoppers the bottle but does not give it back to her. She would seem ill-mannered, she thinks, if she were to lean across the desk and take it. But she must not leave without it.

'I'd like to count your pulse beat,' he says. 'Would you mind? It will tell me how quickly your heart is beating.' He takes a watch from the breast pocket of his white coat, reaches over the desk for her wrist and lays two long, slim fingers across the inside of it.

'It's beating very fast now because I've just been visiting those poor men in Angela's ward and—'

'Shhh,' he says, holding her wrist and looking at his watch. His lips move slightly, as if he were a child counting. He blinks rapidly, smiles at her, then counts the beats of her pulse again.

'Your pulse is very slow,' he says. 'Abnormally slow, not fast at all. Tell me about your father, why he gave you this . . . remedy.'

So she tells him. He is a good listener for someone who seems so scatterbrained, so good in fact that she tells him far too much about her father and his studies, his life's work, his famous book on herbalism, the patients who returned to him time and again, his renowned cures, the scholars who came from all over the world, his own trips to far countries for new and exotic herbs to cultivate. She even tells him the story of her mother's engagement ring, which is ridiculous, for the story has no bearing at all on why she is here.

'He sounds an interesting man. But what made him think you had a heart problem?'

'My heart sounded wrong to him the moment I was born. My mother was old when she had me and the birth was a struggle for us both, he said. We were exhausted. If my father had not fed me the drops I would have died.'

Seb gazes at the surface of his desk for a while, tracing patterns in the trails of dust on it. 'Maybe your heart was beating faster than usual after your birth,' he says, 'but many babies are born with what is called a murmur to the heart, a slight sound defect to someone listening through a stethoscope. It goes away quite soon usually, within a few days. Did your mother recover well?'

'She died,' Non says. She has often wished that she could

remember something about her mother, a touch, a smell, a sound, something a young baby would have recognised and held on to, but she cannot. 'I was all my father had; my sisters had died except for one, and she was grown by then and had a child of her own.'

'I'm sorry,' Seb says, contemplating his desktop again.

Non looks around his room, his consultation room, she supposes. It does not inspire confidence, she thinks, yet in some way, despite the odd-coloured shoes and the lack of gravitas, the man does. There are books and journals piled haphazardly on the floor. The walls have large drawings of men flayed so that the gruesome secrets below their skins are visible. She averts her eyes but not before she sees the heart in several of the drawings. She recognises it from having cooked so many of them. How strange that the human heart should look so like an animal's heart.

'How do you feel, generally?' Seb suddenly asks, making her jump slightly. 'How is your health from day to day?'

'I couldn't manage without my drops,' she says. 'My father called them my lifeblood – did I say? I get very tired, exhausted really, and I haven't much strength. I find I'm having to take more of my drops in this heat. The heat makes me feel much worse.'

'Do you suffer from headaches?' he asks.

Non shakes her head.

'Nausea? Faintness?'

'The heat has brought on some faintness recently And blurs my eyesight. I'm sure I shall be better once the heat breaks.'

'Hallucinations?'

Hallucinations! She shakes her head again.

'Do you mind if I listen to your heart? With my stethoscope.' He takes the stethoscope from around his neck as he speaks.

Non is not sure what to answer. Where is all this leading?

Seb takes her silence for assent. 'I'll call my nurse in,' he says.

He leaves the room, and returns almost immediately with a nurse who wears a hat as white and starched as Angela's.

'Nurse Reynolds will help you get ready,' Seb says, 'and you can lie down on the couch.'

Nurse Reynolds unfolds a screen between the couch and the rest of the room and, when it becomes obvious that Non does not know what is expected of her, she helps her to take off her blouse and to lie down on the high couch. Then she calls Seb, to tell him that they are ready.

'Now then, just breathe normally,' Seb says, 'and don't speak.' He places the stethoscope over her heart and listens intently, moving the instrument to different positions and listening as intently each time. Non sees the concentration in his narrowed eyes and compressed mouth. 'Thank you,' he says eventually, 'you can get down from the couch now and Nurse will help you dress.'

Non does as the nurse tells her and wonders what is to come after all this examining. What has Seb being trying to tell her – that her father had made a mistake? She sits in the chair before the desk again.

Seb leans forward and says, 'You are poisoning yourself with this.' He raps the vial with his pencil.

Non gasps and strains back from him in the chair. Is he saying that her father was trying to kill her? No, she thinks. No.

'I'd like to keep some of this distillation to test in my laboratory,' he says. He takes a glass tube from a drawer in his desk and drips some of her lifeblood into it, then stoppers the tube and the vial. 'But from what you've told me, and from my examination of you, I would say that the symptoms you describe – the fatigue, the weakness, the faintness, the blurred eyesight, and the abnormally slow heartbeat I've just measured, come from these drops.

You are doing yourself a great deal of harm by taking this medication. You will have to stop taking it.'

'But . . . my father . . .' She stumbles to a halt and feels tears gathering in a lump in her throat. What is she to do? Believe this man that she does not know, or believe her father who loved her and cared for her?

'How old are you?' Seb asks.

'Twenty-nine,' she says.

'So, you see, though twenty-nine years is not that long ago, things were quite different then. Medical and other advances have meant that we know a great deal more about how the heart works, for instance. But I do feel that your father probably . . . misdiagnosed your condition in his fears for your life and in his pains to save you.'

Non stares at him. She cannot just stop taking her drops. She needs them, she depends on them to carry her through each day. He must be wrong. She reaches out for the vial but he stays her hand.

'You must stop. But do it gradually. Take less each day. You are bound to feel strange, you will think your heart really is racing. But it means it is beating as it should in a healthy person. I am as sure of this as I have ever been of anything – you must stop taking these drops if you want to live. You'll find, quite quickly, that you won't be so fatigued nor so weak. You must do it.' He releases Non's hand, and she takes hold of her vial and places it in her bag.

'Take a drop less each day until you are taking none. I shall write to you with all I have diagnosed and the results of the laboratory tests. Angela has your address? Fine.' He scribbles on his pad of paper and looks at his watch. 'I'm afraid I have to see another patient now. Maybe you should find somewhere to sit for a little while. The hospital grounds are cool in the shade.'

He leads her to the door of his room, 'Goodbye. I'll be in touch as soon as I have results for you, I promise.'

She stands outside his closed door, resting against the door post, until Nurse Reynolds walks along the corridor with an elderly woman leaning on her arm, and Non has to move out of their way.

25

Non had not wanted to come out this evening. It was only the desperation spilling from Angela – a softer, less high-handed Angela – that persuaded her. She had wanted to go to bed, to go to sleep, to forget about the whole day and wake in the morning just in time to catch the train home.

The room into which Angela has brought her is dim and crowded, Non's seat is hard and too small, and she is jammed up against a large woman sitting next to her on one side and Angela in the aisle seat on the other. She refuses to be drawn into conversation by Angela. The noise is already at a pitch, every single person must be chattering. It is too much.

Today has been one tribulation after another. First, that dreadful ward with those poor men. How could Angela use them in that way as a lesson to Non? Is that how a nurse should behave? And for her to end hating them, or at least hating what they represented, that was wrong, too. Then Seb – her cheeks burn at having mistaken his name so stupidly, he must have thought she was foolish from the start – and his diagnosis; she is still not sure what to think about that. And third and worst, her visit to Burlington House.

After coming away from her consultation with Seb she had done as he suggested and found a seat in the shade of the rose-red building. People – patients and their visitors, she supposed – milled about as they seemed to do everywhere in this huge city, reflecting the turmoil in her mind. The young doctor was brilliant, Angela had told her. Non remembered people saying that to her about her father. She wished she knew more about Osian Rhys the man, rather than the father or the romantic or the herbalist. After he died she soon learnt that her sister would not talk about him. When the young Non had made even the most innocuous mention of her beloved father, Branwen had flown into a rage. There had to be a reason for that, she had thought, as she closed her eyes and leaned against the back of the seat, and when she next saw Branwen she would find it out. It was here in this great city that her father had bought her mother's ring – the ring that had enabled Non to be here. She had opened her eyes and sat up straight. Had her father sent her here? She had banished that foolish thought the instant it came into her mind, but it had made her consider what she should do. She had not been able to find out much more than she already knew about Davey that was useful – except, and her heart had skipped a beat, that she had cast a spell upon him – but perhaps she would be able to find something out about her father, something that would help her to decide what she should do with Seb's advice. She had heard Branwen's voice telling her to think, for goodness' sake, not to be headstrong, the voice rising to a crescendo until she had closed the doors of her memory against it. She had walked up the stairs to Angela's ward, to ask her for directions to the place where the Royal Society resided, and told her she would be back at the lodging house in William Road in time for Angela's return late in the afternoon.

Go back the way we came this morning, Angela had instructed, as far as that Underground station I pointed out to you – Warren Street – and take the Hampstead line to Leicester Square. You can change there to the Piccadilly line and get off in Piccadilly Circus, it's not far from there – just ask someone on the station. Non had no recollection of passing Warren Street station that morning and had to ask for directions as soon as she left the hospital. But after that her journey was uneventful. The underground train was fast and noisy, and she was curious rather than nervous as the train rattled and screeched through its wormhole tunnels. She was glad to sit down, to rest, to watch the reflections of the other passengers in the windows, to read the posters decorating the carriages, to memorise the information that, last year, underground trains travelled the equivalent of eight thousand times around the world – eight thousand! – to tell Wil when she returned home before she recollected, with a physical jolt, that she could not do that. When she reached Piccadilly Circus she lost her way twice trying to leave the station and find Piccadilly. Eventually, after asking for directions, she arrived at Burlington House.

She saw the cobbled yard, the huge wooden doors with the gold lettering above them on the lintels, the carved stone decorations, all as her father had described to her. The east wing was so large and imposing that the thought of her father being there as one of the many honoured scientists filled her with pride. She had asked the attendant in the hallway for help and was guided to a reading table where she was given books containing the names of all the members during the years when her father had been a frequent visitor. Many of the names were familiar to her; she had heard them on her father's lips so many times during her childhood, some spoken with more admiration than others.

But her father's name was not among them. She went through the lists three times. First reading down the page, then backwards up the page, then down again, putting her finger against each name so that there was no chance of missing one. She asked the stern man behind the desk if it was possible that a mistake had been made but his expression was so incredulous and unforgiving that she felt herself shrink just like Alice in Mr Carroll's book. But she asked again if there were other lists she could consult, told the stern man her father's name and his work. The man informed her that there were other – and here he paused in disdain, Non saw his lip curl – that there were other royal societies of this and that, but this Royal Society was not where her father had belonged, or spoken about his voyages, or been given money from a collection – another curl of the lip – which enabled him to buy her mother a betrothal ring. She had walked away from Burlington House angry with the attendant, angry with her father, angry with Branwen for refusing to speak of him, angry with herself for her gullibility, and utterly confused.

When she had arrived back at Angela's lodgings, she had been exhausted, hot and near to fainting. She was glad to drop into the armchair in the stuffy little room. She was fed pink salmon from a tin and brown bread dry from the heat of the day, food that made her want to gag, and which she washed down with the tea for which she was desperate and grateful. And then she was persuaded by Angela – because she had neither the heart nor the energy to keep refusing – to come out for the evening, to come to this other stuffy, crowded room.

'Shhh.' Everyone in the place seems to be shushing everyone else. Non's neighbour turns to her – who has not uttered a word – and shushes her, her finger against her mouth as if Non were a five-year-old. The shushing is like the sea on the sand at home, and pleasanter than the chattering. The air in the room is stifling and the smell of sweat overlaid by the scent of perfumes and pomades takes Non's breath away. She dips into her handbag to find the thyme oil she carries for Osian, inhales deeply from the vial and feels her breathing ease a little. She wishes she had thought to bring some water to drink in the bottle that Branwen had pressed on her for the train journey, for her mouth is dry already.

The audience falls silent and each member of it gazes towards the stage – a wooden dais at the front of the room, with a curtain drawn across it. In the silence the gas lamps hiss and their flames leap, but their light fails to combat the dark shadow cast by the church to which the hall is attached. Through one of the room's high windows Non can see the bright, cloudless blue of the sky, and thinks she ought to feel less enervated here in this shade, but somehow the dimness is neither restful nor comforting, and takes her back to that other room in Port with Catherine Davies and Elsie. She had been surprised that Angela was so anxious to come to this séance, but now she recalls her mother-in-law's yearning to contact Billy, and Elsie's joy in the train on the way home, and supposes that similar feelings have brought Angela here.

The curtains are drawn back to reveal a small round table holding a lamp, with a chair next to the table on which the medium, dressed in mourning, is seated. At her feet sits a child, swathed from head to foot in white. Despite her disbelief, Non shivers slightly with apprehension at this further reminder of the scene in the little sitting room in Port, and she hears again Ben Bach's voice calling his mother.

The audience seems to hold its collective breath as the child descends the stairs from the dais and walks step by slow step along the aisle looking from side to side at the rows of eager and anxious faces. Gasps follow her – whether of disappointment or relief, Non cannot tell – when she passes people by. Some proffer rings from their fingers, or letters, creased and dog-eared, from their pockets, but they are all ignored by the child. Non wonders if all mediums use children, first Madame Leblanc, and now this one. It is not right to make a child do this kind of dishonest work, this hocus-pocus.

'Yes, yes,' says a voice from the dais as the child stops to take a ring that is held out to her. The woman proffering the ring is close enough to her that Non can see she is young, and pale, and holds her now ringless hand to her breast. To stop hope escaping? The child carries the ring back to the dais, and the medium holds her hand out for it, then fingers it, turning it round and round, while the audience waits in intense silence, broken only by the hiss and stutter of the gaslights and the distant hum of noise from the city going about its business outside.

'You have lost a beloved one?'

The young woman gasps and nods and puts her hand to her mouth, and Non feels fury spurt inside her at what the woman on the dais is doing.

'I have a message to tell you not to worry. He is safe and is watching over you.'

The young woman is hiccupping and crying, and fumbles with the ring when the child brings it back to her. The audience is already watching the child to see who will be chosen next. How can Angela, an intelligent woman, sit here and believe that woman is anything but a charlatan? All these people, desperate – just like Elsie Thomas and Lizzie German, and old Catherine Davies – desperate to think their husbands and sons are safe somewhere and thinking of them. Non decides to leave. She tries to rise from her seat but Angela puts a strong hand firmly on her thigh and forces her to sit back down. And Non sees that Angela, too, has a ring in her hand, which she now holds out towards the child, who walks past without taking it. More rings and letters, a watch, even a mysterious leather pouch, are taken to the dais and their owners comforted by the medium's platitudes. Again, the child walks along the aisle, and approaches Angela; Non can see the tremor in her hand as she offers the ring to the child. It is a ring Non has not seen Angela wear and she supposes it must be a gift, a betrothal gift perhaps, from Edward. Non watches the child take the ring and walk to the dais with it. She is consumed with anger at herself for allowing this, and at the medium when Angela cries with joy to hear that her beloved is praying for her.

'That is just like Edward,' she says to Non, smiling and dabbing at her tears with her handkerchief as the child returns the ring. Angela is desperate to find Edward, Non thinks, but without hope of ever succeeding because he is lying somewhere in the soil of France where already lush grass and red poppies are claiming him. A woman sitting in the row of chairs behind them puts a comforting hand on Angela's shoulder. That small hand in its black glove makes Non instantly ashamed of herself for her lack of understanding and for thinking only of her own concerns. She hears Lizzie German admonishing her, People want to know, don't they, missus? No one speaks of it, she thinks, looking at the people around her in this room, no one speaks of their terrible grief. Angela's face still shines with her tears. She is a woman left on her own to make her way bravely in a world which has no place for women on their own – bachelor girls, is what Non has seen them called in the newspaper, as if it is a choice they make for fun. Non sees that Angela will never recover from Edward's death, and not just the fact of his death but the way of it, the ignominy of it. No wonder she has had to harden the exterior she shows to the world, she has needed to do so in order to survive; but here, now, Non sees the young woman with whom Edward fell in love. In a surge of compassion Non puts her hand out to find Angela's hand and clasps it tightly.

26

As her train whistles and chugs its way out of the grand station at Whitchurch and through the countryside Non begins to feel that she is, at last, going home. Angela, turned once more into the efficient nurse, had seen her to Euston and a train that had been as packed on the way out of London as it had been on her journey into the city. What a vast and confusing place London was, and the station at Euston in its bleakness and blackness, even when the sun had managed to struggle through the grime, was like a conduit to the city, reflecting the variety of its people from the obviously rich, with their maids and their luggage looked after by porters, to the down-and-outs, the tramps and beggars that the policemen were constantly moving on. She had barely caught her train because of an altercation outside the ticket office between a young policeman – he had not looked any older than Gwydion – and a tramp of indeterminate age who was trying to board the train, ticketless. The tramp had been turned away in the end, to the tutting and relief of most of those waiting.

Non wonders about the tramp, about why he was so anxious to board the train. She is ashamed that she did not help him in some way. She could have paid for a ticket for him, she had money left in her purse. Where had her sense of charity been? When the tramps came round at home on their tour – it was like an annual pilgrimage, always with the same familiar pilgrims – they were given tea in their billycans and slabs of bread and butter, or dripping, and even cheese or meat from those who could afford to give it, to see them on their way. The gentlemen of the road were treated with respect. They were treated like vermin in London, she had seen it.

You would have to be blind not to notice the indigent people everywhere, women and children as well as men. Every street corner had a maimed soldier, sometimes in a vestige of a uniform, sometimes smarter in an old suit and hat, trying to sell matches or bootlaces from a tray to passers-by. Sometimes they had given up any pretence at dignity and just sat on the dirty pavements, their despair there for all to see in the heads sunken onto their chests and the scruffy caps upended next to them to hold the few coppers anyone could spare. Ignore them, had been Angela's advice, and in the end that was what Non did, not because she thought they were a stain on the face of the city, as she had heard someone claim, but because when they looked at her to thank her for her pennies, she could not bear the misery and desolation and hopelessness in their eyes. It reminded her too much of the look she often caught in Davey's eyes.

Jane Eyre lies open and unread on her lap. She has scarcely turned a page over since her journey began. She needs to order her thoughts before she arrives home. News of a different kind will be expected there – news of Arianrhod and the expected child, and of Aberystwyth – and Gwydion, no doubt, will want to know if she found an opportunity to speak to his mother, to prepare the way for his own news. She remembers her father quoting a great Scottish writer to her, *Oh what a tangled web we weave, when first we practise to deceive*, and explaining to her that it was always best to tell the truth. She has found out that Osian Rhys taught her one thing but did another. It does not help her now to think of that, but she is determined that Branwen will tell her what she wants to know about their father.

She is glad to sit with her own thoughts. Her rushed stay with Angela has tired her so much she does not think she could converse with anyone. She had been so certain that she would find the reason for Davey's strange behaviour, but she had been disappointed. Angela knew nothing that gave an indication of what might have wrought such a great, and apparently sudden, change in him. Whatever it was must have happened before his second time in the clearing hospital. Angela had been a little vague about the date – and why not, why should she remember one event among the many? – but Non has worked out that it must have been after Ben Bach had been killed. Davey was meant to be keeping an eye on him for Elsie, he had promised her that he would do so. And so, maybe Ben Bach's death, coupled with the extensive damage to his platoon soon afterwards, was the cause of the change in Davey's behaviour that Angela had noticed, that thousand-yard stare. In London she has seen how affected other men have been by the War, and she can partly understand Davey's response, but not the story of what Angela had called the liaison. What led to that? She gazes at her book – the pages may as well be blank – and closes it with a bang that disturbs the dust and the one other occupant of the compartment, an old man who had been snoring gently in the seat next to the other door. The train squeals to a halt in Welshpool, with the usual hiss of steam and the stink of burning cinders that the engine spits out, and the old man gathers his belongings, doffs his cap to Non and leaves the compartment.

He is almost immediately replaced by a young family, chattering like a flock of starlings. In her own language. She smiles at them all, and exchanges Good afternoons. The young mother carries a baby, fast asleep, and the next child in age is a boy – a rascal, Non thinks, when she catches the look in his eyes – and then two girls with their hair in long plaits that must have taken time in a busy day. The eldest girl, the one in charge of this little crew, sits demurely next to Non. Her father pats her on the head and tells her she is a good girl before he, too, sits down. Non thinks she can feel the warmth of the glow coming from the child at the praise from her father. A toy is brought out to keep the rascal occupied, a cup and ball. He concentrates hard on mastering the art of throwing the ball into the cup, his tongue poking out of the corner of his mouth like a kitten's.

Non never managed to do that, catch the ball in the cup, she did not have the patience. Her childhood suddenly seems a long time ago; she must have been about the same age as this eldest child next to her here when her father died. She does not think she was as good. She can barely remember what her father looked like. She has his book, his famous herbal, at home, with his photograph in the front – but he had been young then, and she had never known him young. He seems to have become a figure in a story that she was told, as if he invented himself for her benefit. She does not know if any of the stories he told her about her mother, about his work, about his scholarly pursuits, about his travels and those foreign men that used to visit him – she does not know if any of those are any truer than all the stories of old and the fairy stories he told her. She believed every word, never questioned any of it. Although she does, now, recall occasional puzzling remarks from neighbours, and asking her father to explain them. Ignore them, Rhiannon, he had told her – our neighbours are good people, but because we do not share their belief that there is a God looking down on us, they fear for our mortal souls. Non suspects now that the neighbours had long given up their crusade for her father's soul, they were likely concentrating on saving hers. Her father had left her to her own devices much of the time, to develop her own ideas about life from the information and the teaching she had from him. By now she understands that children can develop strange and perverse notions when matters are not explained to them. She knows she must have been an odd little thing by the time her father died and she was taken in by Branwen – an odd, wayward little thing. She feels bereft, as if something has been taken from her, as if now she has lost her father all over again. She needs to find out what is true and what is not, and she reminds herself that she will insist that Branwen answers her questions about Osian Rhys when she goes down to Aberystwyth for the birth.

She is jolted out of her reverie when the train stops at Newtown and the young father takes his son on his knee to make room for a woman dressed in heavy mourning – in this heat! – accompanied by a young man, her son or, more probably, her grandson. The young family, with the exception of the sleeping baby, is fascinated by the woman, they are all watching her with interest, but Non turns her eyes away – she sees a woman whose heart is compressed by a great sorrow, who is beyond the help of the Sal Volatile her caring grandchild is holding for her.

The heart is a mysterious organ. She thinks of the drawings she saw in Seb's consultation room. How can it be that a lump of flesh – for that is all it is – full of gristle and muscle and tubes can hold our feelings? She should have asked how that could be, if Seb's own heart had felt something when his friend was lost. Would he have an answer? Would his laboratory be able to tell him that? Or tell him why Angela is still alive when her heart is broken utterly?

Last night, still angry with her father's deceit, Non had decided to place her trust in modern medicine and, without thinking too long about it, had taken one drop less of her nightly draught, and this morning another drop less. She is not sure if she feels different, whether she is better or not. She is still tired, exhausted, worn out by the heat and by the city. How can people live all their lives in such places? She hopes Seb knows what he is about. Perhaps she will slow down the rate at which she is reducing the number of drops she takes of her lifeblood, until she receives his letter with the results of the tests that he had promised to send her.

A thought has come to her since he spoke about symptoms. He had asked her whether she had hallucinations and she had laughed at him. But she was not entirely sure that she knew what such a thing was. When she looked at the elderly woman on the seat opposite, or when she saw the child on the way to London, and saw the sickness in them, was she hallucinating? Were these figments of her imagination? They were moments of great clarity and distress to her, but were they real? Branwen is the only living person who knows of Non's gift, and she prefers to pretend it does not exist since one unfortunate diagnosis of Non's that involved a local minister. Non's sister had been – and still is – a great chapel-goer, and she had been mortified.

Non closes her eyes and leans on the glass of the compartment window, cooled slightly because she sits on the opposite side to where the sun is slowly descending into the west, still a red-hot ball, the sky aflame with the certainty of more heat the following day. She is on her own, listening to the rhythmic clatter of the wheels on the final stage of her journey. The young family waved her a goodbye at Aberdyfi, and the mourning woman and her grandson left the train at Barmouth . . .

She opens her eyes with a start. Has she dozed? She looks out at the sea and the lowering sun through the opposite window. Home, she thinks, almost there.

The castle looms above her as she leaves the train and crosses the railway to climb the hill home. The shops are closed, the winding streets quiet. The Saturday evening hush is broken only by the voices of children at play, or by their mothers calling them indoors for their suppers.

She is quite breathless when she arrives at her own house, but that is as usual, neither better nor worse, and she climbs the steps to the front door and pushes it open. Home. She wants to cry for the happiness it brings her despite the worries and problems that await her here.

Gwydion steps through from the kitchen into the hall as she is hanging up her hat on the hat stand. 'Non! Oh, Non, Non.' He takes hold of her and shakes her, then hugs her tightly. 'Where have you been, Non? What happened to you? We've been so worried. Davey's frantic. Are you all right? Oh, Non!'

27

Outside the back door, shaded from the sun, is the only place that is cool. Non stands, leaning lightly against the wall, crushing some of the honeysuckle that scents the air, and surveys her garden. The hens cluck faintly at one another and they are already out of sight, occupying what areas of shade they can find to hide from the relentless sunshine. Her plants are in dire need of water – she forgot to ask anyone specifically to water them every evening when she was away – and now the lemon balm and the mints are paying for her lack of concern. Even from here she can see browning leaves underneath the shrubby tops, and some of the flower heads are drooping. That is the first task, then, although it is entirely the wrong time of day to do it.

She fetches the big watering can from the shed next to the closet and fills it from the cask standing beside the shed. That, too, is almost empty, rain is desperately needed. When she was in London, Angela told her there were rumours that the Government was considering causing explosions in the clouds to bring rain, although Non cannot for the life of her see how that would work. It seems a most unlikely solution; there were never clouds in the sky to explode. She shakes her head. Some people think they can make everything behave the way they want. Some things you just have to let be, some things are stronger than man. Man can't control everything. Her father used to teach her that, Work with the natural world, Rhiannon, he would say, not against it. She is no longer sure about anything he said, the truth of it, the value of it. But it is difficult to stop thinking about his teaching, it is something she has always done, it has been her one constant all the years of her life. She feels now as if the ground is shifting beneath her feet, as if she is standing on the soft sand of the dunes. She is out of kilter with the way things really are, here at home and in London. She knows that the cause of it is the way her father reared her – Branwen often complained of her upbringing. During the ten years she spent with her father she had settled into ways of thinking and behaving that would never leave her. It was no wonder that she had never felt at home with Branwen – nor with anyone else until she met Davey. She wishes now that she had not become so . . . so pliant when she married Davey, trying to suit his ways instead of staying her own self. But she had wanted to be a good wife to him, and to repay him for loving her. During the War she had been more like her true self again, in order to survive. When Davey returned she had reverted to the role of the good wife who does as her husband tells her and does her utmost not to annoy him – though there are times when she forgets. She sighs. She is not absolutely sure where she belongs, whether there is a place where she can belong.

'Yoohoo, Non!' Maggie Ellis bobs up and down beyond the garden wall.

Non lifts the heavy watering can and walks across the garden. She does not want to speak to Maggie this morning, but it is as unavoidable as sunrise and sunset.

'Have to do everything yourself if you want anything done.' Maggie nods at the watering can.

'I forgot to ask anyone to water the plants,' Non says. 'They've managed everything else.' But she knows this is not what Maggie wants to talk about. She can see that something else is biting at her.

'You had everyone in a bit of a tizzy,' Maggie says.

Non lifts the foliage of the balm and waters the roots, careful not to drop water on the leaves where the sun would scorch.

'But you're home, now,' Maggie says. 'And no harm done.' The slight upward inflection invites Non to tell her more.

'A misunderstanding is all.' Non does not pause in her task.

'Ah, your niece had her baby sooner than expected?'

'The minute I left to come home, it seems,' Non says. 'I'm travelling back down tomorrow, so I've got a lot to do, Mrs Ellis.'

'Of course you have.' Maggie Ellis is still bobbing about, still has not said what she wants to say, but seems reluctant to start upon it. And for that Non is glad.

Pandemonium had broken out last night on her return. Eventually she had found out that on Friday, when everyone at home thought she was still in Aberystwyth and everyone at Aberystwyth thought she was at home, a telegram had arrived from Branwen asking her to return immediately. At home, no one knew what to do, they assumed that she was on the train home from Aberystwyth when the telegram arrived and so had not begun to panic until it was obvious she was not. So, yesterday, when she was sitting on the train from London in the heat of the day, telegrams had gone back and forth between Davey and Branwen. They both knew she had lied to them. But neither knew where she was.

Davey's relief at her return was more than tinged with anger at her behaviour. Meg had quietly left to spend the evening with a friend from work, Wil had gone to play a game of billiards at the Institute, and Gwydion had taken Osian for a walk with him though it was well past the boy's bedtime. And Non was left with Davey. Davey had talked to her, no, at her, concerned she could see, and furious, too, wanting to know what she had been thinking of, where she had been.

Even now she cannot believe how calmly she told him half the story. And how he had not questioned it. She told him that she had become anxious about her health, the condition of her heart, that she did not want anyone to worry about it and had conceived this plan to write to a specialist in London she had heard of when visiting Branwen on a previous occasion. Before Davey had time to think of the gaps in this story, she told him the consequences of her visit and what Mr O'Neill – here she had to be careful not to refer to him as Seb – had said about her father's medicine. Davey was uneasy. He was not at all convinced that this young man would know what he was talking about. What were his qualifications? He wanted Non to take no action until he had been with her to see someone else. There must be other doctors, he said, that would know about these things, they would ask Dr Jones to recommend somebody. He said Non must be exhausted, which was true, and that she should go to bed, for which she was grateful. As she lay in bed she had heard Davey speaking to Meg when she returned, then to Gwydion and Wil in turn, about what had happened.

This morning no one mentioned her absence or her illness. Davey said that he had told Catherine Davies that there would be no Sunday dinner today, which Non hoped would bring the habit to an end. Gwydion looked at her in such a way that she knew he did not entirely believe her story. Meg was uncharacteristically quiet, and Wil gave her a hug, which told her he was pleased she was home, before leaving with his father for the workshop where they had yet another coffin to finish for the next day. Osian was Osian, away in his own world. She could expect nothing else. She wondered if he had as much as noticed that she had not been there. Everything as usual, seemed to be the message. But everything was not as usual, was it? In London she had learnt things about herself and about her father that might change everything.

'I said, Non,' Maggie Ellis says, leaning over the wall, 'I said, have you got any more of that plant I can have for the closet? The honey cart's been running later and later this past week, my closet is stinking again. I'm sure to catch something else.'

Non stands up and looks beyond the shed and closet to the far side of her garden where the woody stems of marjoram sticking up from the dry earth have a few green leaves struggling to grow among them. 'It's all used up,' she says. 'Has Meg been giving you some while I've been away?'

'She said to help myself,' Maggie says. 'So I did.'

'You didn't notice you'd had it all?'

'Thought you'd have another clump somewhere, Non.' Maggie Ellis is not abashed.

'And you didn't notice everything was getting just a bit dry?' Non empties the last of the water from the can into the earth under the lemon balm and begins to pull the browned leaves from their stems.

'Too much else to worry about, Non.'

Non does not want to know Maggie Ellis's worries. She does not reply.

'Everyone's talking about these tramps,' Maggie says, reluctant to let the conversation go.

'Tramps? Well, they're here every summer. You know that, Mrs Ellis.'

'More of them than ever, they say,' Maggie says. 'Not just the usual few. All sorts. Not even Welsh, some of them.'

Non pauses in her gardening. She stands up and stretches her back. She thinks of all the beggars and tramps she saw in London, and the poor man trying to board the train. Did he think he would find more help out in the country than he found in London?

'Looking for work, do you think?' she asks Maggie.

'Work-shy, more like,' Maggie says. 'Want something for nothing. Not like they used to be, always grateful for anything we could give them. They knew we were practically as poor as they were.'

It is the War again, Non thinks, all those men with no work, and with no future, after all the terrible things they have been through.

'I only give to the ones I know,' Maggie says. 'Not that I've got much to give. But a billycan of tea and a crust of bread I can still manage.'

'Is anyone helping?'

'Helping?' Maggie says. 'Who is there to help except us? Constable Evans is trying to move them on, the new ones. I don't know where they all came from, all of a sudden.'

Non knows that she has more than most of her neighbours, but even she would find it hard to feed another mouth on a regular basis. She bends to her plants again. She wonders if the advice Seb gave her is beginning to take effect. She had taken one less drop of her lifeblood again this morning – having completely forgotten to take any last night – and she does not feel so weary. But she is being foolish; she is feeling like this because she sat in the train all yesterday, and had a long rest in bed last night. And because she is home.

She reaches the raspberries. They do not seem to be as affected by the drought of the past three days. She fingers their leaves. She will not need any now for Arianrhod, the baby having safely arrived. She wonders what she can usefully take with her when she travels there tomorrow.

'Didn't need the leaves, in the end,' Maggie Ellis says.

'Leaves?' Non struggles to think what Maggie is talking about.

'The leaves you gave me for my niece – she didn't want them.' Maggie shakes her head and looks mournfully at Non. 'What can you do, Non? I think she's making a big mistake. But you just can't tell these young girls anything.'

This is what Maggie has been itching to talk about. Non cannot believe the girl is going to have the baby when there is a way out of the dilemma. She raises her eyebrows at Maggie.

'You can look, Non,' Maggie says. 'But it's the truth. She had a letter from this man to say he's leaving his family for her. Can you believe such a thing? That a man could be so . . . so . . . treacherous? To leave a wife and children like that? I said to her, you be careful, my girl, if he can do it once he can do it again.' She leans right over the wall, squashing the roses flat. 'Divorce,' she whispers loudly. 'He's getting a divorce. Did you ever hear of such a thing? I don't know what the world's coming to, Non, I really don't.'

Non feels the earth shift beneath her feet, a sensation with which she is becoming familiar. Treachery, betrayal, subterfuge – who is more culpable than she? She is trying to make amends to Davey but her efforts are pushing her deeper into perfidy. The penalty, she thinks, of not staying true to yourself. And she has one other she should speak with, to explain why she had abandoned him. While she is at her sister's home over the next few days, she must seek out Owen – to explain, to make things right with him, to assuage her guilt for the way she cast him off.

28

Branwen's house, the house in which Non was brought up after her father's death, was never home, Non realises. Home was always the place she lived with her father in Trawsfynydd, and now it is the place she shares with Davey and their children, her own place. Branwen's house stands on the Promenade, looking out to sea. Through the bay window Non can see the span of the seafront, from the pier in the north to nearby Constitution Hill where the red valerian fights its way through the shale of the old quarry. Non had spent hours on Constitution Hill when she lived with Branwen, trying to race the cliff train to the top, sneaking into the camera obscura amid the paying visitors, spying on life in the town below her through its lens, seeing everything at a remove. She senses that she still does that, as if she is watching other people's lives unfold in a play for which she is the audience, an outsider looking in at it.

She watches the glint of the sun on the sea. The ripples on the sea's surface can barely be called waves, but the tide moves the water constantly back and forth whether there is a wind or breeze or not. It is a little like Arianrhod's hair, that ripple – how she envied her niece that hair when they were young! She and Branwen had spent the morning with Arianrhod and the baby, Branwen fussing over him, repeating her refrain of, A month too soon, you must wrap him up well. Non had seen a baby who was obviously full-term – he had all his eyelashes and eyebrows – but said nothing when she saw the plea in Arianrhod's eyes; her wedding had taken place only eight months ago. Despite Branwen's fears, the birth had not been a breech, but she still insisted that Non should have been there. Arianrhod is twenty-five, Non, she had said, old to bear a first child. And Non had pointed out that she was no midwife, and look, was it not obvious that Arianrhod and the child were in the best of health? She and Branwen had paused and looked at the mother and child, who were bound up in a world of their own for that moment, and Non was caught unawares by the pain of loss for something she had never experienced.

They had walked back along the Promenade and stopped for lunch – Catherine Davies would be pleased to hear that word – with some of Branwen's acquaintances. Non felt as out of place among them as she had in London. She did not know where she belonged, that was the truth, and she did not know how to find it out – this place where she should be, this place that she believed she had found when she married Davey. I was younger than Arianrhod is, she had thought as she watched the ladies at their lunch, what did I know that was of any use?

This room with its big window had been Non's favourite when she lived here. This was where she had squabbled with Branwen's eldest daughter, Gwenllian, who had been a few months older but no match for Non's waywardness. Arianrhod and Nêst they had both ignored, but all four of them adored the baby Gwydion. Non remembers playing with him, crawling after him around this big room, teaching him bad ways, Branwen had said, telling her off, teaching him to be a disobedient little thing like Non herself.

And look at me now, she thinks, as Branwen brings in a pot of tea and deposits it alongside the cups and saucers on the table in the bay of the window. Non sits and begins to pour milk into their cups, then the tea. Branwen walks about the room, plumping up cushions, shaking the curtains at the window, moving books from the writing table to the shelves against the walls then back again, until Non can stand it no longer.

'Sit down, Branwen. Whatever is the matter with you?'

'They know – did you see them, did you see the looks? They all know, Non.' Branwen slaps her hand on the table top.

Non had thought it was odd that Branwen was so blind to what was perfectly obvious. They are having to pretend. 'What does it matter? The baby's perfect, and Arianrhod is well and happy. That's all that matters, isn't it?'

'That is just typical of you, Non. You don't care about the . . . the . . . niceties of life. You know – those little things that make life run smoothly?' Branwen beats a cushion almost viciously; Non can see the dust rise from it and wonders who Branwen thinks it is. 'I know it wasn't your fault you were the way you were, Non, but it took me two years – two years! – to stop you telling people your opinion of them. I tried and tried to explain how you have to consider people's feelings. And all that business about seeing inside them. I will never – never, Non! – forget that time you told Reverend Richards's wife he had something wrong with his . . . his . . . well, you know. It makes me cringe even now. People still talk about it!'

Non smiles into her teacup. 'What happened to him?'

'He died, of course, eventually. But not before he went mad with it, just like that English king, George the something.' Branwen leans down close to Non. 'It isn't funny, Non. And it wasn't funny then. His poor wife! They had to move away in the end. The shame of it was too much. I don't know what happened to her after he died, poor woman.'

'It wasn't funny that he preached the opposite of what he was apparently doing, Branwen. Was it?' Not that Non had understood any of that at the time.

'Oh, you're impossible.' Branwen deflates, and sits in the chair opposite Non at the table and glances down at the seafront. 'You were such a handful. And so righteous. All Father's fault, the way he brought you up like that. And I know you were right about old Richards – but you have to think about other things, too. His wife, and us. We have to live here, remember?'

Non knows her sister, she knows all this springs from her anxieties about Arianrhod and her new grandchild, and that Arianrhod's husband is thinking of moving them all away because he is trying for posts at colleges in Oxford and Cambridge, and is more than likely to be given one soon. He is ambitious, Branwen has told Non. She places her cup in its saucer and goes to her sister and hugs her.

'Get away with you,' Branwen says. But her voice is softer, less anxious.

'It'll be a five-minute wonder, this early baby,' Non says, 'you'll see.'

'Prys,' Branwen says. 'Her father is so pleased that she's named the baby for him. He's telling everyone!'

'Prys Bach,' Non says. 'He looks a bit like Old Prys, did you notice?'

'Old Prys!' And now Branwen smiles, if fleetingly. 'Don't let him hear you call him that.'

The elder Prys had been kind to the little interloper Branwen had brought into their household all those years ago. Non had been fonder of her gentle brother-in-law than of her sister when she had lived with them. 'It must have been hard for you and Prys to take me in.' It is a statement rather than a question.

Branwen becomes serious again. She toys with tongs in the sugar bowl. 'It wasn't you, Non, it was the way you'd been brought up. You were . . . well, almost uncontrollable. You'd do as you liked and say what you liked. I didn't know what to do with you.'

This is an old refrain, Non knows it well, but it may be an opportunity to question her sister. 'Why did you take me in, Branwen – immediately, the way you did? One day Father was dead and the next I was living with you is all I remember. Didn't you take time to consider it?'

'I promised Mother,' Branwen says. 'Poor Mother. She had such a bad pregnancy with you. Well, she was far too old to be bearing another child – but it seems Father was one of those men you hear about who won't take no for an answer. She wanted to be sure you would be looked after. I'd not long had Gwenllian, and she asked me to have you, too.'

'I didn't know that.' Non reflects that she knows only what her father told her about her mother.

'Well, Mother wanted me to take you straightaway if she died, but of course Father stepped right in and refused to let that happen. I don't know how he thought he was going to take care of you. And look at the consequences!'

All these things Non does not know, and here they are all pouring out. It is this baby's birth that has caused this torrent, she thinks, Prys Bach has opened a floodgate that Branwen has kept tightly closed for years. 'You never told me any of this, Branwen. Why not?'

'What for?'

'Oh, I don't know,' Non says. All at once, she feels slightly sorry for herself. 'Maybe these last few days wouldn't have been such a shock.'

Dismay shows in Branwen's face. 'What do you mean? What are you talking about, Non?'

So Non tells her about London, or at least as much as she has told Davey. She does not mention Angela. Lies, she thinks, treachery, perfidy.

'Oh, Non.' Branwen is horrified.

'Yes, well . . .' Non says, 'perhaps I'll be the way I should be when I've stopped taking these drops altogether. But Branwen, why did Father do it? What was he really like? I can't remember what he was like any more.'

'If I tell you, you probably won't believe me. You worshipped him.' She pauses and looks at Non. 'And I don't think that's too strong a word to use.'

'Tell me how you saw him. I only have a child's memory of him, it's like thinking of a character in a story I heard a long time ago. Please, Branwen?'

'Arrogant,' Branwen says. 'He always thought he was right. And selfish – he always had to have what he wanted. He believed his own stories, that was the trouble, it made him impossible. Poor Mother.'

'I loved his stories,' Non says.

'But they weren't true, were they? He was a liar. Everything he told us that I ever found out about was a lie. I expect the rest was, too, the things I didn't find out about.'

'No, I know that now,' Non says, although she still feels that stories are not necessarily bad for not being true. Is it not the nature of stories to not be true? They must hold a truth, but that is a different thing. In fact, that is their purpose, to hold a truth, rather than to tell the truth. In a flash she understands that all her father's stories did that. She will see if she can explain this to Branwen. 'Do you remember his story about Mother's ring? When I was in London, I went to Burlington House so I could see the place where he'd been given the money to buy the betrothal ring for Mother.' She holds her hand up to stop Branwen from interrupting. 'But he'd never been a member there, there was never a collection made that he spent on a ring for Mother. But there is still a truth in—'

Branwen can wait no longer, 'You see? You see?' She leaps to her feet, rocking the table and its cargo. 'That was a complete fabrication, from beginning to end. A big lie, Non!' She begins to pace the room. 'He didn't buy Mother that ring – it belonged to her grandmother. She gave it to me to keep safe for you, and what a to-do he made about that! And she made sure that the bit of money she had would come to you when he died. He only ever got the income from it or God knows there wouldn't have been a farthing left for you.' She paces, window to door, door to window, she thumps the backs of the chairs when she passes them, picks up the cushions and throws them back down again.

Branwen would smash everything, only then she would have to clear it up again. A picture of her sister furious at her for some misdeed comes into Non's mind: Branwen had thrown a milk jug and broken a window and had been even more furious at having to clear up the whole mess. Non has a memory of the house shaking, but, she thinks, that is probably a truth rather than the truth. Non does not feel as shocked as she thinks she ought to be at these revelations about her father. Somehow, she must have been aware of much of this, but it never mattered. She ought to be as furious and horrified as Branwen is – after all this time! – but she never knew her mother, only the father in the stories and she loved him. She is glad he did not teach her to be so narrow and constrained in her thoughts and feelings, even though it has made things a bit, well, maybe more than a bit difficult at times.

'And the worst thing,' Branwen stops pacing, takes hold of the back of her chair by the table and leans towards Non. 'The very worst thing, Non—'

'Is what?'

'The worst thing is that I think Gwydion is far too like him. He looks like him and he's so like him in his ways sometimes, Non . . . well, it worries me to death.'

Non thinks of Gwydion, of his love for her, of his kindness to Meg and Osian, of his passion for Aoife, of his developing political ideals, of his fear of his mother, and does not think he sounds like the self-centred man that Branwen says was her father.

'He's getting on well with the work at Wern Fawr,' she says.

'Well, that's something.' Branwen nods her head. 'Yes, that's good.'

'And he has mentioned that there's a girl he's sweet on – Aoife. I expect Prys knows her father quite well—'

'A troublemaker,' Branwen says. 'That's what they say her father is, a troublemaker. Prys thinks he's a nice man, of course, you know what Prys is like, never a bad word . . .' Her fingers tap frantically on the back of her chair. 'I really don't think there's anything there, you know, with the girl, nothing serious, thank goodness. They're going back to Ireland soon anyway, the whole family.'

This is not the best time for Non to mention Gwydion's plans. And anyway, he has to tell his mother himself, Non had told him that quite firmly. And the longer the silly boy waits, the harder it is going to be. Branwen has a black and white view of the world that Non does not share. She fears that Branwen will never understand what her son wants to do.

29

The walk from Branwen's house to the back lanes of Llanbadarn is a long one of twists and turns and changing views so that Non has passed through seascapes, townscapes and the beauties of the countryside before she stops at the start of a row of small cottages where she has assumed, without really thinking about it until this very moment, that Owen still lives. She had set off early, thinking to avoid the worst of the heat, yet she is hot and dusty, her shoes and the hem of her skirt dirty from the pavements in town and from the packed earth of Plas Crug Road and the path through the cemetery that have brought her here. She looks up the incline along the fronts of the cottages. They are all in the darkest of shade, but their long back gardens, she knows, will be full of herbs and vegetables and flowers, of bees and butterflies busy at their essential work, just like her own garden must be already this morning. Owen's back garden will be the most productive of all.

She sets off again up the slope, counting off the cottages until she reaches the fifth. It is as dark and quiet as the others she has just passed; it is difficult to see even the front door, painted a dark brown, as she knows, so that it merges with the shade, and if she did not know it was there she might easily have tripped into the well before the door. When she knocks memories return of how she used to knock three times, pause, then knock twice – a code to let Owen know it was her and no other on the outside. Her face grows hot at the thought of such foolishness.

As she waits the silence settles around her, the air is perfectly still and the heat, as usual, seems to muffle distant noises. A train she cannot see whistles as it passes along the rails and disturbs her thoughts. She can smell the sharp burn of its clouds of smoke and steam as they appear above the houses lower down the hill.

She does not hear the door open. Her first encounter with Owen for two and a half years – she cannot believe the amount of time that has elapsed – is a voice that is still familiar to her saying, tentatively, 'Rhiannon?'

She turns around to the open door. 'Hello, Owen,' she says. That was not all that she had meant to say when she saw him again. But what she had meant to say escapes her; it is as far from her as the seagulls floating up there in the sky as if they were on still water rather than a current of air.

'Still lost in some dream or another, Rhiannon?' Owen asks.

Non is not sure how to reply. This is not the reception she has envisaged from the man she had believed was close to her, the man she had thought wanted to be more than a friend to her. He has not even invited her into his house. What is she to do now? She cannot make things right between them standing here on the doorstep!

Owen stands back from the door as if reading her mind, and her heart gives a little leap that has nothing to do with her life-blood or Seb O'Neill's advice, her heart gives a little leap because Owen had always done this, anticipated what she was thinking.

It was one of the things that had endeared him to her. He says, 'Would you like to come in?'

She walks into the house behind him, and at once feels at home in the long passage that opens straight out through the back door into the garden. It looks like a passage into paradise; it always did. In the garden the plants show no sign of the long summer and the drought it has brought with it. The view is lush and green, the bees drone and butterflies open and close their wings, in ecstasy, where they have settled on the flower heads. Non had almost forgotten the loveliness and peace of this garden, something she cannot completely achieve in her own garden with Maggie Ellis just over the wall. She should do what Owen has done, or maybe it was his parents before him, and grow trees with plants to ramble through them to keep the Maggie Ellises of the world at bay.

'So, what brings you here after such a long absence?' Owen says as they step through the back entrance into bright sunshine.

What does he imagine has brought her? Suddenly, she is not entirely certain of her own motives for coming here. She had not thought he could still affect her when she had all but forgotten him. She says, 'My sister's youngest girl has just had her first child.' She cannot remember if she ever mentioned much about her family to him during her visits in the War. Owen merely nods at her and she is tongue-tied again. She looks around the garden and begins to see signs of neglect; the plants are not as well tended as they used to be, they have been allowed to spread and sprawl in a way she thinks is not likely to be good for their medicinal properties. She steps forward and stumbles and sees she has tripped over what she takes at first to be a dead thing, a rabbit perhaps, and then in the same instant sees it is a child's toy, a stuffed cat or dog, maybe, it is difficult to tell.

Owen limps to her assistance. He still wears the black and heavy boot on his club foot, the foot that saved him from the carnage to which so many of his friends had succumbed. He helps her back to the path, and she looks at him, asking a question with her eyes that she does not want to put into words.

'I'm married now,' is his answer.

Married! Non looks at the toy at her feet, and then at the washing draped over the bigger shrubs further up the garden, bright children's clothing, a woman's underclothes, and small items of bedding.

'She brought a child with her. Her husband was killed right at the end of the War. He never saw the boy, and the boy never saw his father.'

Non cannot think of anything to say. What had she expected – that he would have waited for her, pined for her? Maybe she had been mistaken, maybe Owen had never wanted to be more than a friend to her. She feels her face flush again.

'He's a dear little soul,' Owen says. 'And the odd thing is, he even looks a bit like me.' He smiles at Non; she had forgotten his smile. 'We suit each other well, me and Jennet,' he says. 'We suit each other, Rhiannon, we both answer a need in the other. I never could work out what your need was.'

Non is not sure what her need had been, exactly, either. Someone to assuage the loneliness of being without Davey? She no longer knows. She has no idea what she is doing here visiting this man who has done very well without her. 'I shouldn't have come,' she says, finding her voice at last. 'I was in Aberystwyth with time to spare and thought I would see how you were.'

'I am as you see,' Owen says.

Suddenly Non is reminded of how irritating Owen could be, too, with his enigmatic replies and sayings so that she never quite

knew where she was with him. 'And still tending to your herbs?'
she asks.

'Not as I should,' he says.

'And still tending the horses?'

'Rhiannon, the horses, if you recall, went to war and as far as
I know were slaughtered with all the men that were slaughtered.
None of them came back, anyway. It's something I prefer never
to think about.'

Non knew the horses had been taken, of course she did, Owen
had been so unhappy about it, but she had forgotten. Is that how
much she had cared for him in reality?

'I'm working at the National Library now. I saw your – what?
– cousin, nephew? Gwydion? We were both up there for a meeting.
Did he tell you I was asking after you? Is that why you're here?'

She manages to both nod and shake her head. Does Owen
remember what he told Gwydion?

'I'd just had some good news,' Owen says, 'and had a drop too
much of Evan Jenkins's home brew to celebrate before heading
off to the meeting. It was a lot stronger than any of us expected.'
He smiles at the memory. 'Oh, that was a night and a half! Gwydion
looks exactly like that picture of your father that was in that herbal
you showed me. I thought I was seeing ghosts – the home brew,
you know – then Evan told me who he was. Do you remember
Evan, Rhiannon?'

Owen abstained from alcoholic drink when she knew him, his
Quaker family chose to do so, as her own family had done, and
here he is speaking of having been . . . well . . . drunk on home
brew. And she does not remember anyone called Evan Jenkins.
She has walked all this way, through the heat and the dust, for
nothing, for no reason. But she knows she has no right to feel
piqued. 'I'm glad to see you well, Owen, and happy,' she says, and

is pleased to hear her voice say the words so calmly, as if she meant them, the little niceties of life, Branwen would be proud of her. Or maybe not, given the situation. She turns for the back door to the house, to see a young woman walk through with a small boy in tow. He has a mop of red curls, and freckles on his nose like Owen's. The boy runs ahead and launches himself into Owen's arms.

'I'm sorry for his bad manners.' Jennet, for it must be she, follows the child into the garden.

Non looks at her in amazement as she comes out of the shadow of the house. She thinks of Owen's description of his celebration – a night and a half, indeed, she thinks, for Jennet is hugely pregnant.

She makes her farewells hastily, refusing the offer of tea, or a cold drink if she would prefer. She almost runs down the hill from the cottage. It is done, she thinks, I need never think of Owen again. She has a more pressing thought that meeting Jennet has awoken in her. If, when she has entirely stopped taking her life-blood, she has the heart of a normal woman, there should be nothing to stop her having a baby – to be sure, if Arianrhod is old at twenty-five to be bearing her first child, then Non is very old already at twenty-nine, but not impossibly old. She is not entirely sure how she feels about the possibility, but her feet give an involuntary little skip as she turns onto the dusty path through the cemetery on her way back to Aberystwyth.

'A baby of my own!' she says to the gravestones, just to hear how it sounds.

30

She is certain it has taken her hours to make the journey home to Branwen's house. When she had reached the Promenade, with its screaming gulls and milling visitors, she wanted more time to herself to consider this new idea. She had sat on a bench, the wooden slats of the seat burning beneath her thighs, and put up her parasol to provide shade from the sun and inquisitive stares and possible recognition. A baby of her own! The phrase had rung like a bell in her head. But only, she had thought, if Davey remembers that he never had a liaison with Angela and does not need to punish himself – nor her – by refusing to be her husband. There had to be a way to help him remember. She still had not spoken to him about Angela's letter – and that, she had thought, would be the way to do it. She had looked out over the still sea and felt a calm settle over her that she had not experienced for a long time. Something has changed, she had thought, something has shifted inside me.

She bought an ice cream from the Lorne Dairy cart to keep the pangs of hunger at bay and enjoyed the contentment it gave her to do such a simple thing. Branwen would not approve, she knew, and was careful to brush any evidence from her blouse and the folds of her skirt before arriving at the house.

Branwen is in the garden at the back, entertaining friends with an al-fresco luncheon that would have delighted Catherine Davies, although – and here Non feels a soupçon of guilt – there is only the debris of lunch left apart from the pristine place-setting laid for the one person who had not been there.

Branwen does not mention the untouched plate, nor Non's lateness, and introduces her to her friends, dust and all. Non bobs and smiles and shakes hands as the ladies leave, and follows them back through the house to run upstairs to change her skirt and shoes.

When Non comes downstairs, Branwen has cleared the table in the garden and laid out the cups and saucers for them, and bara brith on a plate. Non is partial to Branwen's bara brith and her stomach rumbles at the sight of it.

'I've made a fresh pot of tea,' Branwen says. She pours milk, then the tea, into their cups. 'Where did you get to, Non? I was expecting you to come back to have lunch, not after we'd finished eating it. You embarrassed me.'

'I walked further than I intended to,' Non says. 'I'm sorry I didn't get back in time.' And she is sorry to disappoint and upset Branwen yet again, although she had completely forgotten that Branwen was having a luncheon party. Luncheon! She pushes the thought of Catherine Davies outside the boundary of her newly acquired equilibrium. 'But this is nice,' she says, 'sitting here with you.' She looks at the long garden, with its roses blooming and tumbling in every direction, their scent filling the air with a heavy sweetness that she can almost see. She fingers the velvet of a rose petal that has dropped onto the tablecloth and rubs it on her cheek. 'It reminds me of playing here when I lived with you.'

'It's overgrown,' Branwen says. 'Everything needs cutting back, but this is how Prys likes it. He says it's like a bower – a bower, for goodness' sake – and relaxes him. I suppose all the greenery keeps us cool in this dreadful heat.' Branwen fidgets her cup around on its saucer and the saucer on the tablecloth. She shifts the milk jug and the sugar bowl and shifts them back again. 'My friend Eluned Bowen-Pugh came here especially to meet you. You have no idea of how difficult it was to persuade her to come to lunch – no idea, Non – she's an important woman, very busy.' She slides a calling card across the tablecloth to Non. 'She left this for you. You'd better put it in your bag, or you might lose it.'

'I didn't know you'd asked anyone to come to meet me especially,' Non says, ignoring the card and Branwen's instructions.

Branwen carries on speaking as if Non has said nothing. 'You see, Non, you could get Osian into this place her husband runs for boys like him.'

Non sits perfectly still; she feels her calmness dissipate a little. She has had fruitless arguments with Branwen about Osian since the War. 'What place?' she says.

'A hospital or something. Well, an asylum, I suppose, for boys that aren't . . . well, that aren't quite, you know, right. Come on Non, even you can't pretend Osian's right in the head.'

'He's different, that's all, Branwen. He's not wrong in the head, or whatever you want to call him. He's . . . he's gifted.' The word comes to her from nowhere. Gifted, she thinks, is exactly right.

Branwen snorts then turns the noise into a cough. 'Head in the clouds as usual,' she says when she has finished spluttering. 'Well, you pretend all you want, Non, but the only thing to do with a boy like that is to have him put away. He's not even yours, for goodness' sake.'

He is mine, Non thinks, not of my flesh, perhaps, but mine all the same. She is not going to argue this time. Branwen has told her what to do – and what not to do – since the day Non went to live with her. Saying nothing is the best defence against Branwen's hectoring, Non has discovered, as it is with Maggie Ellis's questioning, and Branwen will think she has won the day, when in fact she has not. Non has forgotten how single-minded Branwen can be. She wonders from which parent her sister inherited that trait. She sips her tea and nibbles at the bara brith, her hunger vanished again. A blackbird rustles the leaves of the lilac tree above the table and more petals rain down from the rose that rambles through the branches. When Non thinks enough time has elapsed for Branwen to feel pleased with what she will see as a victory, she says, 'I've been thinking, Branwen, about how little I know about Mother, except what Father told me – and I don't know what to make of that any more. What was she really like? How did she come to marry Father?'

'Oh, how would I know?' Branwen says. She sweeps the rose petals off the tablecloth with her hands. Non wonders if her question will be ignored, but the floodgates, it seems, remain open. 'She was head in the clouds, too. I expect he bullied her into it. She was . . . she was just there, somehow, like his shadow or something. Everything was always about him, about what he wanted.' She brushes some more petals to the ground. 'You see? Everything needs cutting back!'

Non pours more tea into her sister's cup and pushes it towards her. 'What were her parents like, Branwen? Our grandparents. I never heard Father mention them.'

'Well, he wouldn't, would he?' Branwen says. 'I was the only child I knew who had never met her grandparents. I don't know what happened exactly, but Mother's parents were so disgusted with her marriage to Father that they cut her off. And that was that. It was lucky for her that she had some money left for her by her grandmother. And that ring – she would never sell it you know, no matter how much Father wheedled and bullied. She said her grandmother told her the money and ring were to go to her youngest child.' She draws her cup and saucer towards her and picks a rose petal out of the tea and flicks it onto the grass with a grimace.

'She must have loved Father a great deal to cut herself off from her family,' Non says.

'Love!' Branwen snorts again, and does not bother to disguise it. She jumps up from her chair and marches into the house. 'I'll show you,' she calls back over her shoulder. 'You'll see!'

Non knows her father loved her mother from the stories he has told her, and that her mother loved him in return. The stories may not have been true, she thinks, but the truth was in them.

Branwen returns into a flurry of petals as the blackbird takes flight from the lilac. 'Here,' she says, and holds out an opened envelope to Non. 'You read that. She sent it to me when Prys and I married. She couldn't come to the wedding – can you believe that? And why? Because she'd just had another miscarriage! Father again!'

Non draws the letter out of the envelope. The paper is a pale cream and carries a faint scent that she thinks she recognises. Maybe Non the baby had captured a memory, after all. She unfolds the letter and reads it.

It is clear to Non what the letter is saying: that her mother had seen in Osian Rhys what others could not see, and that she had always, all her married life, loved him, even when she was not happy with some of the things he did. And she hoped Branwen would know the same love.

Non closes her eyes. She is thankful to have read her mother's own words, to know for certain that the truth was present within her father's web of stories.

'She loved him.' She smiles at Branwen.

'What are you talking about? She says she hated the things he did. She says it there in black and white, Non. How can you be so . . . so blind?'

Non sighs. She gazes at the letter with its roughly cut edges and fading ink. She folds it and puts it back inside its envelope. She and Branwen will never agree. They look upon life too differently.

'You weren't there, Non, the way I was.' Branwen pushes her cup and saucer away from her so violently that the tea splashes onto the tablecloth, but she does not notice. 'You weren't there watching those little girls die, and the miscarriages Mother had. She was too delicate to have all those children. But did he care? And you know why he insisted on keeping you when Mother died?' Branwen's voice has risen until she is shouting. 'All that nonsense he used to bore everyone with about Mother seeing things, seeing what was wrong with people – he was convinced you'd be the same, wasn't he?'

Non is surprised to feel relief at this information, she had no inkling of it, but it explains the way she is. 'But I was, wasn't I?' she says. 'I am, Branwen.'

Branwen screams. She picks up the cup from her saucer and smashes it into the nearest rose bush and runs into the house.

So who is Branwen like? A grandparent, maybe. Non can see that she herself is a mix of both her parents. From her father she has inherited a way of seeing the world that is different to the way most other people she knows view it. And her mother's bequest to Non was her gift. She wishes she did not find it a burden, she wishes she could thank her mother for it; she wishes she did not hope the gift was the result of hallucinations brought on by the May Lily. She shivers to think it is a curse she may hand down to a child of her own flesh. Then her heart lightens when she thinks of another inheritance from her mother: her spontaneity. She had married Davey – in a haste of which Branwen had disapproved – for the same reasons her mother had married her father. She had seen in Davey those qualities she admired – steadfastness, quietude, loyalty. Qualities he still possesses. She has, unlike her mother, forgotten why she married her husband, but she will not forget again.

31

A moment ago Non had been fast asleep and dreaming, though the dream has already escaped through the open window, and now she is awake and alert. Something must have woken her but when she lies still to listen she can hear only the hush of a Sunday morning.

Without thinking she stretches her hand out to the cool sheet and empty place beside her and finds Davey still there. She rests the back of her hand on his bare skin and feels the steady rise and fall of his chest beneath it. He must be exhausted to be sleeping this late in the morning. She should not have left him for all those days to carry everything, to look after them all. Especially Osian. She has been worrying about this since Gwydion told her yesterday that when she was away in London, and then in Aberystwyth, he had risen early to help Davey with some of her tasks and had found him one morning aiming an imaginary rifle at an imaginary enemy in uncanny silence, and another time crying and shivering under the table. Gwydion had not known what to do, and so had done nothing, and Non assured him that he had done the right thing, that there was nothing to be done,

Davey had to be left to return to normality by himself. It had been frightening, Gwydion had told her, and he had thought it best not to mention it to Wil or Meg.

After her conversation with Gwydion, when she had the house to herself during the afternoon, Non had decided to look through all the letters Davey had written to her over the years he had been away. She would read them differently now, she reasoned, she would read them with the benefit of hindsight, she would know what to look out for. The small travel case they were stored in under the bed was dusty, and the letters inside had already taken on a look of age and fragility, their envelopes brittle, their ink fading. In those bundles she could see the playing out of her distancing from Davey. The first few bundles, the oldest, were bound by a ribbon tied in a bow to hold them together. The last of the letters she had received had been thrown on top carelessly. She could remember doing that, just lifting the lid and throwing them in, resenting Davey for writing so impersonally, so infrequently, and she felt the tears gather in her throat as she looked through them.

At first, Davey's letters had to be written in English to get past the censor, and she remembered her disappointment as she read them. But the content was, she knew, much as other women of her acquaintance had received, the ones who had asked her to read their letters to them – jokey comments about the food and the weather, a longing for the recipient of the letter, a report of meeting with somebody's brother or cousin. They were letters written by rote in a foreign language, not real feelings and thoughts. She picked through them in the hope of finding some nugget of information that she had missed at the time, anything that would help explain Davey's distress. But she could see no connection in his words to anything that she had learnt since she had first read them about the ordeals men had endured during the fighting. She kissed each letter, in an apology to Davey, before she replaced it in the box.

Davey's voice had surprised her. It wasn't like that at all, Non.

She had not heard him coming home or walking upstairs and had no idea how long he had been standing in the doorway, watching her. He had come into the bedroom and she had looked up at him as he said that everyone wrote letters that would not worry or demoralise the people they had left behind; those had been the instructions they were given.

Non was astonished. This was the first time Davey had voluntarily spoken about the War since he had confessed his – false – infidelity to her. It was the first time since his confession that he had spoken to her without avoiding her gaze. She had risen to her feet and held her hand out to him in delight.

That had been too much for him. He had backed away from her. Burn them, Non, he had said, and returned downstairs. But she could not. She had finished packing the letters and pushed the case back under the bed.

I wish I had known, she thinks, lying next to Davey, listening to the silence. I do not know what I could have done, but I wish I had known then what I know now.

She turns on her side to look at him. He is awake, watching her. She smiles at him.

'I'm glad you're home, Non,' he says.

Something has happened. Something has changed while she was away in Aberystwyth. She had sensed it yesterday. Davey has not lain with her like this since he told her he was not fit to be her husband. She is almost afraid to speak in case the moment vanishes like one of the perfect little worlds inside Osian's soap bubbles. She is filled with gladness. She does not want to be anywhere else. This is where she belongs. This is her place.

'This business of your medicine . . . Are you sure it's safe? Cutting your drops down like that after taking them all your life? Are you sure you wouldn't like to see another doctor?'

She rests her hand on his shoulder as he talks to her, and he puts his own hand over hers, the callouses scraping her skin, his palm like the sandpaper he uses every day. And she feels as she did the very first time he touched her.

'I feel better already, I'm sure of it. I'm cutting down on them very slowly, Davey.'

'But, this doctor . . . He will write to you, will he? He will think about it all and say that what he told you was right?'

'He said he would, and he seemed the kind of man to keep his word. I expect it takes him a while to do these tests in his laboratory that he was talking about.'

Davey shakes his head, 'Sounds like magic, doesn't it?'

'I think it was Father who dealt in magic. Mr O'Neill seemed very . . . scientific.'

Davey squeezes her hand. 'It's difficult when the things we've been so certain about get knocked away.'

She wonders which certainties he is talking about: her father, Wil, Osian, old William Davies? Is it Angela? Or is there something she does not even know about yet? She waits in silence. The Sunday hush is broken by the sound of birdsong, the squeal of a door opening and shutting, somebody softly singing a hymn as the morning brightens.

'What did you sell to get to London?' Davey says. 'I hope it wasn't something you didn't want to part with.'

He would know that she had no money unless she sold something. She should have realised that he would be anxious about how she had funded the trip when they were only just managing because of the money he gave to his mother every week. 'Mother's ring,' she says. 'To the pawn shop in Port. So I had a chance of getting it back.'

'I thought it might be the ring,' Davey says. 'You shouldn't have had to do that. I have managed to put a bit of money by, Non – in case of an emergency, you know, though I don't know what sort of emergency . . .' He pauses, as if it is a wonder to him.

As it is to Non. She is sure they never used to think there might be emergencies. She supposes it is the War that has made these changes in him, in them all. Davey saving! She moves her hand slightly under his. She can feel his pulse, the beat of his heart in his wrist, and feels tears threatening to overwhelm her. And I never used to be a cry baby, she thinks.

Davey tightens his hand over hers. 'But we can use it to buy the ring back, Non. This counts as an emergency. And then . . . Do you think it would be as if I gave you the ring?'

Non nods. She does not know, she cannot imagine, what all this means. She listens to the comforting sounds of the day beginning outside their window.

'And I've remembered . . . well, you know, Non, I don't know why I thought I had all that nonsense with that nurse. I just can't understand it. These last few days I've known more and more that it never happened. And it is such a relief, Non, to know that it didn't – but why did I think it had?'

Non does not think Davey is expecting her to answer him. She waits for him to go on. The morning is rapidly becoming noisier. The crows roosting in the copse beside the farm across the road have started calling one another, their cries raucous and demanding.

'See, Non . . .' Davey shifts his position so that her arm is uncomfortable where it is and she slips it around his waist. And he does not pull away and pretend it is not there. 'See, I've been trying to puzzle it out. She looked a bit like Grace, the nurse. But I don't think that was what gave me these . . . well, these false certainties. Because – and I never said this to you before, Non, and I don't really know if I should now – but I knew even before Wil was born that I'd made a mistake marrying Grace. So did I dream this nurse thing? Or was it the gas – the gas was bad, Non – or, there was an attack on our trench. Maybe I got a knock on the head or something. I don't know, I can't remember. I think I've forgotten a lot of things, Non. But it has upset me so much, thinking I had been untrue to you.'

The letter, Non thinks, it is Angela's letter that has brought the truth to the surface. She waits for him to mention the letter, but he does not. But then again, neither has she mentioned Angela's letter, and she has not mentioned, and has no intention of mentioning, that part of her visit to London. Does that make them equal? Equal in deception, she thinks. Can they live with it? She does not know what the answer might be.

'You are all I want, Non,' Davey says. He looks into her eyes.

She curbs a desire to look away in case he can see her deceit. Now, she understands why he found it difficult to look at her when he believed he had wronged her. She puts her arm around his waist and her other arm around his neck and draws herself to him. She feels his limbs relaxing and his breath deepening. And he puts his arms around her and begins to stroke her back with the long, languorous strokes that she loves and has not realised until this moment that she has missed so much.

As she murmurs her appreciation a loud clatter makes them jump apart as guiltily as if Catherine Davies had entered their bedroom. Herman is balancing on top of the open sash, cawing raucously, his beak wide open.

Davey begins to laugh. He laughs and laughs as if he will never stop, this man who has not laughed since he returned home to her from the War. And then his laughter turns to sobs as raucous as Herman's caws, and Non holds her arms around his heaving body until her own body quivers with the effort.

32

'Them crows are a bit loud this morning, missus.' Lizzie German heaves the dolly into the washtub as she speaks, and begins pounding the clothes with it.

'From first thing,' Non says. 'And yesterday the same. Herman's around somewhere. He flew in through the bedroom window yesterday morning. What a fright he gave us, Lizzie.'

'That bird,' Lizzie says. 'Just like my poor Herman was. Loud and clumsy.'

Non laughs at Lizzie's expression, then begins to scrub in earnest at the cuffs of the shirt on her washboard. The suds float into her face. She can taste the soapiness when she licks her lips to moisten them. We are almost getting used to this heat, she thinks, it is as if we have never experienced anything else. No rain, no wind, no cold, no snow, no sleet, just sun from one year end to the other. She tries to remember how many weeks the heatwave has lasted. It is not tiring me as much as it did, she thinks, this weather.

'Saw your Davey on my way up here this morning,' Lizzie says. 'Looks better than he's done in a while.'

'I think he's feeling better.' Non thinks maybe she ought to cross her fingers as she says it, touch wood; for luck, just in case. Yesterday she had scarcely been able to think about anything all day except that she had Davey back. She had been unable to stop smiling at him, touching his face or his hand whenever she walked past him, until Meg noticed and began to groan whenever it happened. Non smiles at Lizzie.

'You, too,' Lizzie says.

'What?'

'Looking better.' Lizzie stops the pounding and leans on the dolly to watch Non. 'And feeling better? You're not having to stop every two minutes to draw breath.'

'It seems to be working, Lizzie, cutting down the medicine, drop by drop.'

'Two-edged sword, missus.' Lizzie surprises Non with her insight, as always.

'Yes. I can't help feeling I'm somehow letting my father down.'

'Hmm,' Lizzie says. 'You look to the living, missus. You've got plenty of them to look after without worrying about the dead.'

'Life goes on, you mean, Lizzie?'

'It does that. Full of life, your lot, too. I saw young Meg this morning after I saw your Davey, running down the hill. Looked a bit cross.'

'Poor Meg,' Non says. 'I'm surprised she didn't have steam coming out of her ears. The boys had been teasing her because she had a letter from her French penfriend.'

'French!' Lizzie begins to work the dolly again, as if she's taking out her astonishment on the tubful of washing.

'Yes, she thought it was a girl she was writing to, but it's a boy, and he sent a picture of himself. She turned scarlet when she saw it, and those boys wouldn't let up. It's a good thing she had an excuse to go out – she's working at the St David's, she's a chambermaid.

And they're teaching her to serve at table, too. Just imagine, Lizzie – Meg having to be polite to people!'

'Won't do her no harm,' Lizzie says. 'Bit of hard work. Having to mind her manners.'

'They're all working,' Non says, 'even little Osian, with his carvings. I'll show you his latest, Lizzie, when we stop for dinner. Meg is secretly pleased, I think, that she's his model for almost every carving so far.'

'I saw him going off with your Davey,' Lizzie says.

'He's going to spend his days at the workshop during the holiday,' Non says. 'I think he'll like that. Though it's hard to tell with Osian.'

'Told you he'd surprise you all,' Lizzie says, echoing Gwydion's words.

Non smiles and passes Lizzie the shirt to drop into her tub. She blows the suds from her arms and smoothes back her hair with her forearm. Gwydion, she thinks. I hope he goes soon to tell Branwen about what he is thinking of doing. The letters from Aoife and from his friend in Ireland seemed to arrive more and more frequently. Jackie Post had complained to her that morning that her family kept him busier than any other in the town. She wonders how long it will be before Gwydion begins to prepare actively for his departure. It is all talk at the moment, but he really needs to tell his mother. Non sighs. She knows how difficult that is going to be for him. She pulls another shirt from the soak and begins to rub the cuffs on the washboard. Every item of clothing Wil possesses has to be mended, washed and ironed, or sponged and pressed, over the next two days.

'When's he off, then?' Lizzie nods at the shirt Non has in her hands.

'Thursday,' Non says. 'He only heard yesterday. Eddie brought him a note from the Captain. They finished the work on the ship quicker than they expected. It's just as well, Lizzie. It keeps us all too busy to think about him going. Meg and I thought we'd make a special supper for him on Wednesday, to wish him well on his travels.'

'Your Davey'll miss him in the workshop,' Lizzie says. 'What's he going to do for an apprentice?'

'Albert's dragging his feet a bit,' Non says.

'That's Albert all over,' Lizzie says. 'Too mean for his own good, let alone anyone else's.'

'Davey can't think of anyone who'd make a good apprentice,' Non says. 'He's thinking maybe one or two of the tramps would be glad to take on a bit of casual work for a roof over their heads and their food. They could sleep in the loft at the workshop. Just for the summer, you know. It wouldn't cost Albert much.'

'Oh, I wouldn't do that if I were Davey.' Maggie Ellis's voice comes floating over the garden wall.

Lizzie rolls her eyes at Non, who tries to keep a straight face.

'No, I don't know if any of them can be trusted,' Maggie says. 'I could tell you some tales, you know. Oh, the stories I've heard!'

'I think most of them are looking for work, Mrs Ellis,' Non says, 'not out to make mischief.'

'I blame the War,' Maggie Ellis says.

'So do we all,' Lizzie says, adding under her breath so that only Non hears her, 'you silly old besom.'

'And talking of the War,' Maggie says, leaning over the roses, 'did you hear about Elsie Thomas's letter from the War Office?'

Non stops scrubbing and looks first at Lizzie, who shrugs, then at Maggie. 'No,' she says. 'A letter about what, Mrs Ellis?'

'Well . . .' Maggie Ellis settles her bosom on the roses. 'Elsie got someone to write to the War Office for her to ask if she could have

Benjamin back from that grave in London, and they wrote back to her and said the soldier in London was unknown and that Benjamin had a grave in France, and they sent a picture of it. It was a cross with a number on it, I saw it, it's better than the one she's got, but you still can't read the number. Elsie thought it was lovely.'

'I thought she'd given up on all that after seeing the woman in Port,' Non says.

'Ah, well,' Lizzie says, stopping to stretch her back. 'She had, missus, but someone persuaded her different.' She turns to Maggie Ellis, 'Didn't they?'

'Nothing to do with me, Lizzie,' Maggie says.

'Not what I heard,' Lizzie says, and returns to her pounding.

'And,' Maggie says, 'a lot of people went to see that woman in Port after what happened to Elsie. Seems she's a foreigner, would you believe. Her own husband was killed in the War.'

'She's still there, then?' Non says. She shakes her head. 'Well, I think she was a fake.' And yet, she thinks, fake or not, she did bring Elsie some comfort – though she seemed to have frightened herself! Then that séance in London – what a sham that woman was, too – but what she told people seemed to comfort them. In her mind's eye she sees Angela weeping with happiness. People are deceived because they want to be, she thinks.

'Ah, but Non, did you know . . .' Maggie Ellis leans so far over the wall that Non thinks the roses that were blooming earlier must be completely destroyed. It is a wonder they keep growing at all. 'Did you know that it's the child who has the gift?' Maggie looks from Non to Lizzie and back again. 'It's not the woman, it's the child.'

The child! No wonder Madame Leblanc had been so astonished. Non feels the hair rise on the back of her neck, and begins to scrub with vigour.

'I told Elsie it was the child,' Maggie Ellis says. 'But she doesn't want to go back there again. No, it's all about the war memorial with Elsie now. That's what I've heard, anyway.'

Maggie picks up news like a terrier scenting a rabbit, thinks Non. And at that, Maggie points her nose in the air as if she has scented another piece of gossip.

'Someone's at my front door,' she says, and heads back for her house.

'Is old Mrs Davies still after putting her Billy on the memorial?' Lizzie says.

'Oh, I don't know, Lizzie. I've lost track of where we are with that. I hope not. I hope Davey's managed to persuade her to leave it alone.'

'A bad lot, that Billy,' Lizzie says.

'You mentioned that before, Lizzie. And just lately, I heard something – I didn't know about this – I heard what Billy was like, you know, with the girls and the babies. And I wondered – did you ever hear anything about that, Lizzie?'

Lizzie looks up from her tub. She nods. 'Heard something about it, missus. Got a cousin in Tremadoc.'

'What about Osian?' Non says. 'Is he one of Billy's? I don't want details, Lizzie – I just want to know.'

Lizzie nods again.

'For sure?'

'Yes, missus, for sure.'

'Thank you, Lizzie,' Non says.

'He were like an old goat.'

'Who's that?' Maggie Ellis bobs up again behind the wall. 'Who are you talking about? That William Morgan? Real old billygoat, that one.'

'Looks like one, too,' Lizzie says, 'with that sorry beard.'

They cackle companionably, a pair of old crows. Non knows exactly what William Morgan is like from helping Gwen Morgan out so many times over the years. Until Davey put a stop to all that.

'He's a sour one, too,' Maggie says. 'Did you hear about Gwen dressing up like Charlie Chaplin and walking down Tryfar swinging a walking stick just like he does in that film I saw in Port? Did you see it? And William Morgan's best black shoes on her feet. Laugh? I thought I'd die. It was better than a circus. But old William didn't think it was funny. 'Specially when he saw his shoes. You should have seen his face.'

'She paid for that, Maggie,' Lizzie says.

Maggie Ellis stops laughing and leans on the wall. 'Men!' she says.

'Her Emlyn's a good lad, though, looks after her,' Lizzie says. 'I dare say your Wil knows him from the golf, missus. He goes caddying down there, too. He'd make your Davey a good little apprentice in a few years. How old would he be, Maggie? Ten? Eleven?'

But Maggie is not listening. 'Someone at your door, Non,' she says. 'Can't you hear? It'll be that tramp I just sent round, the one at my door just now. An Englishman. Said he was looking for Davey. Why d'you think an English tramp's looking for Davey?'

Non's mind races as she hurries through the house, drying her hands and arms as best as she can on her damp apron. An English tramp – could it be someone Davey knew in the War who has fallen on hard times? Someone who could help him remember what he has forgotten? She pauses in front of the looking glass on the hat stand to tidy her hair, then opens the front door.

The man has retreated to the lower step after knocking on the door, so that she is looking at the top of his head. Why did Maggie

Ellis think he was a tramp? His shoes are a little scuffed and dusty, but his fair hair is neatly parted and combed, and he is wearing a lightweight suit that, though it looks a little grubby to be sure, is of a better quality than anyone can afford around here.

'You're looking for Davey?' she says.

'Davey Davies.' The man does not raise his face to look at her and she barely hears what he says.

'Davey's at work. Can I help you?'

'Would you direct me to his place of work, if you please?'

He speaks the way Angela spoke, she thinks, and the way the grand English families spoke who used to come here to their big houses until the War took away their husbands and sons and their money. Maybe he takes her for the skivvy, standing here in an apron.

'I'm Rhiannon Davies, Davey's wife.'

The man makes no response; his shoes seem to be of more interest to him. Non waits a moment, then gives him directions to the workshop.

He says something to his shoes that Non takes for thanks and turns away. She watches him as he walks down the hill until he is out of her sight. He shuffles his feet like an old man, and she sees what it was about him that led Maggie Ellis to call him a tramp – a slump of despair in his shoulders.

She closes the front door and hurries back to Lizzie and the washing. How odd, she thinks, how peculiar. She cannot imagine Davey shoulder to shoulder with someone like that in the trenches.

33

They are having their last supper before Wil leaves them. Here is Wil himself, sitting next to his father and eating his favourite meal: the last of the salt bacon, and potatoes fried to a crisp. Catherine Davies has already objected to eating any kind of pork, even one as well salted as this, because it is summer, and has given her portion to Wil. The time of year does not worry Wil. He will eat most things at any time, like any growing boy. Which is what he is to Non, however manly he may feel as he sets off to his new life.

'I just hope you're not all ill after eating that meat.' Catherine Davies cannot let it go. 'And it's rather extravagant in the middle of the week, Rhiannon.'

'It has to be special to wish Wil well for his journey,' Non says.

'He deserves a good bellyful this evening.' Davey ladles the rest of the potatoes onto Wil's plate before anyone else can take them. 'He's done a week's work today, showing Teddy the ropes.'

Catherine Davies sniffs. She doesn't actually need to say anything, the sniff alone would do it, but she cannot help it. 'I just hope that you won't have cause to regret taking on a vagrant like that.'

It has happened so quickly, one day there was a man at the door looking for Davey, and two days later he is Teddy – Teddy! – and working for Davey, sleeping in the workshop loft and eating their food. Davey told Non he had no idea who Teddy was, that he must be one of the many things that Davey seems to have forgotten, but Teddy said that they met in the clearing hospital and Davey had given him a letter to be sent to Non if he were to die or disappear. Non had shuddered at the thought, and then realised that this must be one of the letters Angela had mentioned. How many more of them were there? Davey said the least he could do was make some provision for the man when he had gone to so much trouble to return the letter to its writer. And it had happened at a propitious time, Davey argued, as if he had to persuade himself. Wil was about to leave, and the amount of work was increasing fast with not only coffins to make, but the new items of furniture the owner of Wern Fawr was ordering. And the carvings he had commissioned meant that Davey had to keep an eye on Osian, too.

'He'll be fine, Mother, and it's only temporary until Albert agrees to a new apprentice for me,' Davey says. 'Don't let your food get cold.'

There is an air of excitement among the diners, and Non knows this is because each has a special gift for Wil to remember them by and to be useful to him on his voyages. How they have managed to keep this secret from Wil, she does not know. Meg is usually the one who cannot hold a secret for long, but maybe she is beginning to become a little more private, a little more secretive, since she had her reply from Jean, because she has not told any one of them anything about him, nor shown them the photograph he sent to her.

Non finishes her potatoes and pork. She has a better appetite than she is used to having, and the salt is welcome in the heat, though she fears they will all be drinking water like fish all evening. She lays her knife and fork on her plate and looks around the table at the faces there. The only member of the family missing is Herman. He has flown in and out of their house all his life, but cannot stay in the vicinity of her mother-in-law without attempting to peck her, and has had to be shut in the kitchen. She can hear his soft, sad caws as he eats the potato she has left him.

Now Meg is signalling to her. Everyone has finished eating. They had decided beforehand, Meg and she, that the gifts would be given to Wil before the pudding came to the table. Meg helps her to clear the supper dishes and cutlery, and Non lights the lamp at the centre of the table. Wil looks at them, from one face to the next around the table, his eyebrows raised in a question.

'It's a surprise,' Meg says. 'But we didn't decide, Non, we didn't choose who was to go first.'

'Shall we begin with the youngest?' Non says.

'You first then, Osian.'

Meg has changed in her attitude to Osian. She has a grudging respect for his carving skills, and there is no doubt that she is quite pleased that he has chosen her as his model, though Non does not suppose it means anything to Osian in terms of love. Which of them can know for sure what goes on in Osian's heart, or head?

Osian is as oblivious as usual to what is required of him, and Meg helps him by bringing from under his chair a small parcel, longer than it is wide, and giving it to Wil. 'This is from Osian and Herman,' she says, and cannot resist adding: 'It will be very useful to you, Wil, to write home.'

Wil peels the paper from his gift and they gasp in unison when they see what it is. Even Meg, who has been supervising the making and the wrapping of it, seems amazed anew at its beauty and the skill apparent in it. 'It's one of Herman's feathers,' she says, as proudly as if she had made it herself.

It is more beautiful than anything Non has yet seen of Osian's work. It is a simple quill pen carved of wood. It is passed around the table for all to see and exclaim at. Osian's carving, in some way Non cannot imagine, has captured the very nature of featheriness. She runs her finger lightly along it, almost expecting to feel the softness, and realises how clever a construction it is, a perfect pen, curved to fit Wil's left-handedness. She marvels at the neat contraption at the end to which the nib is fitted to become part of the feather.

'That is perfect, Osh. Thank you,' Wil says. 'Almost too good to use, really. What if I break it?' He lays it on the tablecloth. And it is true that his hands, already thickened with the work they do, look too clumsy and heavy to use such a delicate instrument.

'It's stronger than it looks. Osian made it specially for you to write to us with,' Meg says, 'and for you to write about your adventures with.' She produces a parcel of her own as if by sleight of hand. 'In here.'

Meg has prepared her own gift to Wil with such secrecy that Non has no idea what to expect. Wil pushes his pen gently to one side, places Meg's parcel in front of him and fumbles to open the knots in the ribbon she has tied around the wrapping paper.

'Open it, open it.' Meg takes the parcel from Wil because he does not obey quickly enough, pulls the ribbon away and folds back the wrapping to reveal a book with an embroidered cover. She opens the volume to show blank pages waiting to be written upon. 'See, everybody,' she says. 'Wil can write all his adventures down here and then we can read about them when he comes home.'

Catherine Davies is watching the proceedings with her eyebrows raised. 'A pen and a notebook,' she says. 'Wil has never been a great one for writing, has he? I should know. When I think of the hours I wasted trying to make him write with his right hand—'

'But this is a special pen for his left hand, Nain,' Meg says. 'It'll be something for him to do in the evenings. Won't it, Wil?'

Wil turns the book around in his hands. 'It's lovely, Meg. It must have taken you a long time to do this.' Wil smoothes the cover, until his rough palm snags the threads on the embroidery. 'Thank you.'

Below Wil's name Meg has sewn a ship in full sail, sitting tipsily on the waves beneath it where fish of all colours swim and leap. Non had not known that Meg was capable of making such a lovely thing. What talented children she and Davey have – though, of course, none of the talent comes from her. But she cannot help agreeing with Catherine Davies that these are not quite the kinds of gifts Wil would best like. She feels reluctant to give her own offering, but after pointed glances and nods from Meg, she hands Wil the copy of Joseph Conrad's new book, which she has only read once since she bought it last year, so it is very nearly new. She had thought reading it would help fill his lonely hours at sea.

'Well,' Catherine Davies says through a cat's bottom of a mouth, which Non is pleased to see Wil has not missed, 'I've never known Wil to be a great one for reading, either.'

'It's a sea story, an adventure,' Non tells him. 'Look at the ship on the cover, Wil. D'you think the David Morris will look like that in full sail?'

'Thank you, Non,' he says. 'But, you know, I'm going to have to work much harder on board the David Morris than you all think. There won't be much spare time to write and read, so I may not fill Meg's notebook or finish . . .' He glances at the cover of the book. '*The Rescue* all that soon. But I shall treasure them.'

There is a small silence as Meg looks at Non, and Non shakes her head at her. They have got this wrong. How could they have done that?

'Maybe Gwydion will give you something you really like,' Meg says despite Non's head-shaking. 'What have you got for him, Gwydion?'

'I'm afraid mine's a book, too, Wil,' Gwydion says.

This is Wil's largest parcel so far, square and bulky so that everything else has to be moved aside to make room for it, and not as meticulously wrapped as Meg's parcel, so it does not take Wil a second to find out what the book is. 'The Times Atlas,' he reads, and begins to leaf through it. 'A map book.'

'But he's travelling on the sea, not on the land, Gwydion,' Meg says.

'Ah,' Gwydion says, 'so, see what the map on pages seven and eight shows, young lady.'

Wil has already found the pages. 'Look, it shows the routes that ships have to follow to get across the Atlantic Ocean. The David Morris used to sail to Newfoundland.' He traces the journey with his finger. 'It looks no distance at all on here, but it takes weeks to get there and back. I didn't know where it was, though, Gwydion. This is good – thank you very much.'

'And look, Wil,' Gwydion says. 'Go back a page – see, it tells you how deep the water is everywhere in the oceans and seas. Can you see those measurements?'

Wil looks down at the page. His lips move slightly as he reads the figures. 'It's very deep in some places,' he says. 'I didn't know it was so deep. I didn't know there was so much water in the sea.'

'That's a lovely present, Gwydion,' Non says.

'Davison's selling a lot of his books,' Gwydion says. 'This was one of them. I thought it'd be just the thing for Wil.'

'It is, it is,' Wil says. 'I just had no idea . . .'

'You'll come safely home with this, Wil, however deep the waters you sail on.' Davey takes off the charm he keeps around his neck on a leather bootlace.

'Your lucky charm?' Wil says. 'The one Taid gave you?'

Catherine Davies rounds on Davey. 'And look what happened to him the minute he gave it to you.'

There is no need for any of them to look at William Davies to see what has happened to him. They all know that over the years and months and days he has removed himself to the land of his childhood.

But Davey will be fine, Non thinks. He no longer needs the charm. Davey the stranger has almost gone and Davey her husband has returned. It does not matter that bits of his memory are missing, they are not likely to be things he wants to remember. He has remembered the important thing, and he will be fine. They will be fine. Sometimes, it may be best not to know everything. Curiosity has its dangers, as she has discovered.

Wil puts the charm around his own neck, and tucks it under his shirt. 'It brought you safely through the War, didn't it?' he says to Davey.

'It brought me home,' Davey says.

'But it's a disgusting thing.' Meg makes a moue of distaste. 'Made out of bone like that. I wouldn't let it touch me.'

'Bone?' Gwydion says. 'Let's have a look, Wil.'

Wil pulls it out from beneath his shirt. It is yellowed and the shape is difficult to discern. 'It's a hare,' he says, 'made from the leg bone of a hare. It's really old. Taid told me the story of it once, his own Taid gave it to him. Hares are lucky.'

'It does look old,' Gwydion says. 'But I don't think whoever made it was as good at carving as Osian.'

'It should have gone to Billy. He was the eldest.' Catherine Davies snuffles into her handkerchief.

'But Uncle Billy wasn't going to the War,' Wil says. 'Thank you, Tada. I'll keep it safe.'

'It's meant to keep you safe, Wil,' Davey says. 'And when the time comes, you can give it to your own son.'

His own son! Non can hardly think of Wil being old enough to have a son of his own. The boy that she brought up and cherished – a father!

'It's your turn, Nain,' Meg says.

Catherine Davies seems to take an age to put away her handkerchief in her sleeve. She bends from her chair to lug her voluminous handbag from the floor. They are holding their collective breath as Catherine Davies rummages in the bag. There is no knowing what she will pull out. Here it comes – it is a small round tin, which she hands to Wil.

Wil turns it around to look at what it says. 'The original and proven glucose travel drops,' he reads aloud. 'They're mints. I like mints. Thank you, Nain.'

'They are to stop you being sea-sick, Wil,' Catherine Davies says. 'I have never, myself, travelled on water but I understand that it is treacherously . . . unstill. I trust you will find them a great deal more useful than books and paper and pens.'

'Well, I hope I won't need them for that, Nain,' Wil says. 'But I do like sweets.'

'And,' Catherine Davies says, 'once they are finished you will be able to use the tin to keep things in.'

'Tiny, small things,' Meg says, under her breath. Non sends her a warning look and she jumps from her chair. 'Why,' she cries, 'this is better than a birthday, or Christmas, Wil. And I helped Non to make your favourite pudding.'

As Non rises to her feet to fetch dishes and spoons, and the bread-and-butter pudding from the warming oven, old William Davies stirs in his chair and produces from his pocket a leather drawstring bag. He leans across the table to give it to Wil.

'What's that you're giving him?' Catherine Davies tries to snatch it from her husband's hand, but William Davies manages to evade her grasp.

Wil opens the bag and spills its contents onto the table. They all count the golden sovereigns that lie there, glittering in the lamplight. Twenty! Twenty golden sovereigns.

'I can't take so much money from you, Taid,' Wil says. 'It's a fortune!'

'You keep it, my boy,' old William Davies says. 'You might be glad of it one day. And good luck to you on that ship.' He nods at Wil, and then winks at him. 'Just one bit of good advice, Wil. Don't let your hair get wet in winter.'

'What do you mean, Taid?'

'Oh, Wil, when I was a bit older than you are now I was courting the prettiest girl in Llŷn – I was the lucky one then! I was going to see her one evening, January it was, bitter cold, and I was running late because we'd had a big blast at the quarry that afternoon and my hair was full of dust, so I had to wash it. But there was no time to dry it by the fire, see, because if there was one thing she didn't like it was anyone being late. So, I jumped on my bike, wet hair and all, and off I went. But my wet hair froze and gave me the most unbearable pain in my head, Wil, and I had to turn round and go home. She never spoke to me again. Broke my heart.'

They all laugh, because the heartbreak was a long time ago, and not a fresh pain. All but Catherine Davies; she glowers at her husband. But even as they laugh and William Davies laughs with them, a vacant look begins to steal into his eyes, like a mist settling on the sea, and then – he has left them. He rises from the table. 'Thank you for the meal,' he says. 'I have to be getting home, Mother will be wondering where I am. She worries, you know, since David my brother was killed. She thinks the rock face is going to fall on me, too.'

Catherine Davies takes hold of his shirt sleeve and pulls him down into his chair where he sits with a slight smile on his face.

He seems to be happy, wherever it is he has gone, Non thinks. It was nice to have a rare visit from him to see Wil on his way; Wil will always remember that.

34

Non is tired of train journeys and this is one she does not want to make. She glances away from the fields and trees and hedges that race by and looks at Wil sitting opposite her. He, too, is watching the passing fields, the sheep-filled meadows and the streams as they journey. She wonders if he is storing them up in his memory so that when he is far away he can take them out, as he would photographs, to remind himself of what he has left behind. Or is he thinking of all the new countries he will see as he sails the oceans, and how different they may be from all this? He is just a boy, she thinks, his cheeks still smooth and a little plump. And then he turns to look at her and she sees the man in his eyes.

Yesterday she spent hours preparing everything for Wil's departure in the morning. Socks were darned, shirts washed and starched on Monday were ironed, new patches were put on jersey and jacket elbows, trouser hems were let down – when did he grow that extra inch? – buttons were double-sewn on everything that had buttons, pots of salves and dark bottles of tinctures for this and that were packed around the clothes into the corners of the old canvas bag found for him by his father in William Davies's garden hut. The bag had held old William's quarrying tools and was full of granite dust, but Davey had shaken it out and scrubbed it thoroughly and laid it out in the sun to dry. They were all surprised to see the bag was coloured green, not grey, a green not unlike the colour of the sea in the bay on sunny days.

When they waved him off this morning Meg had insisted that everyone call out Farewell to him, because, she said, it was less final than goodbye. It was one of those rare times when Non wondered if the County School was entirely good for Meg. She had also read a poem she had written for the occasion, and Wil had turned scarlet and looked at her in horror when she insisted he take the paper it was written on and stick it into the notebook she had given him, which she now called his journal. Non wishes they had been more successful in their choice of going-away gifts for Wil – but this morning she had tucked into his canvas bag the pen, the notebook, and Catherine Davies's tin of mints, which might yet prove to be the most useful.

Wil had asked Davey to take care of old William Davies's money, with instructions that his grandparents were to be given it back if they were in need. He said he treasured Taid's advice about not getting his hair wet much more. It had been a great deal of money, and a shock to them all for they had not dreamt that William Davies possessed so much. It would be a long time before Catherine Davies gave up demanding its return.

'Your father will be sure to keep his eye on Taid and Nain's finances, Wil. You know that, don't you? He won't let them want because Taid gave you the money.'

'I know, Non. But he helps them so much already with all that money for Billy's mistakes. It's not fair, is it?' Wil is indignant on behalf of his father. 'I don't understand why Nain is so . . . nasty to him. You'd think she'd rather he was dead and not Billy.'

Non has thought the same thing herself often and puzzled over why it should be so, when everyone else likes and respects Davey so much and never has a good word for his brother Billy. 'I don't know why she's like that, either, Wil. I'm sure there is an answer, but I don't know it.'

Wil smiles at her. 'But he's looking happier – Tada – isn't he? Don't you think so, Non? He was even making silly jokes in the workshop yesterday.'

'He's relieved that he's remembered what was in some of the gaps he had in his memory. Things are coming back to him slowly.' Davey wants to remember everything that happened to him. He has experienced so much relief from remembering that he had not been unfaithful to Non, he told her, that he would be able to deal with whatever he remembered. He wants to know what and when and why. Especially why. Non understands, her own nature is a curious one, her father brought her up to be inquisitive, but . . . but . . . She is not certain that knowing everything will help Davey, although she cannot explain why she feels this so strongly. Especially when the discoveries she has recently made about her own past have planted her feet more firmly in the present.

'It was bad for people over there, in the trenches, wasn't it, Non?' Wil says. 'I think I'd want to forget, not remember.'

'I suppose your father needs to remember everything that happened before he can make the decision to forget it,' Non says, for who really knows how the human mind and the human memory work. She recalls thinking when she was at the hospital with Angela that doctors of the mind were needed as well as those of the flesh to look after the broken soldiers who returned, and she is surer of that than ever. If only there were doctors who were as clever at treating damaged minds as Seb was at treating damaged hearts. 'He'll miss you, Wil. You've spent so much time together in the workshop.'

'I don't know how he's going to manage, Non. There's something not quite right about that Teddy, but I don't know what it is. He's not used to working with his hands, for sure.' Wil grins. 'You should have seen him with the plane – he had no idea which end was which.'

'I hope he's learnt enough from you to be of help, Wil. But it's only temporary, Albert is sure to want someone your father can train properly. And Teddy'll move on soon, I expect. The tramps never stay long in one place, you know.'

'But he's not a real tramp, is he, Non? He's a bit la-di-da for that.'

'It's just the way he speaks, Wil. He may be someone who's fallen on hard times. And anyway, your father felt he owed him something for holding on to that letter he wrote for all these years.' But it is strange, there must be something they are missing here. She has no sense of what it is, and after all, what could it possibly be? 'Your father can look after himself, Wil. He's much better and stronger in spirit since he regained his memory, you know. It's not just jokes in the workshop – he's generally happier.' Non, not superstitious, wants to touch wood, cross her fingers. She still finds it hard to believe that some fate will not snatch Davey away again. Maybe it is this fear that makes her want Davey to let everything be, not to stir up his lost memories.

'Teddy was trying to be pally with Osian,' Wil says. 'I told him not to bother – you know what Osh is like. Just stared right through him! And then Teddy got hold of his arm, just being friendly, I suppose, and Osh began that scream. It always makes me think of the banshees in some of those Irish stories you used to tell us – d'you remember? – and Teddy didn't know what to do. He didn't have the sense to just let go of Osh. Then his face went empty – you know, as if he'd gone somewhere else inside his head. I had to pick his fingers one by one from Osh's arm, and Osh never stopped screaming the whole time.' Wil shivers. 'D'you remember Bobby Hughes, Non?'

'Aggie's grandson? The poor boy who hanged himself?'

Wil nods. 'Teddy looked just like Bobby the night before he did it, Non. Eddie and I were at the Institute that night. We saw him.'

'What?' Non says. 'You think Teddy could do the same?'

'I'm just saying,' Wil says. 'Something isn't right about him. Osh knows it, too.'

Non does not know what to say to Wil. She will speak to Davey about Teddy in light of what Wil has told her; she will see what Davey thinks now that he has worked with the man for a few days.

'Will Osh get better, do you think?' Wil has left Teddy behind.

Non wishes she knew what the answer was. 'You never know, Wil. He's clever in some ways, isn't he? Look at the skills he has – those carvings are absolutely incredible. But he doesn't seem to feel anything, does he? He's never sad or happy, or pleased or cross. I don't know. Sometimes I think the only one of us that causes a little spark of feeling in him is Herman. But just look at how well I am now I've found out I don't need my drops. Maybe something will turn up that will mend Osian.' But she suspects this is how Osian will be all his life.

Wil nods at her. 'Fingers crossed, hey, Non?' he says. 'I'll send him a picture postcard with a ship on it, or maybe pictures of birds, and fish, and maybe a mermaid, and he can carve them all.'

Non laughs at him. 'Wil, you're only going to Belgium on this first trip.'

'But after that . . .' Wil says.

Non thinks, he is looking into a future where he will sail to all four corners of the world on the *David Morris*, across the seas and the oceans, through storms and into the doldrums, under searing sunshine and starry skies.

35

Non realises that she is sweltering, as everyone is in this weather, but she is not breathless, she is not aware of the beat of her heart, she is not so tired that she can barely stand up, she is not fearful of falling over because she is faint. And she has not had any hallucinations. Were all those illnesses she saw a result of taking the May Lily? She decides not to dwell on it. She has often enough wished she did not have her gift. Be careful what you wish for, she thinks, an echo of something Branwen used to say to her, although now she cannot think what it was said about.

She pauses in the shade of the trees in the small square park in the main street, and looks back in the direction of the harbour. It is only a short distance away and yet seems to have vanished almost without a trace. Here, there is little to remind anyone that this is a port, and still a busy one, still providing work for the variety of trades and unskilled labour in the town. As well as Wil, she thinks.

When they stepped off the train she had told him that she would walk with him as far as the harbour. Wil said she could come to meet the captain if she liked, although she must not expect to be asked aboard the schooner – sailors believed it brought bad luck to have a woman on board. It took Non the whole of the walk to the harbour to recover from the nonsensical superstitions of the sailors, and to promise Wil she would not set foot upon the *David Morris*.

The schooner was beautiful. It was larger than she remembered from seeing it in the distance the last time she came to the harbour with Wil. Its gleaming wooden sides were long and sleek and sat low in the water, though its masts reached up for the sky, all three of them. The sails were furled but she could see that when they were all unfurled the *David Morris* would be a magnificent sight – and not at all unlike the ship that had been on the dust jacket of *The Rescue*. Pennants and small flags drooped from the masts and the rigging. She shielded her eyes from the sun to look up at them. Wil told her that the pennant on the central mast bore the ship's name. The *David Morris* was meant to sail from Port the next day. What Non knew of ships and the sea could be written on the head of a pin, but she was sure a breeze that would set the pennants fluttering was necessary to fill the sails before the ship could go anywhere.

Captain Griffiths had not asked her to board, but he had shaken her hand and told her Wil was a fine young man, which made her proud, and that she looked far too young and pretty to be the mother of such a strapping lad, which made her blush.

She had taken a last lingering look at the schooner once Wil had boarded, and thought it suddenly seemed far too fragile a vessel to take her strapping young lad so far away. Then she had turned and walked away without looking back.

She feels refreshed by the cool green shade cast by the trees. She has a sense of déjà vu when she realises that on this second visit to Port with Wil she has two errands of her own to run, as she did when she accompanied him for his first visit to the *David Morris*. The streets are as dirty and noisy as they were the last time, and she is certain they are the same two dogs circling one another in the dust. Today, she does not need to furl her parasol to use as a walking stick to support her across the street. Today, she does not linger before walking up the steps into the pawn shop.

The proprietor recognises her, she can tell, but lets her present her receipt and explain to him that she has come to retrieve her ring. He tells her that he has a customer who is most interested in buying the ring. She replies that she has no interest in selling it. To redeem her mother's ring costs more than she and Davey had anticipated, but she has extra money with her – Take it, just in case, Davey had said – and she pays what is asked.

She had to learn to manage her money through the years of the War, but she does not care enough about it, she knows. She will need to learn to care. She and Davey have a family to look after and feed and clothe, she has a daughter to educate, and education is not cheap. She has seen what a lack of money can do to people, and how much difference not having a farthing to pay for baking a loaf can make. And here she is, throwing away guineas. She examines the ring, puts it back in its box, and puts the little box safely in her bag. It is no longer her mother's ring, no longer her grandmother's ring, it is hers, given to her by the kindness and thoughtfulness of her husband. And by his love. Her world has changed since she left the ring here.

She leaves the shop and has to pause to get her bearings. She intends to visit Madame Leblanc, but has to work out where it was that Catherine Davies took her and Elsie. She has decided that she will give the ring to Madame to hold and see what she makes of it. She is curious to find out Madame's methods. And she is curious to find out why Madame and her child are doing their kind of work, why they think it is right to gull people in such a cruel way. Branwen used to say to her, Curiosity killed the cat. She knows its dangers now, but it can serve a purpose. Satisfying her curiosity about Madame and her child is not an end in itself; she wants to prove that Madame is a charlatan.

Davey knows nothing about her interest in Madame Leblanc, and this visit is something else she will have to keep to herself. She fears that the list of things she keeps to herself is overlong, and not something a good wife should have. But here she is, already standing on the uneven pavement outside Number Thirty with her hand raised to knock on the door, hoping she has not allowed her curiosity to triumph over sense once again.

Madame Leblanc herself opens the door. She does not look unduly surprised to see Non, which makes Non a little uncomfortable, especially when Madame stands aside, holding the door open for Non to enter and says, 'You are expected.' Expected! What nonsense, Non tells herself, the woman is just a good actress.

'You are expected,' Madame says, once more, 'and welcome.' She holds her hand out towards the shadows in the corners and around the edges of the parlour and the child, Esmé, comes out from the gloom. What kind of child hides away in such odd places? And then Non thinks of Osian sitting in the coffin.

'Esmé said you would come,' Madame says. 'But we do not know the reason for your coming.'

Esmé is not dressed in white today. Instead, she wears slightly old-fashioned clothes, as if she is wearing cast-offs from the generation before hers. Non smiles at the girl, whose face is serious as she stares intently at her.

'Curiosity,' Non says. 'That's the reason I've come. I'm curious about you, both of you. About why you do this kind of work.'

Madame Leblanc turns to Esmé and flutters her hands at her. The child nods. Madame says, 'We have to make a living, you know, like anyone else. Esmé thinks you will understand. She says you, too, have a child who does not speak.'

Non is puzzled, then understands. The girl is deaf, she thinks, and mute, too. Her mother was talking to her with her hands just then. She has heard of this language, but had not realised what she was seeing. But how do they know about Osian?

'My son can hear,' she says. 'His affliction is different to Esmé's.'

'But you understand how necessary it is for us mothers to make provision for them, these children,' Madame says. 'They will not fare well in the world without our support. It would abandon them to the darkest corners without a thought.'

Non thinks there are plenty of dark corners in this house and cannot see a reason for that. She looks back at Esmé and watches the child sign to her mother, her hands like tiny, fluttering birds, thin and fragile.

'You take me too literally,' Madame says. 'Esmé has to have the light dimmed for her powers of clairvoyance to manifest themselves.'

Can the child read minds? Non says, 'Clairvoyance?'

'She can see clearly,' Madame Leblanc says, 'the things that you and I cannot see at all.'

That is also true of Osian, Non realises, in the magical way he makes the wood come alive with the essence of whatever it is he is carving.

'I took her with me to a séance,' Madame says. 'She was a tiny child. Her father had been lost in the fighting.' She pauses for a moment to take a long, deep breath. 'Emile was never found, you know. He has no grave, no place where we can mourn him. I thought he would come to visit his daughter.'

'And did he?'

'No, never. We – she – have had visits from many of those who have passed over, but never from Emile. It was at that first séance we discovered this gift Esmé has of holding an object and taking from it some information or feeling about the person who wears it or owns it.'

The way Osian draws that feeling of being alive from the wood, thinks Non. But this is somehow not so healthy, this delving into the unnatural. She thinks that, on second thoughts, she will not offer the ring to be held. There may be things she would be told that she would prefer not to hear, and then she would never be able to forget them. Not so very curious after all, she tells herself.

Esmé is again signing to her mother. Her hands flutter more quickly. Distressed birds, thinks Non.

'She asks me to tell you that your own gift is not unlike hers,' Madame says.

'What?' Non says. 'What does she mean?'

'I can see none of this, you realise,' Madame says. She watches the child's hands again. 'She says, do not deny your gift, do not push it away—'

Non's chair scrapes back along the floor as she jumps up from it. She has seen and heard enough. She has no quarrel with this child, she and her mother have to eat, have to have a roof over their heads, have to prepare for Esmé's future, and have to employ what skills they have to enable them to do so. She and Davey are lucky that Osian has a gift of a different kind. Non opens her bag and draws from her purse the rest of the money Davey has given her, and puts it on the small round table next to her chair.

'Esmé says, be true to yourself!' Madame's voice follows Non through the front door and up the quiet street. She is glad for once to hear a horse and cart clatter past her, the hooves and wheels throwing up dust into the dense air to form a curtain between her and the occupants of Number Thirty.

36

Davey is busy and distracted when Non arrives at the workshop. Osian sits as usual in one of the coffins ranged along the back wall, and there is no sign of the tramp, Teddy. Teddy, Non thinks, is a childish name for a man who has gone through a war, and then through heaven knows what afterwards to bring him to this. She sits on the one chair in the workshop, first brushing the sawdust from its seat. She wonders if Davey has found it strange to be without Wil today. It is hard to tell with men, she thinks, sometimes they do not seem to have feelings the way we women do. And then she remembers her father who had, it seemed, feelings in abundance, and never held back from expressing them. She smiles at the thought.

It seems a little cooler inside the workshop, shaded as it is from the most intense heat of the sun by its thick walls and the shadow thrown by the high wall of the yard at the back of the Castle Hotel across the road. A little sunlight dribbles in through the dust on the window at the side. She watches the sawdust swirl in the faint light; no wonder Davey's clothes and skin are powdered with it. How lucky that there is a tin tub here where he can sluice off the dust before he comes home. Otherwise, she imagines, there would be dusty footprints all over the house, as if ghosts had visited.

Davey is working at twice his usual pace. She watches him; he does not even glance in her direction as he concentrates on his task. Eventually he stops, straightens his back with a groan, and reaches for a fresh piece of sandpaper.

'Where's Teddy?' Non says.

'Teddy?' Davey wraps a strip of the sandpaper around his block, making sure its edges are not sticking out to catch and tear. 'I can't get used to calling a grown man Teddy. But he won't have Ted, or Ed, or Eddie.' He begins to sand the coffin again. 'I've sent him to meet the train. I'm expecting a parcel of coffin handles.'

'He's making himself useful, then?'

'He's more of a hindrance than a help. I don't think the man has ever done any physical work like this. But what can I do, Non?'

Non is not sure she has an answer and stays silent. Fine dust flies from under Davey's sanding block, and she has to pinch her nose to keep from sneezing. She wonders if it is bad for Davey to be breathing in all this dust, day in and day out. But the scents of the sawn wood, the sap and oils, are redolent of the living forests where the trees once grew, and it is impossible not to breathe them in deeply.

Davey stops and stands back to look at the coffin. 'This heat is a killer, Non. Albert's busier than he's ever been. I pity old Byron having to dig the graves in this heat, he's old enough for it to kill him.' He rubs a bit of sawdust that Non cannot see from the coffin. 'Maybe Teddy'll make a better job of the polishing.'

'Maybe Albert will get you an apprentice soon,' Non says.

'And maybe pigs will fly,' Davey says. 'I think I'm stuck with

Teddy for a while yet, Non. And, you know, I do feel obliged to him. Carrying my letter around with him all that time and then bringing it all the way here.'

'It seems to me a strange thing to do,' Non says. 'Excessive. He could have posted it.'

'He says he felt he had to bring it himself,' Davey says. 'I still can't remember him, Non. He says I gave him the letter when I was at the clearing hospital that last time. I can't remember anything about being there, and I can't think why I would do that, give my last letter to you to a stranger. How would he know if I was killed, or hurt? He wasn't with our lot.'

Non thinks of what Angela told her, about Davey's thousand-yard stare. He would probably not have known what he was doing, nor remembered it afterwards if he had been in the state Angela hinted at. He would not have written the letter over and over, if he had not been in such a state. She thinks, Teddy, Ted, Ed, Edward? Is Teddy the man Angela said was in a very bad way? Become a tramp? What can it mean?

'If he's a tramp, he'll be moving on,' she says. 'That's what they do.'

'He's not really a tramp, though, is he? He's not travelling. He's come here to give me the letter, or so he says.' Davey shakes his head. 'But I don't know what he is, Non. Anyway, I've got more work to do than I can manage, and I haven't got time to puzzle it out. But he seems to know things I've forgotten. He assumes I know what he's talking about.'

'Tell him you can't remember,' Non says. 'And then he'd explain.'

'I can't,' Davey says. 'Something stops me doing that, Non.'

He is squeezing the sanding block, and Non can see that he is trying to stop his hand trembling. It takes her back to early this morning when she had found him once again under the table just as Gwydion had described – crying and shivering. She almost wishes she did have the clairvoyance Esmé had accused her of having; maybe she would be able to see clearly what was troubling Davey, then and now. She gets up from the chair and puts her hand over his. 'Davey?' she says.

'I'm afraid, Non,' he says. 'Something is making me afraid that I've forgotten whatever it is because it's too terrible to remember.'

'Oh, Davey.' Non reaches to hug him but he pulls away. She feels a surge of panic. Oh no, she thinks, not again. 'Davey, I think you'd remember if you had done something terrible – because you're a good man.' But she recalls that she, too, had wondered what could be so terrible that it would cause him to lose his memory like this.

Davey stares at the coffin. 'Some things I've forgotten are coming back. I remember more about Ben Bach, but not anything I can tell his mother, so don't tell anyone this, Non.'

'Of course I won't.' Surely Davey knows he does not have to say that to her?

'I remember how terrified Ben was – all the time, Non, shouting for Elsie. It put the wind up everyone in our trench. I was trying to get the high-ups to send him home. They were sending back the under-age boys by then, and Ben was under-age when he volunteered – he lied about his age, Non, you wouldn't think he'd have the wit – and it was obvious he wasn't fit.' Davey makes a circular motion with his forefinger by his head. 'I thought I could get him home that way.'

Non is not surprised to hear of Ben Bach's terror. He had always been a fearful boy, large and tall, but a brain the size of a pea was what the school's headmaster had told her when she went there as a young teacher. Poor Benjamin.

'Is that what you think Teddy's talking about? Ben being so scared? How would he know about it?'

'I don't know how he would know about anything to do with us. But maybe some connection will come back to me, Non.'

She squeezes his hand. She smoothes the planed and sanded wood of the coffin. It is lovely to touch, like stroking satin. 'You're a craftsman, Davey. You do your best work always, no matter what you're making.'

He bends to kiss her hair. That will do, she thinks, that will more than do.

'I'd better get home,' she says. 'I need to do some shopping on the way. I'll see you when you're done, Davey. I expect it'll be late.'

'Oh, Non,' he says, 'there's a Labour Party meeting straight after work. But it shouldn't be long.'

Labour Party!

'It's important to us all, Non – it's the future.'

'I know,' she says. And she does know that Davey believes this as fervently as Gwydion believes in his way to the future. 'Shall I send Meg with something for your supper, then?'

Davey catches hold of her hand and kisses it. 'Thank you,' he says.

'And shall I take Osian with me?'

'I'll send him back with Meg when she brings my supper,' Davey says.

They both turn to look at Osian who extricates himself from his complicated position in the coffin and comes towards them bearing a carving, carrying it on the flat of both his hands.

'Look at that,' Davey says. 'It's Teddy!'

Non has only had a brief glimpse of Teddy – when she opened the door to him a few days ago – but she recognises him instantly, the lean, slouched body, the dipped head. She marvels again at Osian's skill. She takes hold of the carving and through the wood feels the nature of this man that Osian has captured. He is damaged. Badly. She hears Wil describing his empty face. Something clutches at her heart in a way that has not happened since she began to take fewer drops each day, and her hands of their own volition let go of the carving. She watches as it seems to float down into the sawdust on the floor.

37

Jackie Post had been late on his first round that morning, so only Non knows that the letter has arrived. She has read it so many times she really does not need to take it out of its envelope and read it to remember what it says. But she sits at the table and unfolds the pages, smoothing them flat.

Someone, maybe Seb O'Neill himself, has typed it, badly, with xxxxx crossing out several words, on a typewriter that is missing half its lower-case letter a. The whole thing is hard to decipher, but easy to understand. Seb hopes that she has followed his recommendations and is feeling well. His tests on her tincture have proved what he feared, that it is a particularly strong Convallamarin, which, he explains in brackets, acts like the Digitalin found in the foxglove, and which she does not need, underlined. Seb thinks he has saved her life, and he probably has.

The bad typing continues to tell her that she can lead a perfectly normal life, like any other young woman of her age. He means she can have babies, she supposes, without their births killing her any more than they would kill any other normal young woman of her age. She can think of several normal young women she knew who died in childbirth. Seb would like, the letter continues, to see her again, so that he can check that she is as well as he hopes. And that, she thinks, is highly unlikely to happen. As highly unlikely as normal young women not dying in childbirth.

Seb has added a postscript in his own handwriting under his signature, which is as difficult to decipher as the typing, to say that he has told Angela the results, and he hopes that she, Non, does not mind, and that Angela sends her best wishes and hopes for a visit from Non when she goes to see Seb. Oh, dear, she thinks, I cannot show this letter to Davey. Not with that P.S. She wonders if she can cut that part off the letter, but thinks that it would look suspicious. She folds the letter back into its envelope and puts it into her skirt pocket.

It is official now: she is a normal woman and she can do what normal women do without fear of dropping dead. She has realised that until she slowed down the taking of her father's remedy she lived her life in some kind of dream where she saw the world through a haze which was not unlike the muslin curtains Madame Leblanc employed to separate this world from the next. She is not altogether certain what being a normal woman entails. She hopes it is not entirely about being a competent housekeeper and having babies. Babies! The thought makes her heart leap, but she is not entirely certain that she wants to bear a child of her own. It is a chancy business. What if the child inherited her curse? Or Catherine Davies's character? Or Osian's affliction? And is she able to bear a child? Since Davey returned from the War convinced of his unworthiness as a husband she has not needed to think about precautions. But before he went away the precautions she took because she dared not conceive had been entirely effective. She does know several women, Gwen Morgan for one, who have not found these precautions quite as effective. She wonders if this means that she can never be normal, that she can never conceive and give birth. And how would Davey feel about having a baby? He is supporting his parents as well as his own family, and another mouth to feed would put a strain on their resources – although Wil has left them now, and that will make a difference.

She thinks of Wil, already six days into his first voyage. Is he still at sea or berthed in some foreign harbour already? It will take her longer than a week to become used to his loss! Her thoughts turn to other losses.

Yesterday Gwydion had received a letter from Aoife that had sent him racing away on his motorcycle early this morning to Aberystwyth, to see his parents. But I'll be back tomorrow, he had told Non before putting on his aviator's hat and goggles and running down the front steps to leap on his bike as if it were a horse champing at the bit. Non smiles at the memory, though she wonders what in Aoife's letter had required this urgent action.

And Meg no longer stays at home on her half days. She has gone to the beach this afternoon with her friends, to dip her toes in the water and squeal at how cold it is. And Davey and Osian are at work as usual. Non wonders idly what Osian makes of Teddy, then realises that she knows, and a shudder overtakes her as she thinks of the carving she dropped into the sawdust. Osian had carved a man who had lost everything. What had happened to Teddy to cause him to feel such despair – was it the War? But there was something underlying that despair that had frightened Non – an indifference? a ruthlessness? – she is not sure. She shudders again. What is Teddy doing here? What does he want?

The clock strikes the half-hour. She glances at it; it is half-past three, the time that she expects Catherine Davies to tea. She has invited old William Davies, too, but is certain that Catherine will not bring him with her. The little round table under the shade of the large butterfly bush is laid with the tea things, but the plate of bread and butter is in the kitchen with a cloth over it, to keep it safe from the birds and the sun.

Non can hear the crows cawing, their harsh calls echoing from the stone walls of neighbouring houses. Herman has already visited her today, and though she probably will not see him again, she will need to keep an eye out for him in case he takes umbrage at having Catherine Davies in his garden.

Inviting Mrs Davies to tea is part of the strategy that Non has in mind for dealing with her mother-in-law. She knows that she is interfering between mother and son, but Wil's indignation at his grandmother's unfairness towards his father will not leave her. It is not fair, the way Catherine Davies treats Davey, when he is so good to her. Non knows that nothing he ever does will be good enough for Catherine Davies, and she is curious to know why.

Non has not seen her mother-in-law since Wil's leaving supper. She wants to know if she can still see the woman's illness. She wants to know what Seb cannot tell her, for all his experience and his laboratory tests and his badly typewritten letters: she wants to know if she still has her gift, the gift she has inherited from her mother.

Catherine Davies is late, which is unlike her. Non lights the little paraffin stove – the joy of not having to light the range! – and balances the kettle on it to boil. Nedw in the hardware shop had disapproved of her delight when she discovered he stocked them: they were all the rage among the visitors, he had told her, but normal women who had fires and ranges at home that they could use were not interested in such fripperies.

Non feels she ought to wear a placard, like the suffragettes in the photographs that were in the *Daily Herald* before the War, a placard that says, I am not a normal woman, which she knows is the truth, whatever Seb has written.

At which point Catherine Davies arrives, puffing and panting, and drops into a chair by the kitchen table.

'Is William Davies not with you?' Non says.

'I despair of that man.' Catherine Davies fans her scarlet face with her hand. 'He is deliberately aggravating, Rhiannon. I've had to lock him in the little bedroom.'

Non looks intently at her mother-in-law, searching for those signs of her illness that she usually sees. Non needs to remember that Catherine is ill so that she, Non, does not become too angry with her and her ridiculous way of looking at life with herself at its centre. But she has no sense of the sickness. What does that mean? Does it mean that what she saw was never real, a hallucination caused by the May Lily, or does it mean that she has lost her ability to see what is there, lost her gift? Has she thought all her life that people were dying when they were not? She thinks of all the people she has seen with terrible illnesses and of what happened to them, and she realises that she did possess the ability, but has lost it. She is glad it has gone. Esmé's voice comes back to her, telling her not to push her gift away, to be true to herself. She thinks, What does a child know of these things? But it makes her uncomfortable, as if she is doing some wrong.

'Rhiannon, Rhiannon.' Catherine Davies thumps the floor with her black parasol. 'You are not listening to me. I cannot possibly, not possibly, sit out there at that table in the open air with all those dreadful birds flying around. What if that nasty one of yours was among them?' She clutches at her breast. 'I fear for my life when he is in my vicinity.'

Non takes the big tray outside to the table, loads everything onto it and brings the tea party – tea party! – indoors.

'What is that contraption?' Catherine points with her parasol at the kettle burbling on the paraffin stove.

'It saves lighting the range in this heat,' Non says, busying herself with the tea-making.

Catherine Davies sniffs. She leans across the table and takes the cloth off the plate of bread. 'Butter! You are so extravagant, Rhiannon. You must remember that Davey does not earn a great wage from that menial work he does.'

Non knows this. She also knows that too much of his small wage goes to his mother. So, whose money does Catherine Davies think pays the rent for this house, and bought all the furniture in it, including that chair she is putting so much strain upon this minute? It is a blessing that they have Non's inheritance to draw upon.

'Maybe he could give you a bit less, Mrs Davies, and then we would have more.'

Catherine Davies stiffens, and puts the slice of bread that was eagerly on its way to her mouth down on her plate. 'It is his duty,' she says. 'I am his mother.'

'He is dutiful,' Non says as she pours the tea, with a steady hand, too, she is pleased to notice. 'He is the kindest man I have ever known. Don't you think he is kind, and dutiful?'

Catherine Davies sniffs harder. She helps herself to a spoonful of sugar, which she stirs into her tea, briskly.

'Why are you so hard on him when he is so good to you?' Non says.

'Hard on him?' Catherine says. 'What are you talking about, Rhiannon? He is my son.'

Remember her illness. Non's conscience is a small, fading voice. She unclenches her hands and takes up her teacup.

'If Davey had died in the War, he would not have brought back that terrible influenza, and Billy would be alive today. And I would not need Davey's money. You see how it is, Rhiannon?'

'That doesn't make sense, Mrs Davies. And it's unkind. Especially given Billy's behaviour.'

'I don't know what you mean, Rhiannon. Really!' Catherine Davies's cup clatters down on its saucer.

Non can hear Branwen somewhere at the back of her mind warning her to curb her tongue, to think about what she is saying, to count to twenty, to stop before she has offended. She ignores her sister's voice. 'I mean the reason Davey has to give you his money,' she says.

'I've told you, he is my son, it is his duty. And it is not your business.'

'I think it is my business when I'm bringing up Billy's son,' Non says. 'Haven't you noticed how like the family Osian is? Everyone else has. Everyone else knows whose son he is.'

'I'm not going to sit here and listen to this . . . this filth,' Catherine Davies says. 'You are smirching Billy's good name! He would never have fathered an idiot like that.' She manages to stand up, and leans over the table, her bulk towering above Non. 'Have you not thought, Rhiannon, that the boy looks more like Davey than anyone? You were a disgrace, setting your cap at him the way you did. So brazen. And with no intention of being a proper wife to him, giving him children. No wonder he had to look elsewhere.' The bulk shakes as the voice rises into a screech, and spittle sprays from Catherine Davies's mouth.

Too late, Non realises this is not a good idea, nor a kind one. She ought to know by now that a sensible conversation with her mother-in-law is impossible. She should have listened to Branwen's voice. Catherine Davies is obviously unwell. Non has been uncharitable. Cruel, even.

'And no good to him for anything else, either, all that reading, no idea how to do anything in the house, refusing to go to chapel. What kind of wife are you, setting a son against his mother?' Catherine Davies pushes herself upright. 'I am not a quarrelsome woman, Rhiannon. I have lived in this town since the day I was married and I have never quarrelled with anybody. And I am not going to start now.'

Behind Catherine Davies, on the sash of the open window, Herman is perched with his head on one side as if he is engrossed in what is being said. His feathers ruffle as Non rises to shoo him out, and he flies at Catherine Davies and circles her head, his wings flapping close to her face and hair.

Catherine screams and falls back into her chair and then topples to the floor, a dead weight. Herman lands beside her and begins to pull at her hair with his beak, rapidly loosening the bun she wears at her nape.

Non fails to shoo him away and picks him up instead and runs out with him, throwing him into the air, so that he takes flight with an indignant caw. She runs back into the house and finds the bottle of Sal Volatile in the remedy cupboard, unstoppers it and waves it about under Catherine Davies's nose.

Catherine begins to cough and thrash about on the floor. She opens her eyes and sees Non kneeling over her. 'Keep away from me,' she screeches. 'Don't touch me, you . . . you . . . witch.'

38

Davey had gone to visit his parents when supper had been eaten, at Non's request. She felt guilt for her part in her mother-in-law's collapse yesterday. She had fetched Maggie Ellis to help her lift Catherine Davies and walk her home, by which time Catherine seemed herself again and slammed the door in their faces. Maggie Ellis had dashed into her house, then promptly dashed out again in her monstrous sun-hat and scurried off down the hill to town where she no doubt told everyone she met about Catherine Davies's fainting fit.

But now, Davey is home. Non rests her head on his shoulder. It is not altogether comfortable sitting on his lap in the old kitchen armchair, with one of its wooden arms digging into her back, but she would not change it for the softest of down beds. Davey's arm is around her waist, stopping her from slipping off, and his other hand strokes her hair and her face, his hand rough with callouses, but she would not change that either.

The nights have begun to draw in, and she is sure the air has cooled a little today. The kitchen door is open and the phlox she seeds either side of the doorway each year, which seems to thrive in the heat, is spilling its scent into the approaching dusk.

Osian has long been in bed and Meg had taken herself off upstairs earlier than usual, complaining that the pair of them, Non and Davey, were too old and long married to be behaving like a courting couple. A courting couple! Non snuggles up to Davey as best as she can in the old chair.

'I am sorry, Davey,' she says. 'You have enough to worry about without me upsetting your mother.'

'She's difficult, Non. It's the way she is.'

'Maybe she's not well, Davey, have you thought about that?'

'She's like she's always been, Non. No way to do anything except her own! A bit worse because she's older, perhaps. I tell you – I wish Katie and Bess lived a bit nearer so they could help out.'

Non smoothes Davey's tufts of hair flat, then ruffles them again. 'They are rather far away,' she says.

'Well – who can blame them, really, for wanting to get as far away as they could from Mother. She was always telling them what to do.'

'I think your father used to miss your sisters, you know. But he doesn't even remember them now, does he? I was so glad when he came back to us for that short while when we were having Wil's leaving supper. Wil said he appreciated the advice not to get his hair wet more than anything!'

'Mother wasn't too glad,' Davey says. They smile at each other at the memory of Catherine Davies trying to take the money bag back. 'Poor old Father. I don't know what to do for him, Non. We need more help, really, to keep an eye on him, and to follow him and bring him home if he wanders off. I can't let Mother go on locking him up.'

'Lizzie German could do with more work. Now the English

families aren't coming here to their big houses in the summers like they used to, the work isn't there. Which means she'll be short of money. And none of her grandchildren are old enough to earn much except a few pennies on the golf course. She's too proud to take anything without working for it.'

'Lizzie,' Davey says. 'I don't know what Mother would say about that.'

'Well, if you pay her she'd be working for you, not your mother. And she's no gossip, you know – she knows when to keep her mouth closed. And—' Non yanks at a lock of Davey's hair. 'You could pay her with the money your father gave Wil.'

'But that's Wil's money. Father meant Wil to have it.'

'Yes, but you know what Wil said about it. He'd be far happier knowing that you weren't struggling and his Taid was well looked after than he would be thinking he had a nest egg in a drawstring bag at home.'

Davey squeezes her waist. The dusk deepens until the firelight casts flickering shadows on the kitchen wall and the moths come fluttering through the door to play in the flames. Is this happiness? Is this contentment?

'I'm sure it's cooler this evening,' Non says. She gets down from Davey's lap to close the door and turn the key in the lock. People have started to lock their doors since the tramps began to appear in their dozens in the town. 'Perhaps this heat is breaking at last.'

'That'll mean fewer coffins,' Davey says. 'That must be good.'

'Maybe you could manage without Teddy, then.'

'I'm managing without Teddy as it is,' Davey says. He pulls her back onto his lap. 'Seriously though, Non, I think he's got a bit of a problem – he's a drinker. I can smell it on him, even in the mornings. He rambles on, you know, and something he said made me think he'd been in hospital for a while, I don't know if that was to do with the drink. Anyway, I don't let him near any of the woodwork now. He does the polishing. And he's not very good at that. He let slip he knew Robert Graves the other day. I wonder if he was an officer, you know. It would make sense.'

'Is that why he's here? Something to do with the Graves family?'

Davey shakes his head. 'I really don't know, Non, what he's doing here. He maunders on and on, as if he's dropping hints, but I don't know what he means by them.' Momentarily, his hands clench into fists.

'Why does it bother you so much, Davey?'

'Because I don't know what he's on about. Something about him – something about the way he talks about what happened, but not really telling you anything. I don't know. It brings things back, things I'd forgotten.'

'What sort of things?'

'Little bits of things, parts of things. Like – it came back to me that I couldn't remember Ben Bach being with us that last night in the trench, before the attack. I've gone over it and over it, Non, like watching a film. It was bedlam. The night was pitch black, the duckboards were long gone under the mud and . . . other things, so we were all slipping and sliding everywhere, and so exhausted I don't know how we kept going. And the stretcher parties were running backwards and forwards along our trench as best they could, so it was hard to keep track of people. Everyone was terrified there'd be a gas attack, the wind was just right for it, and we all knew the gas masks weren't much use by then. But see, Non, what was missing was Ben calling out to his mother. There was no sound, we were keeping quiet as we could, even the stretcher-bearers, pretending we weren't there – the blooming rats were making more noise than we were, squealing when we trod on them. But no Ben. No Ben.'

Non shudders at the thought of the rats. She holds Davey tighter.

'He should have been there, Non. So, where was he?'

'Does it matter, now? Poor Ben, perhaps he was killed early on in the attack. The letter Elsie got just said he'd died.' What did it mean, what help was it, a letter like that? Didn't they all die, the ones who didn't come back? Poor Ben Bach. She remembers, now, thinking that Ben had been killed earlier. She had tried to work it out from the date of the letter to Elsie. It was hopeless to try to make sense of any of it.

'He'd have been at the clearing hospital if that's right, Non, where we all ended up that night, the living and the dead,' Davey says. 'But he wasn't there, I'm sure of it. I'm fearful, Non, of what I may remember. I'm fearful of what Teddy knows.'

Non tries to clutch at the contentment that had stolen over her, but it slips out of her grasp. 'I wish Teddy would just go away,' she says.

'I wish it was as easy as that.' Davey kisses her hair. The clock begins to mark the hour. 'Look at the time. It's past our bedtime, you know. We'll never get up in the morning!'

They are halfway up the stairs, hand in hand, when someone plays a wild rat-a-tat with the knocker on the front door. They cast startled looks at one another, and Davey takes the lamp from Non and runs back down to see who it is making so much noise at their door at this time of night.

'Gwydion,' Non says as Davey opens the door. 'What is it? What's happened?'

Gwydion is speechless. He pushes past them into the house and paces the kitchen floor, back and forth, around and around, while Non and Davey look on, not sure what to do.

'Tea,' Davey says. 'I'll put the kettle on that little stove. Get the cups and things, Non. A strong cup of tea is what's needed. And some food.'

Non has never seen Gwydion in this kind of state. It will take more than strong tea to resolve whatever has caused this agitation. But she takes the bread from its bin and butters thick slices of it. Davey makes the tea. He takes Gwydion by the shoulders and propels him to one of the chairs by the table.

'Sit,' he says. 'Here – food, tea. Just calm down, Gwydion, and tell us what the matter is.'

Gwydion crams the bread into his mouth as if he is starving and gulps down the tea that must be far too hot still. Then he leans his elbows on the table and cups his face in his hands. 'How old am I?' he says. He looks up at them. 'I'm so furious with Mother. I explained to her what I wanted to do, what I planned to do, and why, and to Father. She wouldn't listen once she realised what I was planning. She said I was silly, Aoife was silly and worse, her father was incompetent and a troublemaker – hah – and then when I got up this morning, ready to talk to her again, try to persuade her I know what I'm doing, I found she'd gone through my pockets when I was asleep – can you believe it? – and taken Aoife's letter and read it and torn it to pieces. That was it, Non. I told her she'd never see me again, and left.'

'Oh, Gwydion.' Non strokes his hair. She does not know what to say to him. She wonders where he has been all day. Riding about on that motorbike, I expect, she thinks, no wonder he is so hungry.

'I feel bad about Father, I really do, she's such a tartar, she wouldn't let him say anything. And to think how we laughed that day on the beach – d'you remember, Non? – how we laughed at Taid giving her that name when she was so different to Branwen in the story. But it's not funny at all.'

'What did you tell Branwen you were planning, Gwydion?' Davey says. 'What are you thinking of doing?'

Gwydion looks at Non as if she has asked him the question. He holds his hand out to her and she takes it and sits down in the chair beside him at the table. 'I'm going to Ireland,' he says. 'Next week, if not sooner.'

Non has been expecting news of this kind, but Branwen had not. She has some sympathy for her sister. 'I'm sure Branwen will come round, Gwydion,' she says. 'I expect it was a bit of a shock for her.'

'I don't care whether she comes round or not,' Gwydion says. 'I will never see her again, Non. Never.'

Davey raises his eyebrows at Non – what are they going to do? 'How will you manage?' he asks Gwydion.

'Aoife's father's found a post for me at Trinity,' Gwydion says. 'In Dublin, Davey. Doing research. That's what the letter was about. Mostly.' He turns to Non. 'It was a private letter, Non. She had no right . . . no right to . . .' Words fail him. He buries his face in his hands again.

Non lays her hand on his head, stroking, wishing she knew how to repair the damage that has been done. 'What about you and Aoife?'

'We'll marry,' Gwydion says. 'And live with her parents. They've got a huge house. Plenty of room.'

'You get on well enough with Aoife's parents, do you?' Davey says.

'Same ideas, same ideals, Davey. All the changes that are happening over there, I want to be part of it all. It's an exciting time for Ireland. We could learn from them about being in charge of our own fate, we're too slow about it.'

Davey lets that go, Non is glad to see. This conversation is not about politics. She can see from Gwydion's grey face that he is exhausted. Emotion is so exhausting. 'Go to bed, Gwydion,' she says. 'We'll talk in the morning. You know you have our support if you are doing something you really and truly believe is right.'

'You two are good to me,' Gwydion says. He stands up and hugs Non and shakes hands with Davey. He has gone already, his head and his heart are over the sea in Ireland.

Non knows she will miss him almost as much as she misses Wil. 'Don't wake Osian,' she says as Gwydion heads for the stairs. He turns back and smiles at her – she is so glad to see that smile – and goes on up the stairs.

She and Davey look at one another.

'Well,' Davey says.

Non shrugs. What can she say? She knew this day would come. Though not quite in this way.

'I hope Branwen and Gwydion don't leave it at this,' Davey says. 'She has to let him go – he's a grown man, Non. Surely she can see that?'

'Branwen can be stubborn,' Non says. Black and white, that is how everything is for Branwen.

'That doesn't help, does it?' Davey shakes his head. 'See, Non, any man will do a better job if he's doing what he wants to do, it stands to reason.'

Non wonders if he is speaking from experience. 'You're good at your work,' she says.

'It's what I chose to do, that's why. I like working with the wood, the feel of it, the smell of it, making something with my hands. It must be in the family somewhere. I could never work in an office, Non. That's what Mother wanted for me and Billy – I disappointed her.'

And Billy did not, Non thinks. Billy spent his working life

making things as difficult as he could for people from that office of his in Port, but he did not disappoint his mother.

'Mind you,' Davey says, 'I don't think our children will disappoint us, do you?'

Our children! Non has wondered for days now how to broach the subject of children with Davey. No moment has seemed right. The ardent Davey who courted her was adamant that he wanted no more children. And yet, he had brought her Osian. Non has been unable to decide what she wants, her heart and her head have been telling her different things. Maybe it will help her to know what Davey thinks now. She hugs him. 'How would you feel about having another child, Davey?'

Davey stares at her. He lets out a whoop. He picks her up by the waist and swirls her around until she is giddy and he is breathless before he sets her down again. He says, 'But, Non? You can't possibly be . . . ?'

'No. No, of course not,' she says. 'But it can't be too difficult, can it?'

39

The rhubarb pie should really have been eaten with a spoon, but she and Meg were too soporific from sitting in the green shade to go indoors to fetch any. If only every day was as calm and pleasant as this one.

'How long,' Meg says, as she licks her fingers one by one, 'before Maggie Ellis comes creeping out to listen to what we're talking about? She'd have made a good spy in the War. If she didn't hear what the enemy was saying, she'd have made it up.'

Non smiles at her. Meg has begun on a metamorphosis from a scowling child to an open-faced, pretty young woman. They have the spectacular monthly bad tempers to prove it. Non thinks Meg's holiday work, the responsibility, the money she earns, the new friends she has made, have all helped. Along with the fright she had when Catherine Davies demanded she go back to live with her.

'It's good of the housekeeper to let you have the afternoon off,' Non says, as she licks a couple of her own fingers free of the sticky rhubarb juice.

Meg swings round from the table and lifts her feet onto the

chair opposite. 'Saves the hotel my wages,' she says. 'It's never busy on Saturday afternoons, especially when the weather's like this.'

'Still,' Non says. 'You get to rest a bit.' She pours lemonade into their glasses and swats away the wasps that gather greedily around the rims.

'I thought Gwydion would be here,' Meg says. 'Where's he gone? He hasn't left for good already, has he?'

'He wouldn't go without saying goodbye to you, Meg, would he?' Non says. 'But he has gone up to Holyhead today on the motorcycle to book his boat passage and find out how to ship his books and other things over. He knows someone he can stay with on Angelsey. He'll ride back again tomorrow.'

Meg sips her lemonade. 'This is a bit sour, Non.'

'It's nice like this, sharp, it quenches your thirst better,' Non says. 'And sugar is still a bit costly, you know.' She feels a little smug; she is beginning to care about money.

'Well, I don't like it,' Meg says. 'I didn't think he'd go, did you?'

'Gwydion? Yes, I think I did. He seemed more serious about it all – Aoife and the politics – than I've ever seen him about anything else.'

'I wonder if she's as pretty as he says.' Meg pushes her glass in Non's direction.

'I expect he thinks she is,' Non says.

'What about Wil – d'you think he'll find a sweetheart?'

'Not on the David Morris, he won't,' Non says. 'They don't allow women on board, Meg, did you know? We're bad luck.'

Meg seems to think about this, dropping her head back and closing her eyes. Eventually she says, 'Are you sure? How would a woman get to France, then, or some other country across the sea?'

'I suppose we're not bad luck on passenger ships,' Non says. 'Which just shows you what a silly superstition it is.'

Meg opens her eyes and laughs at Non. 'You get so cross,' she says. 'You should have been one of those suffragettes you were always reading about in the paper.'

'I might have been if I hadn't had you and Wil and Osian to look after,' Non says.

'I wonder if he's written anything in his notebook yet,' Meg says. 'Wil, I mean.'

'I expect he was right when he said he wouldn't have much time,' Non says. 'It's only a six-man crew, and they have to keep the ship moving all the time, night and day. At least, I think they do. I suppose they take turns.'

'It's exciting to think of going so far away, Non. It is adventurous, isn't it? I hope he writes at least some of his adventures down.' Meg pushes her glass nearer again to Non. 'D'you want my lemonade? It's much too sour.'

Non finishes her own glassful and draws Meg's glass towards her. It is pleasant to sit here with Meg. They are all always so busy. She waves a wasp away.

'Listen!' Meg holds up her forefinger. There is a prolonged rustling in the shrubbery at the end of the wall between their garden and Maggie Ellis's. Non expects Herman to emerge at any moment, it is sometimes the way he announces himself, but he does not.

'Maggie Ellis,' Meg mouths at her. She whispers, 'Let's invent a story and see how soon it gets back to us.'

'Meg!' Non speaks quietly. 'Poor old Maggie would have an unexciting life without her gossip. She spends hours looking after her husband.'

'What's wrong with him?' Meg says.

'Well, I don't exactly know,' Non says. 'We never see him out nowadays, though, do we?'

'I've never seen him at all. D'you think she makes him up? So we'll all feel sorry for her?'

'What a thing to say, Meg. She has a hard time of it with him.'

'Well, I'm never going to get married and be somebody's slave,' Meg says. 'I'm just going to take lovers.'

Take lovers! Non cannot imagine where that has come from. Is it that new teacher of English, she wonders, letting them read all kinds of novels? Or the French teacher – maybe they were allowed to read racy French novels. *Madame Bovary*, she thinks. 'What a notion, Meg,' she says. 'I think you'd have to earn a lot of money and be independent to do that.'

Meg waves her hand about airily, a woman of the world already. 'I know that, Non. I'm not going to be kept, don't worry. I'm going to work hard at school and go to university, like Gwydion.'

'To do what?'

'Learn French,' Meg says.

'French?'

'Yes. Did I show you my French penfriend's photograph?'

'No,' Non says. 'You didn't.' And Meg knows perfectly well that she did not.

Meg takes her feet from the chair and a box from beneath the table. She lifts the lid and draws out a photograph that is already dog-eared. 'Don't you think Jean's very handsome, Non?'

The boy in the photograph is older than Meg, maybe as old as Wil. He has dark hair and dark eyes, and his eyelashes are ridiculously long. He is handsome, Non thinks, but she says, 'You can't really tell from a picture, can you, Meg? It depends what the person is like.'

Meg snatches the photograph back. 'Well, I know that,' she

says. 'But he looks as if he's very nice, doesn't he?'

Non smiles at her, and Meg blushes. 'Jean's father runs a lycée,' she says. 'What's that, Non, a lycée?'

'A school, I think,' Non says.

'Oh.' Meg seems slightly disappointed. 'A school. I thought it was something more . . . romantic than a school.'

'Well,' Non says, as seriously as she can, 'it is a French school.'

'That is romantic, isn't it?' Meg says. 'Jean said I could go there and teach English. I thought he meant teach him English, but maybe he didn't. I'll have to ask him. I don't want to teach a whole school.'

'But, Meg,' Non says, 'you're Welsh, not English.'

'It doesn't matter. I can speak English, can't I? And read it. And I can write it a lot better than Jean. You should see his letter.'

Non holds out her hand, and Meg looks puzzled for a moment, then she grins at Non. 'I haven't got it in here,' she says.

'So, you're planning on leaving, too?' Non says.

'Will you make me a special leaving supper and make everyone give me presents? Like Wil had.'

'Only if you say you're going for good,' Non says.

'You don't mean that, Non. You'd miss me. You miss Wil, don't you?'

'I do,' Non says. And she does, far more than she even feared she would. 'But that's the way it is. Children leave home like birds fly the nest.'

'Herman didn't,' Meg says. 'He fell out of it and broke his wing.'

'You're the one learning French,' Non says. 'You should know about the exception that proves the rule.'

The rustling shrub waves its laden branches at them as if a wind is trying to blow through it. Several angry wasps fly out from it. Non wonders if they have a nest in there. Meg throws the beaded cover over the lemonade jug and nods meaningfully at the waving shrub. Non shakes her head at her, and Meg turns her attention to her box again.

'Look what else I've got in here,' she says. 'You'll like this, Non.' Meg unwraps tissue paper from the round object. She holds up between her thumb and forefinger the most exquisite carving Non has ever seen.

'It's you,' Non says.

'Osian gave it to me this morning. I don't know why. He's gone a bit silly with this carving, Non. It's all he ever does.'

He is rather obsessive about it, but Osian is like that with whatever he does. That's just Osian. Non turns the tiny carving this way and that. He has made a head and shoulders portrait of Meg, and caught her resemblance to Grace. Non is surprised by the detail Osian has captured in such a tiny piece.

'It's perfect, Meg. It's lovely. I don't know how he does it.'

'Well, he just picks away with that little knife, doesn't he? Pick, pick, pick. It could drive you insane. It's really sharp that knife, Non, all I did was touch – just touch – the blade, and it cut my finger. It's a bit dangerous.'

'He's been using it for years, Meg, and he hasn't hurt himself,' Non says. 'What I meant was, how does he capture the person he's carving? Look at this – it's more you than you are, somehow. What do you think it tells you about yourself?'

Meg takes the carving from Non and studies it. 'It tells me I look a lot prettier when my freckles don't show.'

'Oh, Meg,' Non says.

'Well, at least I'm not brown like you. That's a bit common, you know, Non. If you had a baby it would probably be brown like you, wouldn't it?'

'What?'

'I heard you and Tada talking the other night. D'you think you'll have a baby, Non?'

Non begins to wonder what else Meg has heard up there in her bedroom. She and Davey will have to be careful in future when they are sitting in the kitchen discussing matters they want to keep private.

'We'll have to see, Meg,' she says.

'It won't bother me, you know, a baby. And I would be leaving, anyway, wouldn't I, before it was very old?'

Is Meg jealous? Or is she stating the obvious?

'Who will Osian carve when I've left, I wonder.'

The baby, maybe, Non thinks.

'He won't change, will he?' Meg says. 'He won't get better. You've only got to look at him sitting in that coffin in the work-shop to see that.'

'No, Meg, I don't suppose he will,' Non says. 'So it's lucky he's happy doing his carving, isn't it?'

'He's not so happy since that Teddy came, is he? He really, really doesn't like that Teddy.'

'How do you know, Meg? How can you tell?' Maybe that was what she had felt when she held the carving of Teddy. She had felt Osian's own fear and dislike of the man.

'I don't know how I know,' Meg says. 'I just do, that's all. I don't like that Teddy either. It's his eyes. Haven't you noticed his eyes, Non?'

Non has not seen Teddy's eyes. When he came to the door, looking for Davey, he'd looked down when he spoke to her, dipped his head. She thought he was embarrassed, ashamed even, of his state. And he has not been in the workshop when she has visited Davey there.

'You look at him,' Meg says. 'He's not . . . right in the head.'

Non laughs at her expression and Meg demonstrates the look in Teddy's eyes by giving Non an empty stare that is so unnerving it stops her laughter instantly.

'See?' Meg says. 'It scares me – and Osian.'

The rustling shrub gives a frenetic shake and keels over into their garden with a crash, carrying Maggie Ellis with it until she is lying on her belly on its branches, beating away the wasps that gather around her head.

'I was wrong,' Meg says. 'She'd have made a useless spy.'

40

Davey has been quiet all evening. It is not a companionable quiet. This is more akin to a white-faced, thousand-yard-stare-into-the-distance quiet that means Davey is troubled.

He had sat at the supper table with her and Meg and Osian, had pushed his food around the plate and then pushed the plate aside. For the rest of the meal he just stared at the place on the tablecloth where the plate had been. Meg had looked enquiringly at Non but not taken it further. They had both regaled Osian and Davey with the story of how they had lifted Maggie Ellis out of the shrub and helped her home full of excuses about how she had come to be leaning so heavily on it that it had fallen over, ripping its roots out of the ground. They did not expect a response from Osian, but they did not have one from Davey, either.

Once the apparatus of supper had been cleared away, Non had sent Osian to bed, after telling him that he had made a wonderful carving of Meg, which also elicited no response. It would be so easy to entirely forget that he was there and never to speak to him. And what kind of mother did that make of her? A mother fit to have her own child? Meg had rolled her eyes at Non about her father's behaviour and flounced off to her bedroom. No doubt to bury herself in *Madame Bovary*. In French!

Davey sits now in the kitchen armchair, staring into the small flames that flicker in the range. Non closes the door into the hallway, she closes the window, she closes the door into the garden. She can make it no more private than that. She has shut out all but the loudest sounds of the evening; the hoot of an owl out hunting is all she can hear. She has shut out the scents of the phlox and the roses that linger on the air. She has shut out the world and made a safe place for her and Davey. There seems to be a need for a haven tonight. She pulls a chair from under the table and sits on it beside Davey by the range. She takes hold of his hand.

'What's wrong, Davey?' she says.

Davey shakes his head. 'Nothing,' he says. 'Tiredness is all, Non. Albert's fussing about this coffin for Calvin Edwards, it's such a big thing – I'll have to go in tomorrow to finish it.'

'You need your day of rest,' she says.

Davey shakes his head again. 'Funeral's on Monday morning. There's no family to want a viewing so Albert wants to get Calvin in the coffin, seal it up. Best thing, anyway, this weather.'

'And?' Non says. 'There's more than tiredness here, Davey.' She gives his hand a little shake, as if to shift him into speech.

He shrugs, as if it is nothing. 'Bit of trouble with Teddy, too,' he says.

She has been expecting something of this kind.

'There's something serious wrong with him. You know . . .' Davey taps his forehead. 'Like war damage. Can't talk sense, just looks at you half the time as if he's not all there. The drink can't help. He reminds me of Aggie Hughes's grandson. Maybe that's the kind of hospital he was in.' He taps his head again. 'They had places like that for the officers.'

'Wil said he reminded him of Bobby,' Non says. 'And everyone who's met him thinks there's something wrong about him.' These last few days, whenever she has been in town, Non has been accosted by people asking after Wil, telling her it must be quiet without him, what a nice boy he is, just like his father, and then a quick change of tone to ask how Davey is getting on with that tramp, shaking their heads as they speak of him. Non has never been so popular.

'Not his fault if it was the War. But I'm not sure there wasn't something before the War, something else. As if he's never been quite right. It's the way he talks about things.'

'What things?' Non says.

'Everything,' Davey says. 'It's just the way he says everything. Anyway, I started asking him questions today – I got a bit tired of him going on and on. He'd got hold of some story about someone from here being court-martialled. Said he heard it when we were in the clearing station.'

Non gasps and holds Davey's hand as tightly as she can.

'Well, I said that was nonsense, if anyone from here had been court-martialled I'd know about it, but he insisted he was right. Then he got upset, and said a pal of his had been shot for cowardice and it had been a big mistake. This lad's village weren't going to put him on their memorial, or something. He got in a real state, Non, telling me all this, crying and shaking, saying it was his fault, he was the one should be dead. I couldn't understand half of it. But I got the idea they were a bit more than friends, which might account for any trouble before the War. He had our address on that letter I gave him to send you if . . . well, you know, and he's got some connection with the Graves family here, and in his head it made sense for him to come here and find out about this man who was court-martialled and shot, like his friend had been. It made no sense at all to me.'

'That's because it doesn't make sense,' Non says.

'I tried to talk to him – to make him see that he'd upset every-body if he went around telling those sorts of stories. It's hard enough for everyone as it is.'

Out of doors the owl hoots, and another answers in the distance. A hunting party. The corpse birds, she thinks.

'Everyone's on edge in this heat,' Davey says. 'Teddy could find himself in trouble if he starts telling those sorts of tales.' He stares through the window.

The dusk gathers out of doors and the light from the rising moon puddles on the floor between their chairs, and lights their joined hands and Davey's face.

'There's more, Davey,' Non says. 'What is it? D'you think he'll make trouble?'

'Hold my hands tighter, Non,' he says.

Non does as he asks. She holds both his hands, his rough work-man's hands, as hard as she can. He rocks slightly in the old chair and it creaks along with him. She looks into his face but he will not meet her eyes. Panic wells in her breast and makes her breath-less. This must be the memory Davey has been afraid of remembering. She wonders if his mind has tried to rub it out because it is unbearable, but left behind an imprint that sends him crying and shivering under the kitchen table. The colour has drained from his face.

Time passes. The moon brightens as the darkness deepens, and its light shines on them as if there is no one else in the world for it to shine down on except the two of them here in their mortal fear, one because he knows, one because she does not.

'Davey?'

'I killed Ben Bach.'

'What?' Non loosens her grip on his hands.

'Don't let go. Don't let go, Non.'

She tightens her grip. 'Davey, that can't be true. Are you remembering wrong again? Like with Angela. Are you?'

'I killed him, Non. I killed Ben Bach.'

'No,' Non says. 'No, that can't be right. You'd never kill anyone. Not you, Davey.'

His hands jerk in her grip. He groans. He speaks through his clenched teeth. 'Oh, Non, Non, what do you think I was doing over there for nearly four years?'

Non's tears brim over and run down her cheeks. Where has their safe haven gone now?

'I was walking home tonight, thinking about what to do about Teddy, and the Pentre'r Efail boys were out in the road playing soldiers – I've passed them playing like that dozens of times, Non, and never thought, never remembered before. They were marching one off with a rag tied over his eyes – they'd captured him, you know – and it hit me. I thought I was going to throw up right there.'

Davey pauses, seeming to listen to the owl's mournful hoots. Non waits.

'Ben was court-martialled for running away, Non. He didn't – well, he did, but you should have seen the state of him by then, he wasn't fit to be there. Nobody would listen, Non. They sentenced him to be executed. He's the one Teddy was talking about. And I shot him. Shot him just as the sun was coming up.'

Non wants to scrub the tears from her face, to be brave for Davey, but he is clinging too tightly to her hands. 'Poor Benjamin, poor boy,' she says. A brain the size of a pea, says the headmaster's voice from the past. 'You tried your best to get him sent home – you told me that.'

Davey carries on as if Non has not spoken, not tried to make it right. 'The way those firing parties worked, Non, was they picked ten men from the unit and then the officer put bullets in the rifles and a blank in one of them – so you could spend the rest of your life pretending it wasn't you fired the killing shot, I suppose. It's stupid. You can tell if it's real when you fire.'

Non holds on to Davey's hands as if she is saving him from drowning. The room tilts around them, the ground shifts beneath their feet, as if they are being rocked on board a ship on a wild sea.

'They bound his eyes, Non. He didn't understand what was happening. He kept calling, Where am I, Mam? Some of the men were crying. We were all jittery. It seemed to go on and on, the waiting for the signal to fire, though I don't suppose it did. I hoped I didn't have the blank in my rifle, and I fired before the signal was given. You're not supposed to do that. I wanted to make sure Ben didn't suffer, that he died quick. You heard some terrible tales about those executions, botched shots, prisoners in terrible pain, officers refusing to finish them off. I knew from the recoil I had a real bullet, Non. It was a good shot. I killed him cleanly.'

Non does not know who she is crying for. Davey, Ben Bach, Elsie, herself, the whole of human kind? She cries and cries.

At last, she says, 'Who else knows?'

'Nobody here,' Davey says. 'Our boys were all scattered by then. There was only me and Ben left in our lot. I should have looked after him better, Non. I promised Elsie I'd look after him.'

Non says, 'Elsie must never know.'

Davey grips her hand tighter. 'No,' he says, in a whisper.

'And we will have to live with what we know.'

'Nothing I ever do again will be as hard and as terrible as shooting Ben Bach, Non.'

'You're a good, good man, Davey. You saved Ben from suffering.' And he is, has been always, a good man. As his memory has returned, so has the old Davey with his kindness and humour, but he has brought with him for ever that other Davey who has been irrevocably marked by what he has seen and done. That is something else she and he will have to learn to live with.

Davey stares into the range. The fire has long died, leaving cold coals and ash to mark the place it burned.

Non takes a deep breath. She says, 'And Teddy will have to go away. How can he be persuaded to—?' She stops as a loud noise from outside startles her, though Davey does not blink. 'What's that?' she says, as someone bangs hard on their front door. 'It can't be Gwydion back already, surely?' She lets go of Davey's hands and rubs the snail trails of tears from her face.

Someone begins to call Davey's name in accompaniment to the knocking.

He pushes himself up from his chair as if he is sleepwalking and goes through from the kitchen into the hall. She hears the click of the latch as he opens the front door.

'Davey, thank God. Come quickly. That Englishman of yours has been causing trouble. Calling us all cowards. Drunk as a lord. He got in a fight and the Constable hauled him off to the police cell to cool off. Told us to get you.'

Non recognises the voice, it is Tommy from the Blue Lion. Another voice mutters something but she cannot make it out, and cannot place the voice.

'Thought they were going to lynch him,' Tommy says.

'He deserved it, insulting us. Who does he think he is? Might have been a bloody officer in the War but he's a nobody here, a nobody,' says the second voice. 'Twenty-two boys we've lost! He's got a bloody cheek talking like—'

'I'll be right there,' Davey says. He comes back into the kitchen. 'You heard all that?'

Non nods at him.

He gives her a bleak look. 'I'd better go. You're right, though, Non. Something must be done to send Teddy on his way.'

41

Non wishes she had been able to keep awake until Davey's return last night. The loud banging on the door and the shouting had woken Meg and Osian, and by the time Non had cut bread and butter and made a pot of tea, then chivvied them back into their beds when they had eaten, she had been so tired that she had taken herself to bed – not intending to sleep, but merely to rest.

This morning they were all late. Davey had slapped some oatcakes and cheese into his tin and rushed to the workshop, herding a dreamy Osian ahead of him clutching a lump of half-worked wood and his penknife, and Meg had raced away to the St David's with a breakfast of bread and jam in her hand. Non made a pot of tea and now sits at the open kitchen door, a cup and saucer in her hand, listening to her hens and watching Herman who is making her head spin as he walks around and around the saucer of water she put out for him. She closes her eyes for a moment, raising her face to feel a promise of coolness in the air. Maybe the great heat is about to break at last.

She is lazy, she should be attending to her housework – there is always housework to be done – but her mind is busy, and she has stolen this time to sit and think. Thinking is as important as doing, Rhiannon, her father would say to her when she used to try to pull him from his chair to help her with some childish task. What she learnt last night requires careful thought.

When she had wondered about what it might be that Davey had forgotten, she had not imagined it could be a thing so terrible. She had no idea that such executions took place. She wonders how many soldiers like Davey had to execute men they knew and had fought with side by side. Anyone's mind would try to erase such a memory, she thinks. She had not wanted Davey to remember what had happened, but now that he has, surely there will be no rubbed-out memories struggling to re-appear, and Davey will no longer suffer those waking nightmares when he is back in the trenches.

But she knows that it will always haunt them, the death of Ben Bach – the foolishness of it, the grievousness of it, the burden of it. They will always carry it with them. She lifts her cup to her lips and realises that she has let her tea grow cold; she bends forward to put the cup and saucer down on the floor. It is as well that she is adept at keeping secrets, she thinks, and that Davey is not one to talk for the sake of it. The manner of Ben Bach's death is something that can never be told, never be shared.

'The War has changed everything,' she says to Herman. He struts towards her and dips his head into her cup. He takes a sip of the cold tea, lifting his beak high to swallow it. Even he had his difficulties in the War – some silly boys had made a game out of saying he was a German spy and tried to shoot stones at him with their catapults. They were poor shots and had missed, but Herman had been frightened. Does he remember any of it? She puts her foot out to ruffle the feathers on his back with her toes until his affronted look makes her stop. Sometimes she wonders if Herman thinks he is some higher being and not a bird at all.

'Maybe you can tell me what ought to be done about Teddy,' she says to him. Something, as Davey said, has to be done to send Teddy on his way. The man seems determined to tell the whole town about Ben Bach's death. She wonders, if Davey were able to explain to Teddy the circumstances of Ben's court-martial – that Ben was under-age, and had the mind of a young child – if Davey were to tell him the truth of it all, then surely Teddy would see the cruelty to Elsie, to Ben's memory, to the survivors of the War, of telling it. Davey is able to speak so persuasively to people when it is needed – she has only to think of the people he has recruited to his branch of the Labour Party – that surely Teddy will listen to him. She will talk to Davey after supper, when Osian and Meg are in bed; she will ask him what happened to Teddy last night and if he had an opportunity to persuade Teddy to keep quiet about Ben or, even better, persuade him to leave the town, to go on his way again. But even as she ponders these sensible ideas she knows that there is no sense to the reasons Teddy has for proclaiming Ben's cowardice and execution to the whole town. Oh, she cannot bear to think of Elsie hearing such things about her boy. She scrubs away the tears from her face with the back of her hand. Crying is not the answer, but she cannot think what is.

A sharp pain in her foot makes her jump from her chair. Herman is pecking hard at her toes. She pushes him away. 'You're quite right, Herman,' she says. 'I should have given you your bread and milk instead of sitting here so uselessly. Come on.' She picks up her chair and takes it back to the table, Herman fluttering in her wake.

42

'What happened here, missus?' Lizzie German points at the ruined shrub.

'Maggie Ellis was a bit too anxious to hear what Meg and I were talking about when we had tea out here on Saturday,' Non says.

'That woman needs something to do, don't she?'

Non assumes this is a rhetorical question from Lizzie, but she herself is curious about what Maggie Ellis does. 'I thought she had to do a lot for her husband,' she says. 'Isn't he bed-bound? I haven't seen him about since before the War ended.'

'He was ill with something one time. Something he didn't ought to be ill with – always after the women, that one. He's just lazy by now. Lazy and a bully. He were always a bully, mind.'

'Poor Maggie.' Non feels guilt at the fun she and Meg made of Maggie on Saturday.

Lizzie shrugs. She and Maggie Ellis have known each other all their lives. They each know how the other has suffered. But life has been exceptionally hard for Lizzie. Non cannot imagine being Lizzie's age and bringing up three young grandchildren. Everyone has had to be stoic because of what the War has done to them, but some more so than others.

'I'm glad you're going to help out with old William Davies,' Non says.

'Puts food on the table,' Lizzie says. 'And I always liked old William.'

'It's a pity about what's happening to him. Life isn't fair, is it, Lizzie? I don't know how I would have managed through the War without his help. Little things, but they made a difference.' Non picks up the basket with the dirty washing in it, and tips the contents onto the table. She and Lizzie begin to sort them.

'You needed help then,' Lizzie says. 'But look at you now, missus. Funny them little drops making all that difference.'

'I feel like a different person,' Non says. She leans her hip against the table. 'Well, not a different person, more like I've come out of a dream or a daze.' She has not had the leisure to think about the difference, but she knows that she gets through her housework more quickly, without such effort and tiredness. She knows her thoughts are quicker and more lucid. She hopes her gift has gone, but she suspects it has not vanished entirely.

'Give me that towel there,' Lizzie says. 'It'll go in with the whites. That doctor knew what he was doing all right, didn't he?'

'He did, lucky for me.' Non watches Lizzie sweep the white articles towards herself along the table top.

'Has old Mrs Davies been to the doctor yet? We both know she needs to, missus.'

'I'm sure we'd know if she had, Lizzie – we'd have had chapter and verse of his failings. She's probably better off not knowing, don't you think? I'm not sure there's anything to be done for her.' Non begins to sort through the remainder of the washing. 'I don't see those things any more, Lizzie. That . . . gift. It's gone.'

Lizzie stops picking over the clothes. 'Those sorts of things are always with you. Either you've got them or you don't. You'll see.'

Non does not want what she suspects confirmed by Lizzie. She does not want to think Esmé was right. She believes that her father had mistakenly diagnosed the condition of her heart out of his love for her, and she believes that if he had lived, and seen the longer effects of the lifeblood he made for her, he would have changed his diagnosis. She would like to believe that he was mistaken about her gift, too.

'Best thing for old William to be going the way he is, maybe, given how she is.' Lizzie resumes her work, dropping some of the whites into the tub at her feet and handing others to Non to scrub on the washboard.

Osian runs over to Lizzie and blows at the soap bubbles that float up from her tub.

'Bit of a breeze blowing up this morning,' Lizzie says as she watches him. 'Look at them bubbles go.'

'I think the heat's breaking at last, don't you?' Non begins to rub the collars vigorously on her washboard.

'Good thing, too,' Lizzie says, 'before something else breaks first.'

'Davey feels as if he's been making nothing but coffins lately,' Non says.

'Mmm,' Lizzie says. 'It's true a lot of the old ones have gone. Not before their time, most of them, mind. Burying old Calvin today, are they?'

'That's why we've got Osian,' Non says. 'The funeral's this morning. Davey had to go in to finish the coffin yesterday. Albert wanted to get the body into it and the top nailed down as soon as he could.'

'Don't keep in this heat, the dead don't.' Lizzie lifts the dolly up and down, round and back again, pounding the clothes in the tub.

Non scrubs collars and cuffs and the fronts of aprons, and drops each article as she finishes it into Lizzie's tub. There is something soothing about this ritual of doing the washing every Monday with Lizzie German. It puts everything in its place, it enables her to see a way forward. She is certain, this morning, that Davey will be able to persuade Teddy to keep quiet, to go on his way, to seek help elsewhere if that is what he needs, if he has not done so already.

'That Calvin were the kind you think'll live for ever, mind. Outlived all his family,' Lizzie says. 'Built like an oak, he were.'

'Davey's making the coffin in oak,' Non says. 'He says it's the biggest he's ever made. Albert was complaining about the cost of the wood for it.'

'That Albert!' Lizzie shakes her head.

'So Davey said he'd pay for it,' Non says. 'He couldn't bear to see a man like Calvin in a pauper's coffin.'

'Heart of gold, your Davey,' Lizzie says.

Non wishes she had found an opportunity to talk to Davey yesterday about what he had said to Teddy, and about what Teddy was going to do. Gwydion had returned just before supper from his trip to Holyhead and had spent the evening telling her about his plans, and by the time she went up to bed Davey was fast asleep. She did not have the heart to wake him, and instead kissed his dear face and lay with her arm around him. As if she could keep him safe.

'Is that all the whites, missus?' Lizzie looks down into her tub. 'Have I got them all?'

'There's not so much now we're not doing Wil's washing, is there?'

'To think of him,' Lizzie says, leaning back to stretch herself, 'sailing away across them seas. It's a marvel. It really is.'

'He was ready to go, Lizzie. We gave him a good send-off, though

I think maybe we chose the wrong kind of presents – more the sorts of things we'd like ourselves.'

'Good to try new things,' Lizzie says. 'Stops you getting stuck in one place like an old wagon wheel in a rut.'

Non laughs at her. 'Meg's talking about going away, too. She liked the idea of getting presents.'

'Go far, that one,' Lizzie says. 'Looks after herself.'

Meg seems very self-possessed, Non thinks. She seems to know what she wants from life and even how to get what she wants. But she says, 'She's still a child, though, Lizzie, in many ways. She won't be leaving us for a while.'

'Help me get the mangle in place, missus,' Lizzie says, and between them they manoeuvre it between Lizzie's tub and the rinsing tub. Lizzie draws the whites one at a time from the tub and gives each a quick wring and shake before putting them between the rollers for Non to turn the handle.

She did not have the strength to do this not so long ago. She has written to Seb to tell him of her gratitude and her growing normality. He will be waiting to hear if there is a baby on the way. Or, more probably, he will have patients with far more pressing needs and have forgotten about her – though she does not imagine he has many patients who are medicating themselves with recipes from the Middle Ages.

'Keep turning that handle,' Lizzie says. She holds one of Gwydion's shirts between the rollers. 'I dare say your nephew will be off soon, though. That one's got itchy feet all right.'

'He's sailing for Ireland this Thursday,' Non says. 'I can't believe it, Lizzie. Going off to a completely new life, without a backward look.' She hopes that Gwydion will be happy, contented, that everything will be as he would wish; she hopes he will have no regrets. She wishes Branwen would yield a little.

'The only Irish I know are them pan-mending tinkers that come round,' Lizzie says. 'Rough lot, they are.' She turns round from her work to wave her hand at Osian who is trying to work up some bubbles in the tub. 'Stop it,' she says. 'Here, missus, have you got a saucer I can put some soapy water on for him?'

Non fetches an old saucer from the kitchen and a wire Davey had bent into a circle for Osian to make bubbles when he was younger that had been hanging in the kitchen ever since.

'But,' Lizzie says as she takes the apparatus from Non, 'I don't s'pose your Gwydion's going to live with the tinkers.'

'He's got a job at the university in Dublin,' Non says, 'and a sweetheart over there he's going to marry. Still, Lizzie, it's hard to see him leave.'

Lizzie stops mashing soap onto the saucer and looks at Non. 'O' course,' she says, 'there's some we'd like to see the back of.'

'You heard about Saturday, then?'

'Who hasn't?' Lizzie says.

'Maybe the Constable will just ask him to move on. He did with some of the other tramps.'

'He's no tramp,' Lizzie says. 'He behaves as if he's got nothing to lose, that one. Need to tread careful with him, don't want him telling what he knows.'

Non feels the hair prickle at the back of her neck. How does Lizzie German know these things? But the manner of Ben Bach's death is something Non can never discuss even with Lizzie; it is a burden she and Davey have to carry on their own.

Lizzie gives Osian the saucer of soapy water and reminds him how to make bubbles from it. He blows them high and the breeze that has been whispering incessantly through the trees and the grass floats them away.

Non hears sneezes from the other side of the garden wall and

Maggie Ellis appears rubbing energetically at her nose. 'Stop sending those bubbles my way, boy,' she tells Osian.

'Sorry, Mrs Ellis,' Non says. 'We didn't know you were there. Nice to have a bit of a breeze blowing through, isn't it?'

'It'll clear the air a bit, won't it, Non?' Maggie leans on the wall. 'You all right there, Lizzie?'

'Fine, Maggie. And you? Got over your accident?'

Non can see a long, raw graze on the side of Maggie's face, which must be sore. But Maggie Ellis does not hear Lizzie, or she pretends not to.

'I've got a few things to go in the wash. Any chance of putting them in with yours, Non?'

'Don't you ever do your own washing?' Lizzie says.

'Of course I do,' Maggie Ellis says. 'Only one or two bits, Non. Shall I pass them over?'

Non sighs, though she should be used to this by now. 'Just one or two things then, Mrs Ellis. They'll soon dry for you today.'

'Don't need much ironing if they get a good blow, do they?' Maggie bends down behind the wall and re-appears with a pile of clothing and towels that she puts into Non's waiting arms.

'You old besom,' Lizzie German says, 'you had them there all the time.' She stands with her hands on her hips and gives Maggie Ellis a hard stare. 'One day missus here'll say no instead of yes, and then where will you be?'

'Neighbours help each other out, don't they, Non?' Maggie says, then sneezes as several of Osian's bubbles land on her face. Maggie's hands flail at them as if they are angry wasps.

Osian is unmoved by the commotion he has caused. He watches the bubbles, and Non and Lizzie stand still to watch him. His concentration is total. Something is different about him today, but Non cannot put her finger on the difference.

Maggie staggers back to the wall, rubbing her eyes, which are red from the soapy bubbles. 'Strange boy,' she says.

'Clever boy,' Lizzie says. 'Knows not to like people much. Knows not to trust them.'

'I heard he doesn't like that Teddy your Davey's taken on,' Maggie says to Non.

So Maggie Ellis was listening to her and Meg on Saturday. Non tries to recall what else they had talked about.

'Did you hear about him on Saturday?' Maggie says. 'He did upset people, talking a lot of nonsense. As if we haven't all got enough to upset us already. Didn't I say, Non – weeks ago – didn't I say those tramps would be trouble? Not even Welsh, some of them, I said to you. Didn't I?'

'You did, Mrs Ellis,' Non says. She stirs the contents of the rinsing tub. And Lizzie pounds the washing Maggie handed over the wall, along with the rest of the wash. Non watches the vigour with which Lizzie wields the dolly; anyone would think it was Maggie in there. 'But he can't help it, you know – some sort of war damage, Davey thinks. And he can't help being English, can he?' Non is relieved to realise that Teddy has not said anything in particular; if he had, Maggie Ellis would have been bound to hear of it. A surge of certainty floods through her: Davey is sure to persuade him to leave before he has another opportunity to tell everyone, anyone, about Ben Bach.

'Did I say he can help it, Non?' Maggie Ellis says. 'But he should have stayed in England to do his begging, instead of coming here to cause trouble.' She turns sharply to Osian as he blows more bubbles her way. 'Stop that!' she shouts at him.

Lizzie German takes hold of the edge of Osian's saucer and draws him away to the other side of the garden. When she returns, she says, 'He's taken with them bubbles. They do look like little worlds when you see them close.'

'I don't expect Non's paying you to look at bubbles, Lizzie,' Maggie says.

'She's not paying me to do your washing, neither,' Lizzie says, and she pulls Maggie's clothes and towels out of the washtub one by one and slaps them on top of the wall in a sopping wet heap.

Non feels helpless. She has never known how to deal with the altercations and arguments between Lizzie and Maggie. All she can do is stand here watching them. As if they were in a play.

'At least they're washed,' Maggie says. 'I can put them through my own mangle here.'

Under her breath, Lizzie mutters, 'Silly old besom. Like to put you through the mangle, so I would.' Maggie looks at her through narrowed eyes, but Lizzie begins to wring the clothes left in the tub, turning the handle of the mangle as if it really is Maggie Ellis she is wringing between the rollers, and not Davey's faded work trousers.

Maggie begins to pluck at her washing, pulling away one item after another into her basket. She nods at Osian. 'Look – he's blowing those bubbles as if his life depended on it.' She watches for a moment, then says to Non, 'At least it's safer than carrying that old knife of his around the garden. Used to give me the shivers, that did.'

Non realises what it is that is different about Osian. It is a long time since she has seen him without his penknife, whittling obsessively at a piece of wood.

43

The heat has definitely broken. A breeze blows over them through the open door, carrying the scents of the phlox and roses in its pleasant warmth. The washing had dried beautifully by the time Non had fetched it in. Maggie Ellis was right – it will be a great deal easier to iron it all tomorrow than it has been for weeks.

'It'll probably rain soon,' Meg says. She looks towards the door and grimaces. She and her friends have taken to going down to the beach in the early evening; rain would put an end to that.

'We could do with some rain,' Davey says. 'And thank goodness that great heat is at an end. It'll be easier for everybody.'

'Not for me,' Meg says.

Davey looks up from his supper plate. 'Maybe it's time you started thinking about other people a little bit, Meg.'

'I am,' Meg says. 'I'm thinking about my friends, too.'

Davey does not reply. Sometimes there is no arguing with Meg, she has an answer for everything. But Davey is subdued this evening. Non wonders if he is weighed down by the memories he has recovered. In some ways he seems like his old self, what she has always thought of as his true self, but she supposes that now his true self will be part the old Davey and part the Davey that fought the War. He and she will have to become used to one another all over again. And that is not necessarily a bad thing, she thinks, watching him concentrate on eating his supper. It will be . . . an adventure.

She looks around the table. Gwydion is also subdued this evening, no doubt thinking about his impending move to Ireland. And Osian is always quiet, his face inscrutable, there is no telling what his thoughts are. He has been watching Davey since they sat down to have supper, Non realises, and she wonders if something is troubling him. She is reminded of his penknife. 'Has Osian left his knife in the workshop?' she asks Davey. 'Or has he lost it?'

Davey stops eating. 'I'm going to have to get him another one,' he says. 'Maybe we can go to Port on the train, Osian. We'll go to Kerfoots – they always have a good selection.'

'Port on the train! You're getting a bit adventurous, Davey.' Gwydion raises his eyebrows in mock amazement.

'I've had enough of adventures, Gwydion. It's your turn now.'

'I'm looking forward to them,' Gwydion says.

His tone causes Non to look more closely at him. He does not sound so sure. Or is she imagining it?

Davey also looks enquiringly at Gwydion. 'It's not too late to change your mind, you know.'

'Don't do that,' Meg says. 'If you change your mind, I won't be able to come to stay with you and Aoife.'

'I didn't know you were planning on staying with us, Meg. You'd always be welcome. All of you. The Irish are hospitable people, you know.'

'Maybe I won't be coming until I go to university,' Meg says. 'You can find out what Trinity is like. Find out if they teach French. Maybe I'll go there. Maybe I'll stay with you. And Aoife.'

Meg is not so much following her destiny as making it. And her destiny looks to become more expensive every day.

'You'll have to work hard at school,' Gwydion tells Meg.

'Why is everyone always telling me what I know?'

They laugh at Meg. Except Osian who stares at his father without blinking. Osian is not eating, his food barely touched on his plate. What is this about? Non says, 'When can you take Osian to Port, Davey? I think he misses his knife.'

'Tomorrow,' Davey says. 'How about it, Osian?'

Tomorrow! Non has never known Davey take time off from his work.

'You're not going to leave that Teddy on his own to work on your precious coffins, are you?' Meg says.

'There are no more coffins to be made, Meg, not at the moment anyway. And long may the moment last! And you'll be pleased to hear that Teddy has gone.'

Non stops eating, her knife and fork poised above her plate. Teddy has gone. Without making any more trouble. She knew Davey could do it. She smiles at him. She wants to get up from the table and hold hands with him and dance around the room until they are reeling, the way her father used to do with her whenever he received good news.

Meg gives an exaggerated shudder. 'Osian and I are very glad about that. We didn't like him one bit. Did we, Osh?'

Osh. Meg has taken him under her wing. Non did not expect that.

'Wasn't he up to much, then, this Teddy?' Gwydion says.

'Worse than that.' Meg gives another shudder. 'He was very peculiar. He won't come back again, will he, Tada?'

'No,' Davey says.

How can Davey be so definite? Doubt begins to shade Non's

relief. Won't there always be a danger that Teddy will come back? That sooner or later he will tell someone what happened to Ben Bach?

'Non,' Meg says, rising from her chair, 'please may I not wash the dishes tonight? I've got some schoolwork to do. I should have done it right away when the holidays started, and I don't want to forget it.'

'French, I suppose,' Non says, imagining *Madame Bovary*, in French.

'No. Why would you suppose that?'

Non smiles. 'Go on, Meg. Gwydion can help me. Take Osian up with you, it's time he was in bed.'

Non and Gwydion clear the table, and wash and dry the dishes. It is already twilight beyond the window panes. Non watches their reflections in the glass, busy at work. It is quieter tonight, there are no owls about. They must have found better hunting elsewhere. She stands still at the sink below the open sash, listening to the breeze rustle through the roses that climb the wall around the window.

'Look at that moon rising,' Gwydion says. 'It's a lovely evening. And cooler at last. I think I'll go for a walk, do a bit of thinking, Non. I'll see you both later. I'll take the key so I don't disturb you, shall I?'

Davey flaps his *Daily Herald* at Gwydion to wave him on his way.

Non dries her hands. She closes the back door and the door to the hall and the window. Davey watches her. She feels his gaze following her as she moves about the room. She sits opposite him at the table; she takes his newspaper from his hands and lays it down.

'Davey, is Teddy really gone?'

'He is, Non.'

'But . . . what did he say? Is he going to stay away? What if he turns up again? What if he tells everyone about Ben Bach the next time he comes back, or the time after, or the time after that? Are we always going to be waiting and wondering?'

'He won't be coming back, I promise. There's no need for you to worry, no need for you to ever think of him again.' Davey leans across the table and cups Non's face in his hands. He looks into her eyes. 'We can just forget about him.'

Non holds Davey's gaze for a long time. 'Davey?' she says, 'what—?'

Davey takes one hand away from her face, his calloused palm stroking her cheek. He smiles at her and lays his forefinger against her lips. He shakes his head. 'Shhh . . .' he says. 'Shhh . . .'

44

Non has not slept. Scarcely a wink, she thinks. The window had
rattled until she could stand it no longer and had climbed out of
bed to wedge her handkerchief between the sashes and the frame.
She wishes it were as easy to quieten the thoughts that have rattled
in her head all night. It is noticeably cooler. She should have
slept well on the first cool night for months, but she has heard
the clock strike each hour throughout the night. Now, she hears
it mark the quarter hour. Quarter to six, and the dawn has broken,
tingeing the sky rose-pink, sung-in by a choir of birds.

A whimper comes from Davey who has slept all night. Like a
baby, she thinks, a little resentfully. She leans on her elbow to
watch his face, the blush of the dawn reflecting from the bedroom
walls to colour his skin. She thinks how strange it is that colour
vanishes in the dark. She has always been able to see clearly at
night, but it is always a monochrome world she sees, shades of
grey.

Davey's eyes flutter beneath his eyelids. He is dreaming, but of
what? It does not appear to be a bad dream, his face is reposeful,
a slight smile on his lips. But it is early days yet, she reminds

herself, to think that he is . . . cured. It is only three nights since he remembered what it was his nightmares were trying to bring back to him. It seems strange that knowing what he had done – which seems to Non an act that would haunt her all her life – has brought some kind of peace to Davey. It must, then, be best to know, she thinks, rather than not know; it is something she has always thought to be true in principle. But to kill someone she knows, deliberately, in cold blood, whatever the reason – could she do that? She does not know the answer. Would it not depend on the circumstances? War changes everything, she thinks. Everything. Everyone in the country must know that. We will never be free from it.

When the clock strikes six she will wake him, she decides, laying her head back on the pillow. Why could he not have said what happened to Teddy? He could have said he promised he would go away and not come back, or whatever it was Teddy did say to him. She will not allow entry to the thoughts that have hovered about her all night, waiting to pinch and prod her into the wrong conclusions.

She turns her head away from Davey. Her bedside table still looks a little bare to her without the bottle of tincture on it. It seems to have left a large gap for such a small object. She is hardly ever aware of the beat of her heart now, which is far pleasanter than feeling it leap and flutter in her breast throughout the day, as it often used to do.

The kitchen clock chimes the hour before it begins to strike. She counts: six o'clock. She turns back to Davey and lays her hand on his shoulder to shake him awake. I have not done this since before he went away, she thinks, when he was impossible to wake in the mornings. She had given up trying eventually, she remembers, and used the time before Davey tumbled out of bed to keep up with her reading. So much of our knowledge is in books, her father used to say to her, though she doubts he meant the novels she loves to read. They are like her father's stories – not true, but holding truths within them.

She shakes Davey again, and he grunts and opens his eyes to peer at her as if she is a stranger and he does not know where he is.

'Wake up, Davey,' she says. She watches him remember; it is as if his thoughts are being poured back into his head after being absent all night.

He glances over her shoulder at the window. 'It's early, Non,' he says.

'I want to talk to you, Davey,' she says. 'Before everyone's up.'

'Talk?'

She knows Davey is a doer rather than a talker. He has talked to her more than he has ever done in their few hours of revelations.

'About Teddy,' she says.

'What about him?' Davey's eyes close again as he speaks.

'I want to know what happened to him.' She shakes Davey by the shoulder. 'Please, Davey.'

'He's gone. What more do you need to know?'

'The manner of his going,' she says.

'The manner of his going!' Davey laughs, waking himself properly. 'Oh, Non, you sound like someone in a drama. He just . . . went.'

How can he laugh when this is so serious? She will make him listen. 'Did someone make him go, Davey? Did you?'

Davey turns to stare at her. He shuffles himself into a sitting position, pulling his pillow up behind his back. 'So, you tell me what you think the manner of his going was, Non.' His steely voice is at odds with his bleary eyes and tufty hair.

She wants to back down, un-ask the question, go back to being the good, pliant wife. But she says, 'Something doesn't ring true, Davey, something doesn't make sense.'

'Teddy didn't make sense a minute of the time he was here,' Davey says. 'The only sensible thing that he did was to go on his way.'

'Why?' Non says. 'What changed so suddenly?'

'Saturday night,' Davey says. 'I had to take him back to the workshop, that's why I was so late. Constable Evans said the boys had been pretty rough with him. I expect he took fright. He was . . . gone by Sunday morning, anyway.'

Non notices the hesitation. 'But why didn't you tell us he'd gone when you came home on Sunday?'

Davey makes a fuss of pulling his pillow into a different position behind his back. 'I didn't know he'd gone for good, did I? He might have come back. I didn't want to raise your hopes.'

She sees immediately that he is lying. It is something to do with his eyes. She cannot put it into words.

'Tell me the truth, Davey,' she says.

A mulish look creeps into the set of his face, so like the expression she had sometimes caught on Wil's face that she catches her breath. She had always thought it was something Wil had taken from Grace.

'It can't be worse than what you told me on Saturday evening, can it?' she says.

'Why have you got to know everything, Non?' Davey says. 'Why can't you let things be sometimes?'

She thinks she has let things be far too much. She is not about to do so again. She waits to hear what Davey will say. Suddenly she is aware of her heart beating fast, and lays her hand over it as if that will calm her agitation.

'I was trying to protect you,' Davey says, at last. He looks at her. 'You and the children.'

'From what?'

Davey shrugs. He looks at the foot of the bed again. 'When Osian and I got to the workshop on Sunday,' he says, 'he was still there, up in the loft. I left him to sleep – he was so drunk when I took him back the night before, he wouldn't have been any use for anything. Albert came to the workshop later and we put old Calvin in his coffin. It was dinner time by then, so I told Albert I'd nail the top down, and he went off for his Sunday dinner. I got our oatcakes and cheese out for me and Osian, and called up to Teddy to see if he wanted any. There was no sound from him, so I went up the ladder and there he was – still fast asleep. I tried to shake him awake.'

Non listens to his story. She watches the sun climb higher in the sky, the gathering clouds scudding across its face, the bedroom becoming lighter and darker in turn.

'I couldn't wake him, Non. And then I pulled him on his back and I saw he was dead.'

Non feels no surprise, but she is saddened. 'Poor Teddy,' she says. 'Poor man.' She remembers all the men in Angela's ward. 'Was it his heart, I wonder?'

Davey turns his attention from the foot of the bed to Non. 'Truth is, Non, his throat was cut.'

Non gasps and covers her mouth. She does not know what she was expecting, but it was not something so . . . so bloody as this. This is the way you would kill an animal.

'You wanted to know, Non,' Davey says. 'The mattress he was on was soaked through.'

Osian, thinks Non. Where was he when this was happening? 'Did Osh see him?'

Davey turns his head away. 'I don't know,' he says.

Non thinks she knows. She thinks of Osian's implacable face. She thinks of him not taking his eyes off Davey, even to eat his food. Was he looking for comfort, or was he wondering what his father had done?

'What happened to him, Davey?' she says. 'Who . . . who cut his throat?' She can hardly bring herself to say such words.

Davey starts. 'No one, Non. No one. He killed himself.'

'Cut his own throat?'

'I saw men do that in the War, Non,' Davey says. 'It's a quick way to go. He didn't have anything to live for, Teddy. He was a lost soul.'

'But to cut his own throat . . .' She can scarcely believe that she is sitting in bed talking about such a thing. 'Poor man,' she says again, though she does not think she feels as much sadness as she should. It is too tinged with relief. 'What did Constable Evans say? There'll have to be an inquest, won't there?' As she asks the questions she thinks it is strange that Maggie Ellis and Lizzie had said nothing of this yesterday. The town must have been humming with the news.

'He was dead, Non. Nothing was going to make a difference to him. I thought the least fuss, the better. What if it all came out – the reason he came here – Ben Bach – what if it came out, Non?'

But no one knows except the two of us, Non thinks. 'What have you done, Davey?'

'Protected us,' he says. 'Elsie Thomas, you, me, Osian, the family, the town – all of us, Non.'

'Where is he?'

Davey does not answer. She sees that the tremor is back in his hands. She should not have questioned him so accusingly. He has been through so much, protecting them, Wales, the world, against the darkness. But she has to know all there is to know, now that she knows half of it.

'Where is Teddy, Davey?'

Davey turns to her. His cheeks are wet with tears. 'I put him and the knife in with old Calvin,' he says. 'He's in the ground, in the cemetery.'

'Osian's knife?'

'Osian's knife,' he says. 'Osian's knife killed him. You know what people would think, what they would say. I had to protect Osh, Non, he can't do it for himself.'

Non instinctively puts her hand out to him and he grasps it as tightly as he grasped her hand when he told her he had killed Ben Bach. He grasps it as if he is drowning and she will save him.

'I had to keep Osian safe, Non, I had to keep us all safe,' he says looking into her eyes.

She looks back at him. That is the truth in his story, she thinks. She nods at him and, tentatively, he lifts her clasped hand to his lips and kisses it.

45

Meg yawns and huddles closer to the fire in the range. 'Why is Tada allowed to stay in bed late and I'm not?'

'You asked me to get you up early, Meg. I thought you were going to spend the day with your Barmouth friends.' Non lays down the wreath through which she is twining strands of ivy. It is difficult to see exactly what she is doing by lamplight. She glances through the kitchen window, but all she can see is her own reflection staring back and Osian sitting across the table to her, Herman nestling on his shoulder. When she first came downstairs this morning there seemed to be as much frost inside the window panes as there was out of doors where it sparkled in the light of a moon only just beginning to wane. The winter has already been hard after such a hot summer, and it is not Christmas for another week. She picks up the wreath again and holds it in the pool of lamplight to find the gaps that need filling.

'Is that for Nain's grave?' Meg leaves the fireside and comes to sit next to Non at the table, shivering and pulling her woollen shawl tighter over her nightdress.

'No – the big one over there by the back door is for your grandmother, and the one next to it for your mother,' Non says. 'If you're going to catch the train you'll have to get ready soon, Meg.'

'I've changed my mind,' Meg says. 'I could have stayed in bed.'

'Won't your friends be expecting you?' Non moves the basket of holly sprigs, heavy with red berries – a sure sign of a long and hard winter, she thinks – out of the way of Meg's fidgety fingers.

'I only half promised,' Meg says. 'Are you taking the wreaths to the cemetery today, Non?'

'Only if I get this one finished.' Non begins to pick out some holly sprigs and push them among the ivy.

'Who's that one for?'

'I thought I'd make one for old Calvin Edwards. Your father thought well of him, and there's no family to remember him.'

'Can I make a bunch of holly to put on Nain's grave?' Meg asks.

Non pushes the basket of holly back towards her, with the big scissors and the ball of twine. What has brought this on? she wonders. It had been a shock to them all, Catherine Davies's sudden death. Lizzie German had arrived breathless at Non's front door one morning in October to say that she had just come up to look after old William Davies as usual and found Catherine Davies still in her bed. Says she's going to heaven to see her Billy, Lizzie had gasped, and she gave me this, missus. The note Lizzie waved was a demand from Catherine Davies that she be buried in the same grave as Billy. By the time Lizzie and Non had hurried to the house, Catherine Davies had died. Non supposes that any wreath laid on Catherine's grave will do for Billy, too, which saves her much heart-searching. Bess and Katie had returned for the funeral, a sombre affair, and not at all the kind of family gathering

Non had once thought of arranging. They had all been shaken by the suddenness of the event, but no one seemed especially sad. Maybe Meg had been more affected than Non had thought.

'It'll be strange this Christmas without her,' she says. 'Your grandmother.'

'Yes,' Meg says. 'But you won't mind, will you, Non?'

Non is chastened. She will not mind, but maybe she should mind a little. 'Taid will be here.' But not in spirit, she thinks, for old William Davies has returned to his past for good. 'And Wil is coming home, he'll be with us – I wonder if he's written down any of his adventures in your journal, Meg,' she says, hoping to change the conversation.

'Ouch!' Meg sucks at her thumb after being careless with the holly. 'You do it for me, Non. I'm going to get dressed. Can I have the rest of the water in the kettle for my washbasin?' She does not wait for a reply before she pours the water into the big enamel jug and carries it away.

Non hears her careful footsteps on the stairs. Osian and Herman raise their heads to listen, then Herman tucks his head back into his feathers and Osian returns his attention to his carving. The cold does not seem to worry Osian any more than the great heat of the summer had done. With his knife – an exact replica of his old knife that he had picked out in Kerfoots' store – he chips away at the block of lime in front of him. Non has laid pages of the *Daily Herald* to catch the curls of wood and to protect the kitchen table. Already from the lime emerges the figure of the Little Mermaid on her rock, with her half-legs half-fishtail curled beneath her, copied from the postcard Wil had sent Osian last week. Non thinks of Osian's first carving of Meg – she wonders if that is why Wil chose the card. She has told Osian the mermaid's sad story, leaving out the moralising at the end as her father used to do when he told it to her. That is not what stories are for, Rhiannon, he would say. She looks over at the postcard lying flat on the table. Cards to Osian, depicting all kinds of wonders, have been Wil's way of keeping in touch with his family. Even Meg looks out for them. Wil is as poor a letter-writer as his father, Non thinks; she will be surprised if he has written anything in his journal – Catherine Davies had been right about Wil's writing skills – and she should not have reminded Meg about it.

Gwydion, on the other hand, has written pages to her – she is his only family contact. Branwen will not even reply to Non's letters except for one long tirade accusing her of turning Gwydion against her. Non had not known whether to laugh or cry when she received it. She senses that Gwydion is finding life with Aoife's family difficult – something he had not anticipated. He had not realised that he would be expected to convert to Catholicism for his marriage to Aoife to take place. I do not want to pretend to be something I am not, he had written.

Non sighs, and draws towards her the bunch of holly sprigs Meg had started to gather together. She can see more clearly, now that the day has started to lighten. The whiteness of the garden appears gradually: the stone walls, the ground, the shrubs, the water barrels, the garden sheds are all encased in a deep frost that in all likelihood will not shift today any more than it has done for the past week. Non shivers, more at the thought of the cold than the cold itself, and pulls the holly into shape and wraps the twine around the stems to keep the sprigs together. She stands up to brush the remains of the ivy and holly into the basket, and lays the finished wreath and bunch of holly sprigs on top. She stretches her arms upwards to loosen her shoulders, puts more coal on the fire, fills the kettle ready to make tea.

'We'll have to put your carving away for a while, Osh, so I can make breakfast,' she says. 'When you reach a bit where you can stop, put it on this tray, and your knife.'

Osian gives no sign of having heard her, but after a few moments he stops, lifts Herman from his shoulder onto the back of the chair, and lays his work on the tray as if he were putting it on display. He vanishes from the kitchen and runs up the stairs. Non can hear him moving about in his bedroom.

My own baby, she thinks. My only baby. Fate – she had left the decision for Fate to make because she could not make it herself – has chosen not to give her a child. She does not think she is sad about this, and Davey does not seem to have thought about it at all since his memory returned and reminded him of the changes the War had wrought in him.

She considers that she and Davey have more than enough to bind them together, secrets that are theirs alone, never spoken, but never forgotten. They are both changed from the young woman and the widowed father who had fallen in love before the War, but they are tied together more strongly than the holly sprigs. Davey is immersed in his work with his branch of the Labour Party – the future, Non, he frequently tells her – and he has an excellent apprentice who is already capable of doing much of the coffin work so that Davey can spend time on the furniture he loves to make. Yet, some nights, Non wakes to find his face wet with quiet tears. And she – she is beginning to know her strengths. She looks into her future the way she had imagined Wil looked into his, with eagerness for what it will bring.

She reaches for the plates on the rack and lays them on the table, puts the cups on the saucers, takes the knives and teaspoons from the table drawer, a loaf of bread from the bread-bin, the butter and jam from the larder. Herman stands up on the chairback and flutters to the floor, ready for his breakfast. Non rattles the coals under the kettle with the poker until they glow red. She hears Davey's morning footsteps on the stairs and contentment steals through her.

For now, she is glad to be content.

Acknowledgements

Thank you to Carcanet Press for kindly giving permission to use, for the title of this book, a line from the poem 'To Bring the Dead to Life' by Robert Graves.

Thank you, as always, to Glenn Strachan, and to Adam Ifans, Llio Evans, Cai Strachan and Rachel Ifans, for their support, their forbearance, and their critical reading.

Thank you to my agent, Lavinia Trevor, for her hard work, support and loyalty.

Thank you to Anya Serota, my excellent editor, and to all those Canongaters, too numerous to list, who work so hard for every single book in their care.

Numerous accounts of the First World War are readily available, including first-hand accounts of trench life in published diaries and letters; the experiences of under-age soldiers; the executions for desertion; the work of nursing staff in the field. By contrast, there is a dearth of information about the period immediately following the War, but I was able to gather bits of information here and there, and I have listed on my website books and other sources that I found particularly useful.

Here, I would like to thank those people who generously gave me their time, shared their expert knowledge, and saved me from making embarrassing mistakes. In particular, thank you to Neil Evans, a respected authority on modern Welsh history, for his initial suggestions, and for his critical reading of the book and his pertinent and invaluable comments on it. Thank you to Kate Strachan, then Archivist for the Meteorological Office, whose research discovered details of the weather during the summer of 1921 and provided me with the heat that I wanted. Thank you to psychologist Dr Theresa Kruczek, Associate Professor of Psychology at Ball State University, Indiana, for sharing her extensive knowledge and expertise during our discussion about the effects that trauma may have on memory, the ways the mind may compensate for lost memories, and the ways memory may be restored. Thank you to Robert Cadwalader, seafarer, expert and enthusiast, for information about the beautiful Western Ocean Yachts and their crews still sailing from Porthmadog after the Great War. Thank you to Glyn Evans, a knowledgeable railway enthusiast from the Cambrian Railways Society, who put my heroine on the correct train journey. Any mistakes that remain are entirely my own.

And thank you, Claude and Yvonne Courtine, for lending the name of your cat to Herman the crow.

A Note on the Type

Goudy Old Style was designed by Frederic W. Goudy, an American type designer. It is a graceful, slightly eccentric typeface, and is prized by book designers for its elegance and readability.

Inspired by William Morris' Arts and Crafts movement, Frederic Goudy designed over ninety typefaces throughout his career, and is one of the most influential type designers of the twentieth century.